Deadly Trifecta

A Charles Reynolds Novel

By D.C. Reed

Thanks to my family and friends for all their support while writing this novel.

Thanks to Milton Lewis for his editing efforts and input.

Front Cover: ©Big Stock Photo.com:Alfonzo76, Alfonzo D'Agostino.

Publisher – Cowboy Bookworks and Loaded Dice Publishing

Prologue:

Lazy C Ranch- Scottsdale, Arizona

Sitting down on the porch of an old ranch house, Charles "Chars" Reynolds asked, "And you're from New Zealand?

"That's right. I recently moved to the U.S. My nanna and nandy owned this land, but moved to New Zealand to escape the Great Depression," Hamish Cain answered in his heavy Kiwi accent.

"What do you plan to do here long term?" asked Chars.

"I have a blue healer that needs a job to do, so I think I will raise some sheep and horses."

"You seemed to have recovered from your injuries," Chars stated.

"It is all good. No worries," said Hamish deflecting the unwanted attention.

"And the boy?" asked Chars.

"It has not been a piece of piss. He's not 100% yet, but he is doing well. He's a tough little sprog. He seems to have adjusted well to the loss of his mum and the shock of losing her in the way he did. But I know it's tough to lose someone, particularly when you are that young," Hamish said with a sense of empathy.

"So has your experience of all this soured your opinion of the United States?" asked Chars.

Hamish did not answer immediately. He thought about the events over the past few months and tried to put together a cogent reply. He threw the stick he had been fiddling with over the rail of the porch.

"I think anywhere you go; Lazy C or New Zealand, there will always be a few bad blokes. We did our part in making that number a little better."

Deadly Trifecta

Chapter One

One month earlier: North Scottsdale, Arizona

In the Four Peaks Brewery, Scott Tivy, a small bespectacled man, sat at a table with his back to the wall. He had selected last table in the back of the restaurant trying to remain as inconspicuous as possible. The Four Peaks was known for their specialty beers and tonight Scott had ordered the Kiltlifter™. His rumpled suit showed the affects of a harried business day. This was his second round, but he did not seem to be enjoying his pint of courage. He was grasping on to both sides of his mug as if he would slip under the table were he not hanging on for dear life. A waiter came by to see how Scott was progressing on his beer, but decided to pass on interrupting the man's deep concentration. The waiter was not sure what his customer was focusing on, but whatever it was, it must have been serious. People at other tables were speaking and laughing. Most people visited "The Four Peaks" to have a frosty one and enjoy some good conversation with others. Not this guy. You could see the sweat beaded up on Scott's substantial forehead. The waiter observed that his customer looked like he was about to go in front of the firing squad. Scott's hands were gripped so tight around his mug, that he might just choke the glass to death.

Scott dabbed his receding hairline and loosened his necktie. Suddenly, his cell phone sounded loudly with the musical theme from the movie, "The Sting" by Scott Joplin

3

and Marvin Hamlisch. Scott reacted so abruptly to the loud sound that he nearly knocked over the table in fright. Several people looked over at him, obviously curious about this peculiar man. Scott recovered and tried to look unperturbed. He clumsily silenced the ring and then pressed the answer button. He did not immediately bring the phone to his ear, but instead waited for the onlookers to return to their own conversations. He recognized the number on his caller I.D.

After a moment he put the phone to his ear and asked in a strained whisper, "Where are you?" Once again he looked around to make sure no one was eavesdropping.

The voice that answered seemed to be in pain, "Tom, I am running a little late."

Scott was immediately confused by being called Tom, but just listened intently.

There was a pause as if the speaker was gathering his strength, "I need you to meet me."

The caller took in a breath and grimaced at the pain of a broken rib.

"Where are you? I have been waiting for almost an hour," Scott said in a whiny voice that irritated almost everyone who knew the bureaucrat.

Scott noticed that a couple sitting one table away peaked over at him. He quickly covered the phone and his mouth to make sure that no one would be able to hear. The couple was clearly intrigued, but the woman gained a sense that it was rude to stare. She shamed her male friend into turning away from the strange little man. When an answer was not immediately forthcoming, Scott's tone took on one of concern and he asked in a whisper, "Are you hurt?"

The caller managed to speak, "No, no, no, I am fine. Just got some bad Italian sausage, that's all."

The phone was muffled, but Scott thought he heard a thud and then a huge grunt of pain. Maybe Scott even heard an "Oh God." But he couldn't quite make it out. It was a full 5 seconds before the caller spoke again.

The caller continued, "Tom, I just need you to meet me at Baxter's Warehouse. That's all. Can you do that?"

"Yeah sure, I'll meet you at the Baxter's Warehouse. I will be there, in... say 25 minutes."

Scott was getting up from his seat, reaching in his pocket for a money clip and taking one last gulp of his ale. He had no intention of meeting anyone at some warehouse. He could be out of the city in twenty minutes. He ended the call and tried to run out the door without appearing to run. The bartender showed some concern about his customer moving quickly toward the door until he saw the ten dollar bill left on the table. Scott walked across the street, while checking for cross traffic. His car was parked in the restaurant parking lot toward the back. He stood on his tip toes in order to see the automobile. When his car became visible, Scott punched the remote and then jumped in. He dialed 911, but thought better of it and hung up before it could ring. The police could trace his call back to his cell phone and then he would have to answer the questions that would almost certainly get somebody killed.

Just like what was probably happening right now. Sure he had given Raleigh Allen, a local reporter, the bait to meet with him, but how could he have known that it would get the guy caught. They had to have been watching him anyway and when Scott called they put two and two together and got four. Scott was not responsible for bad guys already tracking some reporter. Scott could not worry about someone he had not even known. He was on his own and Scott knew he needed to get out of town quickly. Before he could start his car, his cell phone went off with the "The Sting" theme again. He saw that it was the same number as before. Maybe they had let Raleigh go free. Scott really hoped so. No he prayed so. He did not want this man's death on his conscience. Heaven knows that he had enough on his plate of guilt with out feeling like he had led this poor man to the guillotine. Scott closed his eyes and decided that it was better to go ahead and answer. But he needed to get going. As he was starting up his Volvo XC90 he answered almost in the voice of a small child, "Yes?"

But there was only silence. Scott hesitated before hanging up because he felt sure that there was someone listening.

The Volvo's Interactive GPS system turned on and a female voice said "Hello Scott, you are currently at the intersection of North Pima Road and Frank Lloyd Wright Boulevard, where would you like to go?"

Scott was aghast and muttered, "Oh shit!"

Scott struggled to see the correct button to turn the unit off, but it was tough to see all those little buttons. Attempting to silence the GPS, he pushed several buttons, but with no success.

In a throaty Chicago accent, a loud voice came through Scott's phone, "Home."

The GPS responded, "Take Lloyd Wright Boulevard east to 90th ..."

Scott was panicking but did finally locate the correct button. He managed to turn the GPS unit off before it gave a virtual road map to his doorstep.

The person on the other end of the call was actually laughing at his good fortune and said, "Well I guess we know that you are not Tom, don't we Scott. And let's see Frank Lloyd and Pimer." The big man evidently turned and asked over his shoulder, "What's at Frank Lloyd and Pimer?"

A voice in the background said, "Four Peaks."

The man returned to his conversation with Scott, "Yeah and yuz are at Four Peaks. If yuz just stays right there, I'z gots someone who wants to exchange some information wits ya. Nobody has to get hurt." He thought, *no more hurt than they alzready are.*

Scott thought to himself, *Oh my God, they know who I am and where I am.*

There was pause as Scott desperately tried to decide what to do.

Scott stuttered, "I, I called 911. They are on their way."

The person on the other end of the call gave another short laugh and said, "Where'd yuz tell dem' to go, Scotty? Pimer and Wright. Or wuz yuze on your ways to the warehouse? Hey Scotty, does uz work in city hall or are yuz over in code compliance? I bet I can find out."

Scott's face drained white with his sense of dread. Panicking, Scott looked both directions and then over his shoulder. He dared not answer. His voice had abandoned him and his hands were now shaking. He punched the end call button; then punched the accelerator.

To his partner, Luigi Beltrano, Little Don Fratelli said, "Let's go. Throws puss and boots in the trunk."

Little Don was referring to the fact that the unconscious man was wearing Florsheim™ Duke boots.

Luigi said, "Hey, I like those boots. They would give me additional two inches."

Little Don was getting in the passenger side of the dark Mercury Marquis with significant difficulty. He adjusted the seat back to the furthest possible setting. He thought, *now that the body is out of the backseat floorboard, this is much more comfortable.* Little Don said, "I know, I saws yuze looking at them. Luigi, yuze don't want no boots like that. They's way too thin for your foot."

Luigi slammed the trunk lid and came around to the driver's side. Luigi said, "What are you saying, I gots fat feet?"

Little Don looked up and sighed. "I did not saze yuz gots fat feets. I said those boots is too thin. With those heels, alls yuz weight will be slidin down to the toe. Gonna cause foot problems and problems with your back," said Little Don.

"I still like them and they're my size," said Luigi.

Little Don said, "Yuz not taking his fuckin' zip boots, Luigi. You don't think that would give the cops a clues? Yuze got shit for brains."

"Hey Little Don," Luigi was looking like a scolded puppy, "You treat me like a dummy sometimes. Maybe I wasn't thinking about taking his boots."

Luigi looked over at the big man with a pitiful look.

Chapter Two

Key Largo Grande Resort and Beach Club, Key Largo Florida

The sun was well up into the eastern sky and the warmness of the day had begun to infiltrate the air. Charles "Chars" Reynolds, writer for the Miami Express, was already boiling hot. He threw down the paper and cursed under his breath. His story had been neutered. He dialed the number for the Editor's Room at the Miami Express, but got the damn secretary.

"Patti, let me talk to Stanton." Chars ran his hands through his thick, but graying blonde mane.

"Who shall I say is calling?" asked Patti Juarez.

You know damn well who is calling, thought Chars. Chars removed reading glasses, the ones that he was particularly embarrassed about needing, and flung them across the room. The glasses bounced up and off the couch, but were not damaged.

Patti was a single mom constantly on the look out for a new beau, but failed to be impressed with Charles Reynolds, super reporter. Chars was not sure if she was a bitch to everyone or just him. He really wanted to ask her that sometime, but Chars had enough grief on his platter to deal with, without giving Patti some real reason to serve as his persecutor. She seemed to be able to be a bitch without a reason. Chars had figured that to give her cause, would only make matters worse in quantum proportions.

Ignoring her question, Chars said angrily, "Just put Stanton on."

There was ever so slight of a pause as Patti looked over to her boss. Thom Stanton had heard the conversation and stepped out of his office. Stanton gave an almost imperceptible shake of his head, indicating he did not want to talk to this investigative reporter. "Mr. Stanton just went into an editor's meeting and will likely not be out till eleven."

Stanton was actually about to go into the meeting and was in the process of stuffing a doughnut in his mouth. He was watching to see what his secretary's facial reaction to Chars' reply would be. Stanton did not like Charles Reynolds. He, in fact, would have enjoyed firing Reynolds. Reynolds was a rebel and that caused problems in his department. Other people got bad ideas from a rebel. Rebels needed to be brought in line and Charles Reynolds needed some serious corralling. Chars wadded up part of the newspaper that had his story printed (what was left of his story) and threw it toward the trash can. The projectile caught the edge of the waste basket, careened up and harmlessly fell on the floor.

"I know that meeting does not start for another 10 minutes, Patti," Chars said with a significant amount of contempt.

He could not stand her or her mealy mouthed, pathetic conniving boss.

"He is probably standing right there. I want to speak with him now!"

Chars was now yelling into the phone. Stanton could hear Chars' voice on the receiver. Chars was put on hold with no transitional statement such as "Could you please hold" or "One moment,"; just silence. Chars thought for a moment that Patti had hung up on him and thought he could use this bit of disrespect to his advantage. He sat his 6 foot frame hard into a desk chair. He fingered his hair back into place.

Stanton pushed down a button on the phone and said, "Chars, how it is going?"

Chars' eyes were about to bulge out. "You know exactly how it's going. You spiked my story."

"Spiked?" Stanton said with an impatient voice. "Your story ran."

Chars took the receiver and banged it three times on the kitchen counter like you would a hammer. Stanton moved the phone about twelve inches from his ear and gave an almost imperceptible smile. Chars was throwing a fit and Stanton was quite pleased with himself. It was about time and the tables were turning. But, Stanton had enough of this little tirade.

He said, "Excuse me, Mr. Reynolds. Get yourself under control. You will not speak to me or any other employee with that tone."

Stanton was pleased that Reynolds was learning the hard facts of life. Chars was Stanton's employee and he needed to learn, don't screw with your boss.

Chars was infuriated, but took a deep breath and seethed the words, "You cut the guts out of it. That scoop was rock solid."

Stanton thought to himself, *you arrogant prick*. But said in a more conciliatory but patronizing tone, "Chars, what was published **is** a good story, but some of your accusations could not be substantiated. You need to do so more work on it, that's all. So don't give me crap about your lack of thoroughness."

He did not give a shit about what Chars felt or thought. Chars was such a pain in the ass.

Stanton wanted to say, *"If you don't like it, you can damn well quit."*

But the fact was, Stanton could not fire Reynolds, because the big boss liked Reynolds.

So *i*nstead he asked, "Chars, I was expecting you in here today, you're not still in Key West are you?"

Chars was stumped for a second. He stopped pacing the hotel floor.

Ignoring the obvious change of subject, he said, "You sacked the story and you know it. And Stanton, I am going to find out why." Chars stabbed the end button with his forefinger and let out a loud "UHHRA".

Stanton's face hardened as he returned the receiver to Patti, but could not suppress a little smile.

Patti smiled as well and said, "I don't know who he thinks he is."

Stanton slightly shook his head back and forth indicating that he agreed. However, he was thinking about his dilemma. How do you get rid of someone who is a pain in the ass; a pain in the ass, who for some reason, was seen as some type of Bob Woodward? Stanton was in line for a promotion to the Washington office. He was not going to let someone like Charles Reynolds get in his way. Throughout his career, Stanton had seen lots of Charles Reynolds' type. Bold and brash, Chars would burn down the house just to chase out a rat. He was a loose canon, and

Stanton was not going to be called on the carpet of the Managing Editor again. No, Stanton did not want to take the heat for firing Reynolds. He really needed Chars to quit. Or better yet, if Stanton got his promotion to the Washington office, he would not even have to deal with the little Prima Donna.

Stanton, after all, did not hire Reynolds. Stanton thought: *Why does the brass come down on me, when it's Reynolds who totals a company car? Why do I get the call when Chars sets a hotel fire to flush out one of his supposed informants? Why do I have to come up with money out of my budget to pay for the entertainment night that Charles Reynolds hosted for 15 of his closest friends? Why does Charles Reynolds get to make his own reservations and fly first class? I don't even get to fly first class. What kind up pussy name is Chars anyway?*

Stanton walked down the hall, turned in to the large conference room where 15 staff reporters were waiting. He sat at the head of the table and looked down the row of faces and wondered: *Why doesn't Charles Reynolds have to attend this meeting?*

Chars gave the sofa a good kick as he walked from the living room to the kitchenette. He slammed the wireless phone into its holder so hard that the battery compartment cover came loose and skidded across the counter. He had all that he could take from this moron and he could not understand how anyone like him could be promoted to the editor's spot. He had just completed an exposé on a local politician that managed to work himself into a land for vote deal that netted him over a million dollars in profits.

Chars had gone undercover for almost two weeks to get the land developer on tape as well as a city worker in the zoning office. That was just the tip of the iceberg because Chars felt sure that this baby was born all the way back in Tallahassee and there could be several others that were going to fall. Chars had speculated a little, but most everything he had learned had been verified. And he wanted to know why Stanton had nixed some of the juiciest details. The story was going to sell and sell big. Now someone else would surely steal his thunder. He went into the bedroom and began to shove his clothes into his suit case.

Chapter Three

Arizona- Scottsdale

The weeping willows branches looked radiant green in the sunlight and their reflection on Respite Lake was as clear as any picture you could imagine. The water was a rich and healthy dark green and completely still. Not even a gentle breeze from the south could interrupt the serenity of the water. About a hundred yards down the bank of this hidden paradise was a large stand of oak trees that had presumably been in existence for many decades, maybe even centuries. The greenbelt to the north stretched a half mile and reached a ledge that overlooked the Sinai Valley just outside Scottsdale, Arizona. This valley had practically gone unnoticed by the mass of developers that had swarmed into this paradise like locusts coming to ravage a corn crop. Looking out over the edge of Sinai Ridge, one could see for miles and the urban sprawl that was on a march toward Respite Lake, and the Lazy C Ranch. The Lazy C consisted of 238 acres of a combination of desert and oasis. The seemingly undiscovered ranch was bordered to the north, by the Tonto National Forest, and located not quite halfway between Highway 17 and Highway 87 to the east. Cactus and rattlesnakes, coyotes and a whole cadre of other creatures had the run of the acreage. With the ever - encroaching population moving towards them, the wilder animals had moved further to the north. However, this did not preclude an occasional mountain lion or bear from being sighted by the inhabitants down below this huge plateau.

The people in Sinai Valley had been spared encounters or attacks because the animals had not been cornered as of yet. The land to the north was vast and like the American Indians trying to avoid the last influx of the White Man, the wild animals were willing to move to uninhabited wilderness. The acreage included a nice-size lake fed by several tributaries that ultimately could be followed, if it were possible, to Horseshoe Lake.

The land was owned by the Crenshaw family, whose ancestors settled part of the territory and then went to New Zealand during the Great Depression. The family leased the ranch and the small farm houses to many families over the years; generating enough income to pay the taxes and make selling it unnecessary. Of course, with all the building and construction that was going on in the Scottsdale area, the recent offers for the land were constant. Offers as high as four thousand per acre had been floated across the desk of Oscar Aramat, Jurist Prudence. For many years, Aramat had served as the family lawyer for the Crenshaws (and now the Cain family) of city of Ashburton on the South Island. Oscar dutifully contacted the family each time he received an offer, but no one in the family seemed to care or even really give consideration to any of the proposals. Hamish Cain, now twenty five, was the great grandson of Benjamin and Iris Crenshaw. He was the child of the late Joseph and Maggie (Crenshaw) Cain. Hamish was the last of five children born to Mr. and Ms. Cain. With parents in their late years, Hamish had grown up with no actual grandparents, but with parents that had the constitution of grandparents. The last child, obviously quite unexpected, was a ball of energy. Maggie and Joseph loved the child enormously, and Hamish grew into a gregarious young man. Hamish was raised with his nephews and nieces (some older than he was) as his contemporaries and developed a close relationship with all of them, 10 in all.

When Mam and Pop had passed, leaving the family ranch to the older brothers and one sister, it was presumed that Hamish would continue in the ranch and farming business with his older brothers and sister. The last of parents' bequest had changed that. Hamish inherited an almost forgotten or at the very least ignored piece of real estate in United States. It was the Lazy C Ranch in Arizona. Hamish had studied the area and decided that he would strike out on his own. He was a young man, and adventure was quite enticing.

Chapter Four

Washington D.C

U.S. Senator Wayman Kaspar, Russell Senate Building

"Senator Kaspar, Jimmy Fred is here to see you."

"Thanks Bev, send him in," said Wayman Kaspar.

With a disapproving look, Beverly White motioned Jimmy Fred toward the Senators door. At age forty eight, Jimmy Fred looked every bit of his age plus ten more. The tell-tale signs of a heavy drinker were evident. His bulbous nose and the paunch of a gut were all signs that most of the 2000 calories that Jimmy Fred received during the course of the day were courtesy of Jim Beam on ice. Having thoroughly challenged his liver earlier today, Jimmy Fred stood determinedly, put on his best smile, straightened his tie and headed toward the Senator's door. He flashed that winning smile to Bev as he passed. Bev smiled back. As soon as he passed, she rolled her eyes. Bev looked at Jimmy Fred warily as he passed by.

She thought, *even a Brooks Brothers suit doesn't hide your sleaze.*

Bev considered herself a good judge of character and Jimmy Fred was a character. He was definitely well-connected, but sirens went off inside her head every time he came to visit or called. He was shifty or slimy, well not slimy she had decided, but surely not someone to be trusted. Bev thought that Senator Kaspar did not really like having to do business with Jimmy Fred, but in politics the people you deal with out of necessity are not the same ones that you would normally pick on your own.

Bev knew that Jimmy Fred traveled in some heavy weight circles. Just last month, Senator Kaspar was part of three way call with Jimmy Fred and a Premier, Prince or Sultan from Saudi Arabia, or some such dignitary. It may have been a Saud royal family member, Bev thought. That was certainly a possibility since there were so many of the Prince lings. Bev had listened to the conversation on the Senator's end but could only make out a portion of the conversation. It was some funding issue regarding an Indian Reservation. Bev could not figure how that involved Senator Kaspar, but then again, he was on so many committees, it was hard to keep up with all of them. As far as Jimmy Fred, she knew he was important, because the Senator did not stop to see just anyone, particularly someone without an appointment.

The first time Jimmy Fred had arrived without an appointment, Bev remembered bristling and politely asking, "Is the Senator expecting you?"

Jimmy Fred's response was "Not unless he is telepathic."

Then he let out a laugh that sent the message that he was merely amusing himself. She knew that the Senator was not expecting him, of course, because he was not on the schedule. Senator Kaspar had made it quite clear from the start that everyone, maybe with the exception of the President's cabinet member and major committee member in the Senate, must have an appointment to be granted an audience. But, when Bev discreetly called back to the

Senator to check on status of Jimmy Fred, Bev was very surprised when the Senator said, "Send him in."

Then he followed with, "Bev, hold my calls for a little bit please."

Bev also thought it odd that Jimmy Fred never gave a last name. So unless Fred was his last name, Jimmy Fred was famous or infamous enough not to have to go with a last name. Of course, Bev figured that there was not likely to be two Jimmy Freds out there anyway. Bev thought that maybe Jimmy Fred might be a lobbyist, but if he was a lobbyist, he was different. Lobbyists were usually deferential when they came to visit. Most of them practically fell all over themselves while meeting with Senator Wayman Kaspar, head of the Democratic Convention, Chairman of the Ways and Means Committee, and a power broker for a half a dozen others. Kaspar, save two other senators, was the second most tenured Democratic U.S. Senator.

Bev enjoyed working for the Senator, because she was privy to so much that many people never heard about. She knew weeks before anyone that the Vice President was going to assume the Presidency last year. She of course could not tell anyone, but she still knew and when it happened, she would be sure to tell her friends that she knew….but could not say anything. She also knew about the President's resignation before it happened. Her thoughts were interrupted when Jimmy Fred came back out of the Senator's office with a big smile on his face and gave a knowing smile to Bev.

"Have a fantastic day young lady," Jimmy Fred said.

He headed out the office door not even waiting for a reply. Bev took a sighing breath and gave a little shake of her head. That Jimmy Fred was a piece of work she thought. Bev noticed that the light on the Senator's private line lit up and stayed lit for almost a full minute. When the Senator's phone line light went out, Bev interrupted with a reminder that the Secretary of the Interior was expecting a call back prior to their twelve noon lunch appointment.

"Thank you Beverly, please call his office and let him know that I am leaving right now, but may be a few minutes late. You can go grab some lunch if you like."

Lori Turner, a new girl from down the hall, had stopped by to see Beverly when the phone rang. Bev held up one finger that told Lori to wait just a moment while she answered the call. Bev answered, "Senator Kaspar's office, this is Beverly."

Jimmy Fred said, "Hi Bev, Jimmy Fred. Is the Senator still there?"

Bev's face showed a painful look. Her friends called her Bev. She had never given Jimmy Fred permission to call her Bev.

She said, "I am sure he will want to talk to you…uh…, Mr. Fred, but let me see if now is a good time, he is about to leave for a meeting. Hold, please."

Beverly placed Jimmy Fred's call on hold and slowly shook her head. She rolled her eyes, slightly embarrassed at calling Jimmy Fred, Mr. Fred, but she really did not care. He was such a sleaze that she wished he would just go away; crawl back under whatever rock he had materialized from. She covered her mouth with her left hand as if passing on a secret. She said to Lori, "This guy was just in here." Beverly thought, h*ow stupid is the name Jimmy Fred anyway.*

Lori was next to Beverly's desk looking amused at the reaction of Bev to the phone call.

Softly she said to Lori, "This guy is bad news, I just know it. But you watch, the Senator will take his call."

Bev pressed the intercom button on the handset. "Senator, Jimmy Fred is on the line. Would you like me to take a message?"

Senator Kaspar said, "No, I will take it. Thanks Beverly."

Though no one else was in the office, Bev once again held her hand up to her mouth, but this time whispered in a confidential manner. "This guy is way too familiar."

Lori asked "Who is it?"

Beverly rolled her eyes and took in a deep breath, "His name is Jimmy Fred something or other. I don't know what his last name is unless it is Fred."

"What do you know about him?"

"Not very much. He just seems a bit shifty and I don't think the Senator sees that," Bev said slowly moving her head side to side.

"Oh, he's probably harmless. But it is odd, the access he has with the Senator. You know, I bet he is a college friend or something like that," Lori suggested.

Bev did not even have to think about that, she said, "No, he's no college friend. Jimmy Fred's a deal maker of some sorts. He has been..." she did not finish because the Senator's door opened abruptly.

Beverly had not noticed that the phone light was no longer lit.

"Beverly?" the Senator questioned while coming out the door.

When he saw Lori he stopped dead in his tracks and said, "Oh I'm sorry. I did not mean to interrupt. I did not know we had a guest."

Bev straightened up in her chair and said, "No, no, no, Senator you are not interrupting." Bev thought how stupid that sounded.

Trying to alleviate the uncomfortable moment, Lori was quick to step in and said, "Hello Senator, I am Lori from down the hall. It was me who was interrupting. I was just on my way out, but nice to meet you."

And she just walked out without another word. Senator Kaspar had a somewhat amused look on his face. He looked over at Bev. She had returned to her computer not realizing or ignoring that the Senator was expecting an explanation.

Not to be ignored, the Senator asked, "Your friend, was it Laura?"

Beverly pivoted back in her chair to face the Senator. "Yes, but her name is Lori."

There was silence. The Senator was expecting more information, but Bev seemed unmotivated to continue. Beverly was embarrassed that she had been talking about Jimmy Fred and was hoping that the Senator would just go back in his office and shut the door. She hoped that he was not listening to what she told Lori. Maybe he had heard and that was why he was asking so many questions. The Senator recognized Beverly's unease and thought it strange.

Finally the Senator said, "I don't believe I have seen her around. Who does she work for?"

"I think she is fairly new. I believe she is with Senator Todd's staff," offered Bev.

He started to continue his questions, but thought it would appear that he did not trust Beverly. He shrugged and returned to his office. Something was odd though and he picked up the phone and dialed Senator Todd's office.

Chapter Five

Salt Flats Housing Project – South Border of the Lazy C
Ranch

Approximately 10 miles northeast of Phoenix and
near Scottsdale, lay Salt Flats, with a population of about
6,000 inhabitants. In June 1879, President Hayes
established the Salt Flats Pima–Maricopa Indian
Community. Through executive order, Hayes allowed the
Pima and Maricopa people to inhabit about 87 acres of
fertile land. Today the Salt Flats Community included such
modern day conveniences as a drug store, a nearby Wal-
Mart, the Talking Stick Golf Club, as well as one casino.
About 19,000 acres has been apportioned as a natural
reserve. The parcel included the beautiful Red Mountain
which could be seen throughout the community. The Pima
Indians or "River People" made up half of the population,
along with the Maricopa (people who live toward the
water). The Project had provided a home for quite a few
families just outside the Scottsdale area.

On an almost barren piece of land, a group of
children were playing a game of tackle football. The boys
had divided themselves into teams of six. The team that
included Mark, the tallest boy of the group, was getting
ready to kick off after scoring the teams' third score. The
game was now tied at 18- there was no point after- and the
game had occasionally become a bit confrontational, but no

more than usual. The occasional skirmish or argument was to be expected when twelve preteen boys got together for some football. It was almost time for dinner and the next score would win. The kick was a high punt and was fielded by one of the boys named Stevie "Small Feather". He started right, but quickly reversed his direction causing two of the opposition to run past him. He had just a couple more players to beat up the field and he would be in a foot race to score. He was fast, but Mark was bigger and faster. Mark, the kicker, waited to see which way Small Feather would go. He moved across to his right, carefully so as to remain in position to make the hit. Mark watched Small Feather fake and then speed past two of his teammates. Mark was the last defender and had to make sure that Small Feather did not get past him to the end zone. Mark did not like Stevie and the two had been jawing back and forth for several weeks. Small Feather had the goal line in sight, but Mark looked forward to leveling the little puke. The touchdown line was marked by two tin cans at opposite ends of an old rubber garden hose. Stevie had successfully juked around all of his pursuers except one. Mark was shadowing Stevie with the intention of stopping him and maybe hurting Small Feather some too. Stevie appeared to be on a collision course with Mark, when at the last second Stevie veered to the sideline. It looked like he was going to escape for the score, but Mark put on a burst of speed, reached out, and barely grasped Stevie's t-shirt. Stevie kept running even though his progress was dramatically slowed. The faded red t-shirt stretched to the point of tearing; then finally ripped. The tearing sound could be heard by everyone. Stevie "Small Feather" began cussing immediately as soon as he heard the shirt ripping.

"You ripped my fucking shirt, man!" Stevie yelled.

He only had a couple shirts and none to spare. His mother was going to beat him for sure. Stevie recovered his stride, despite the torn shirt and finished his TD return, thus ending the game.

Mark, upset over the giving up the final score, said, "So go to Goodwill and get you another one, Navajo." Mark had a menacing look on his face. He moved up close to Stevie, with his nose almost touching the shorter boy's forehead.

Stevie took one step back and planted a foot and took a swing. Mark ducked and raised his arm to deflect the blow. He threw a counter punch that glanced off Stevie's ear. The power of the swing caused Stevie to step side ways and stumble a bit. Steve instinctively went to a crouch, and then kicked straight out and landed a blow right into Mark's sagging scrotum. All the other players let out a gasp and empathetic groans. Mark doubled over and collapsed onto the ground. He grabbed his crotch and tried to catch his breath. Mark dry heaved a bit and started rolling over and over. He was crying and everyone was standing around just watching.

One of the boys said, "Man, it was just a shirt. You did not have to do that."

Not addressing the comment directly, Small Feather looked at his victim and said, "Screw you Mark, you were asking for it."

One boy standing off to the side said, "That's cold man."

Chapter Six

Miami, Florida.

It had almost been two weeks since his blow up with Stanton. Back at home, following a good night's sleep, Chars Reynolds was sitting at his kitchen table. The Saturday edition of The Miami Express lay unfolded on the table and Chars was sipping on a cup of Millstone Vanilla Cream coffee. He was reading his follow up article to the Key Largo Zoning Scandal in the Miami Express. This time his article had been published just as he had written it. Chars smiled at the thought of the commotion he had caused. Stanton had been trying to get Chars to quit ever since the Assistant Managing Editor had been promoted. Chars' previous boss received a promotion to Managing Editor leaving the void at the number two spot. Charles figured that the corporate big wigs must have owed Stanton a favor, because he was certainly an unimaginative boob.

In retrospect, Chars agreed that a couple of the points Stanton had made were valid. One, he had not provided enough incriminating evidence and two; his work was not quite finished. Chars was still correct in his original assessment. His fear that someone would snatch up his juiciest details had been unjustified. Chars realized now that he was so far ahead of the curve that no one was even sniffing around, much less making any connections to the scandal. The few extra days of tying up loose ends were worth it.

He leaned back in his chair and said aloud with a sense of satisfaction, "Chars, you did yourself proud." He stood, cinched up his bathrobe and topped off his coffee cup.

Thinking about what else he needed to do, he checked his Time Text™. He read his note- "Call Deb in Tampa" with the number written just below. He meant to do it as soon as he returned from Key Largo, but had not really wanted to. Of course he did not mind talking to Deb, one of his old girlfriends, but she wanted him to help out her nephew or brother, he wasn't exactly sure, with some fishing license. That was just going to waste his time and he really did not want to get involved. But Chars would do it because he was a pushover when it came to women asking for favors. Who knows, maybe the story would be more exciting that it appeared on the surface. The more exposure he got the better. He had always envisioned himself at one of the more prestigious papers. He thought the Post might want him to move to Washington D.C. at some point. At least if that happened, he would not have to report to Thom Stanton. Chars picked up the phone to return the call from Deb.

"Chars thank goodness you called back," Deb Coughlin said with enthusiasm. "I just know you can help."

"Thing is Deb, I don't think I can, but let me see if I have this straight," Chars said just trying to be honest. "Your brother is a fisherman..."

Deb interrupted, "My nephew."

Chars corrected then continued, "Your nephew. The new law that was intended to help fisherman out of the Tampa Bay is actually working against him. He missed a deadline and now he can't get a new permit. Is that close?"

Deb jumped right in without hesitation, "That's exactly it and the law was supposed to protect the fisherman by limiting the number of boats that could sail out of the harbor. But they kept delaying the license availability. David went in three times, but each time there was some reason why they would not issue him a license. And Chars," she paused, "both his parents were killed in 911. He really has no one to look out after him."

Chars was now thinking that the 911 attack on the twin towers hook, might work. Who could turn down that story? Chars thought that little bit of information added the human interest that was needed.

"What reason did the Bay Authority give for not giving him his license?" asked Chars.

Deb let out a breath of exasperation and then said, "Well, you should really call David, but he said the first time he went in they did not have the stickers and would not even take his information. The second time they told them that he needed a safety check form from the Bay Authority."

"So they weren't ready the first time but did not bother to tell him that his boat had to be inspected as part of the licensing process?" asked Chars, warming to the story.

He was seeing the same old mismanagement that was famous within bureaucracies. It never seemed to fail that laws passed were well intentioned, but often failed miserably in the application. Chars thought that David might be better served by the local television station. Most of the television stations had troubleshooters that loved to get on the evening news and tell all the world of the atrocities of government. It was hard not to become cynical about the efforts of government. Chars recently completed a story about tobacco. Farmers recently were able to return to profitable farming once the government subsidies and restrictions were removed in 2004. Prior to that time, and for almost 60 years, the United States government had provided payments to tobacco farmers. Even at the same time that the United States government was telling of the evils of smoking. What lunacy: government taking in millions of tax dollars all while extolling the evils of tobacco. Making this scenario even richer were the mandates from federal lawsuits that required tobacco companies to run advertisements that gave people resources to quit using tobacco. What other industry has to run anti-advertisements discouraging the use of the very product that they were selling? It was pure silliness, as if it was some type of inside joke. The politicians thought they had succeeded in punishing the evil doers. It was later determined was the anti-smoking advertisements caused young people to see smoking as a cool way to rebel. Teen smoking rose almost 18% after the "don't smoke" ads began. Chars marveled how our politicians failed to learn that they could not dictate how people would act. Charles realized Debra was still talking.

She continued, "Not only did they not tell him that he needed the permit, but they left out the fact he would also have to schedule an inspector to sign off on his boat. The next time he went in which was almost two weeks later they wanted proof of insurance." Deb was clearly frustrated.

Chars also liked the passion that Deb showed. Chars had a brief flash in his mind about a first sexual encounter the two had shared. He thought it was on a boat of some kind, but he was having trouble remembering.

He returned his mind to what Deb was saying, "So he goes back two weeks ago and they tell him that all the permits had been issued and he would go on a waiting list. In the meantime he would not be able to sail in or out of Tampa Bay."

Chars thought about that for a moment and asked, "Not that I am suggesting this, but how would they know if someone was sailing without one of the new permits?"

"I thought the same thing, But Dave says that the Bay Authority has hired a whole new set of officers that do nothing but ride around looking for these damn license stickers." Deb sounded as if she had just been completely deflated following the lengthy explanation.

Chars remembered that Deb was the consummate crusader against injustice. She once made a trip to Tallahassee to protest a state law that limited the rights of the elderly to vote absentee. Now he remembered it was on a ship. A media party of some sort and ... his memory faltered.

"Where does it stand now?" asked Chars

"I have not talked to Dave this week, so I am not sure. Chars, I know that Dave could give you more information if you called him directly. Tell me you will see what you can do, please," Deb pleaded.

Chars was trying to remember why they had stopped seeing each other and he remembered that the distance between Miami and Tampa had just been too much to overcome. Neither was willing to move or give up their career, so they just stopped contacting each other over the course of a year.

"Of course I will Deb," Chars promised that he would call Dave. Both agreed that it was good to talk.

Chars said, "If I need to come to Tampa, maybe we could get together for dinner."

"Absolutely Charles, I would love to see you. Thanks so much for your help," Deb said with sincerity.

Chars ended the call, took a deep breath, and let it out slowly. He said aloud, "Charles Reynolds, why are you such a pushover? But, lunch with Deb and maybe a just a little afternoon delight!"

Chars immediately called David. After patiently listening to the same story Deb had told, Chars began his questioning. He deduced that Dave had thrown in the towel. He spoke as if he had resigned himself to fact that you cannot fight city hall.

Chars asked, "Dave, have you called one of the television trouble shooters?"

Dave had not called anyone. Chars was having trouble getting excited about this story. Even with the 911 slant, Chars was reluctant to get involved in something that seemed like a local dispute. He envisioned this little fishing boat and the government trying to weed out some of the congestion. But at the end of conversation, Dave said something that convinced him to make a trip to Tampa.

Chars asked, "Are there several other fishermen that are in the same, well, uh, boat?"

Dave gave a pathetic laugh, comprehending the unintended humor. "There are three."

"Three," Chars said thinking aloud. Then he asked, "Are there any reasons why you think you three might have been singled out?"

Dave hesitated a moment and said, "What do you mean?"

Chars exhaled and said, "Is there anything you three have in common? Same type of fish, same type of customers, same type…" he hesitated, "ethnicity?"

Dave thought about this and said, "No I have not thought about that. We catch whatever we catch and there is not a lot of difference in what we go after. I guess all three of have similar equipment, our nets and stuff. What else did you ask?"

Dave was sincerely considering what Chars was asking, but evidently was confounded by the line of questioning.

Chars tried to remember what he had asked. "Any other commonalities: types of customers, or ethnicity?"

"Oh yeah, we all sell to the same people and I guess we are all three white." Dave said.

"Okay, that is something. Were there other white fisherman that got the license?" asked Chars

"Yeah, most of fisherman down here are white," said Dave.

"Then that is not it," Chars stated flatly. He was starting to lose patience with Dave.

"Course, now, Tommy is a WOP and Iggy is a Mick."

"Dave," Chars said trying to get Dave back on track, "can you think of any reason that this happened to you and the other two?"

Dave said, "No, but it almost seemed if the Authority was being paid to be as much of a dick as possible. It seemed like the people there were trying to keep some of us from getting the license."

Something about what David said made him furrow his brow. Maybe there was something interesting going on after all.

"Why do you say that?" asked Chars.

"I don't know. It just seemed like I could have had all my paperwork and they were going to keep coming up with reasons why I could not get the license."

Chars was sure that Dave was leaving something of importance out, but something seemed... well fishy.

"Tell you what Dave, I will come up there on Monday. Give me a place to meet you for lunch."

Chars was thinking that this was probably a dead end but maybe not. Besides it might be nice to see Deb again. Chars ended the call, frowned and said aloud, "So much for the lunch with Deb. Maybe dinner and a nightcap."

Chapter Seven

Tampa, Florida

Monday morning, Charles traveled to Naples and up Highway 75 to Tampa. Charles liked Tampa. It was metropolitan, but at just over 350,000 people it was fairly easy to navigate. Her near tropical climate was far milder than what Miami had to offer. Tampa had so many fun attractions too, Sea World and the Busch Gardens. Tampa was the home of the Buccaneers NFL football team and the Devil Rays, professional baseball team. Tampa served as the spring home to the New York Yankees. Most people did not know that Tampa was the site of MacDill Air Force base. Named for Commander Lesley MacDill, the base had long been a strategic military location as early as World War II. Over the years, MacDill served as the launching point for many operations, but is most well known as the Central Command (CentCom) Headquarters as well as SOCOM, Special Operations Command. Chars was sure that many black ops missions had their genesis at SOCOM.

Chars met David for lunch at Frenchy's South Beach Café. Chars ordered the She Crab soup and the Three Fish tacos. Dave followed suit. The waitress served the steaming bowl with a garnish of parsley and the fish tacos had a side of guacamole. Chars dipped his spoon and took in the rich aroma. He thought maybe this meal alone would make this trip worthwhile.

"Dave, what a great choice of restaurants. I am going to add this to my "Reynolds' top 50 list," Chars said pushing his chair back a little to give his enlarged stomach some room.

Evidently, Dave did not read the newspapers very much and therefore was not impressed. Dave's look of uncertainty verified Chars hunch. Evidently, Dave was ready to get to the point, so Chars began asking questions. When the question and answer session was complete, Chars felt Dave just did not have enough information about why the licenses were being required and what the requirements were. Chars decided he needed to visit the Tampa Bay Port Authority for himself. To properly pursue this matter, Chars needed to get some detailed information about Dave's boat. Following lunch, Dave took Chars over to see the Wampus Cat.

Chars said, "This is yours?"

Dave's face lit up with a big smile, obviously pleased with Chars' response.

"Many people would look at a craft made in 1986 and be immediately turned off." Dave said.

Chars answered, "Well, sure it is no Royal Caribbean, but Dave, this is an impressive ship."

Dave was proud of the Wampus Cat. He was eager to tell Chars all about it.

"It is a 102 foot long Raised Focsle Clammer with a turbo charged CAT D398. This baby can put out 850 horsepower."

Chars still had a look of disbelief. He obviously was not expecting such a big craft.

With a questioning look, Chars asked, "Dave, doesn't something like this run several hundred thousand dollars?"

Dave's chest swelled up with pride and he began nodding his head.

"I got a great deal on her, Chars. I bought her on EBay."

Chars eyes widened in further disbelief. "EBay?"

Dave was smiling ear to ear.

"I had a 58 foot Steel Stern Trawler built in 1977. I put it on EBay and sold it for $50,000. Then I turned around and bought the Wampus Cat using the $50,000 as a down payment. I was able to get financing for the remaining 95%."

Chars did the math in his head and his mouth dropped open.

"This boat cost a million dollars. Dave, I am sorry. I just thought.., but this… this is impressive."

Chars had asked as many questions as he could think of, but some piece to the puzzle was missing. A piece that maybe he could find at the Tampa Bay Port Authority.

Chapter Eight

Tampa, Florida

Chars parked in a Tampa Bay Port Authority, visitor spot and walked through the automatic doors. Inside the smell of the bay had all but disappeared. Chars never really liked the smell of fish and the fresh air was a welcome relief. He was looking for the license and registration department. Checking the marquis, he found the office he was looking for.

Chars wandered down one hall and entered the significant offices of the Tampa Bay Port Authority. He stepped into a line that was about 8 people deep and he waited. Chars hated waiting in lines. He checked his watch. He read all of the signs on the wall. He began fidgeting while looking around for reasons this line was not moving any faster. He thought, no wonder this was taking so long. Only one clerk was serving customers. Chars looked around trying to see other workers. There did not appear to be anyone in the office.

Chars commented to the older man standing in front of him, "Guess it is too much to ask that they hire two people to take care of this line."

The old man looked up at Chars with a distrustful look. Chars was expecting some agreement from someone in the same situation that he was in. Instead the man looked at Chars like he had just announced he was in charge of the voting machines in Dade County.

Not getting any satisfaction from that conversation, Chars turned to the man behind him. Chars shook his head and gave the man a "can you believe this" look. The man just stared ahead without even acknowledging Chars' impatience. Chars turned back around and left out a big sigh. Was he the only one that had other things to do instead of standing in line waiting for some paper pusher? Chars was disgusted that the bureaucracy was so typical of every government agency.

Chars thought: *How fortunate was the person who could go through life and not deal with government bureaucracies. It did not seem to matter if it was a driver's license or a tax issue, government was inherently inefficient. Maybe all bureaucracies should have to run for office like politicians do. If they did a sorry job, we could vote them out of office.*

It was almost 20 minutes before Chars had advanced to the front of the line. It was only then, that Chars noticed a man peer out from behind one of the inner office doors. Maybe it was Chars' frown or disapproving posture, but something made the 35 year old bureaucrat actually step up to the counter and do some work. He was dressed in a tailored suit and his haircut was fresh. Chars tried not to show the contempt that he felt and wanted to say: *Hey buddy, don't lower yourself to help out here. You have sixty people out here waiting and you are sitting in your damn office. But you're right, we have no choice in dealing with your sorry ass anyway.*

Chars thought that this inconvenience alone could be worth an entire 4 inch diatribe in his column. Chars guessed this new man must be the supervisor. Chars thought, *this was good, I can get answers without some flunky having to say, "I will have to ask my manager."* He was getting the top dog, the king "bureaucrap" himself.

The man waived him over to a new window that had a sign that read, "Next Window Please." Chars could not help himself. He picked up the placard, turned it toward the man and set it inside the counter cubicle. The man's look said, "Who in the hell do you think you are?" On closer inspection, Chars could see the man's grooming included the elimination of a uni-brow. The narrow eyes did not do much for the man's look, but Chars would have been willing to overlook his physical flaws had his mental ones not been so grand.

Chars introduced himself, "Hello, my name is Charles Reynolds. I called ahead. Are you Mr. Smalley?"

The man gave a thin smile, reached over to his name tag and tilted up so that Chars could read it more easily.

Chars read Mr. Jones on the man's name tag and gave a little smirk of a smile that said: *Okay smart ass, I should have read your name tag.* To Chars' surprise, without saying a single word, the man did an about face and returned to his office. Chars should probably have been offended, but was actually amused. Chars thought that Mr. Jones must have been in the military some point to have executed that tight turn. Chars could hear the man ruffling through a filing cabinet. He heard the filing cabinet shut with a little more force than was needed. Mr. Ray Jones returned to the counter with a form that he set on the counter in front of Chars.

In a non-distinct mid-western accent, Mr. Jones said curtly, "If you will fill this out, I will give it to Mr. Smalley."

Chars thought, *where in the hell did you come from you little prick?*

Chars tried not to say anything but it was impossible, "Gee…" he looked again at the name tag, "I am sorry if I interrupted your break, Mr. Jones. But lose the attitude."

The young man said nothing. He just looked at Chars with an expression of someone who was going to take pleasure in making another's life absolutely miserable. Undeterred, Chars began reading the information sheet and each proviso with increasing amusement. He checked the appropriate answers to the questions. He answered in the negative to: "infected with communicable disease," "carrying a weapon or firearm" and "member of police or law enforcement". Chars answered positive to the questions regarding his citizenship, residence and official business. Handing the form back across the counter, Chars had a smile that resonated with 'you have got to be kidding'.

Mr. Jones looked over the form, pulled out a large stamp and started to deliver an authoritative blow. Then in the middle of the pounding, he stopped and looked suspiciously up at Chars.

He said very precisely, "You left this part blank, Mr. Reynolds. You must state the purpose of your visit."

Mr. Jones was 100% serious. Chars was just about to bust out laughing at this person's impertinent attitude. Chars had to use all his self-control not to say something that might get him put on some kind of terrorist list. Years ago, Chars had made the mistake of joking with a Miami Airport baggage handler about handling his bags with extra care. When the man seemed annoyed, Chars tried to make a joke by saying, "Got some of the good stuff in there you know." Chars expected the man to give a little laugh and lighten up. Instead the man walked around to the end of his kiosk and called security. Two airport undercover cops appeared as well as a uniformed officer. Chars was led inside, along with his luggage. He was still able to make his flight, but the experience had bridled some of his clever comments to stiff bureaucrats.

Chars was naturally witty. He did not have to work at sarcasm it came naturally, and in volume. Once started, Chars could barely control himself. Some have characterized him as a gum ball machine that lost its exit mechanism. Chars just smiled and wrote, Port Authority Story: TBBA Licensing. Then he added National Security at the end, thinking that might hit home with the stiff necks.

A full ten minutes later, Chars was ushered into the office of one, Milton Thomas Smalley. All three names were engraved on a name plate on the front of his desk.

Chars introduced himself and presented a business card to make it official. Mr. Smalley seemed impressed with the card, looking at it for several seconds. Chars thought that perhaps he was checking the address in his mind to determine if in fact the card was legitimate. Again, Chars restrained himself from making a joke about the man's devouring of the business card's information. While Mr. Smalley was examining the business card, Chars was studying Mr. Smalley. Not a particularly attractive man but like his employee Mr. Jones, immaculately groomed.

Perhaps the older man was a mentor to the young Mr. Jones. Chars could only hope that Mr. Smalley was more cooperative than Mr. Jones. Chars glanced over at the wall and notice a picture of Smalley with the Tampa mayor and Chars made a mental note to mention the picture. Smalley might be impressed that Chars had eaten dinner with the Mayor once upon a time. Instead, Chars got right to the point and when he asked about the impetus of the license requirements, Charles allowed that Mr. Smalley may have misunderstood the question. Mr. Smalley probably confused the word impetus and impotence.

Mr. Smalley's eyebrows went up to show his surprise and he said, "Well nothing is 100% of course, but we do a fairly good job of monitoring the traffic. National security is of the highest priority here and I would say that we are effective."

Chars tried again, "Mr. Smalley, was this new license procedure introduced for national security reasons?

Mr. Smalley seemed cautious in answering this question. He appeared as if he were evaluating whether this was a trap. Smalley decided to answer despite the danger.

Mr. Smalley gave an emphatic raise of both hands. With an expectant smile he said "Why politicians and generals do what they do. Hey, that's way above my pay grade."

When Chars did not seem to be amused by this attempt at humor, Mr. Smalley rephrased. "Well of course," Smalley stopped to look again at Chars' business card and then continued, "Mr. Reynolds, much of what we deal with here in this office is not for public consumption. But what I can say is that license requirements were established to improve security and limit the number of commercial boats in and out of Tampa Bay."

Mr. Smalley was pleased with his answer, took a long sip of coffee and leaned back some in his chair.

Chars asked, "have the new restrictions caused any discontent amongst the locals?'

To which the Mr. Smalley said sincerely, "No, everyone has been quite understanding."

"I see," said Chars. "Mr. Smalley, have you ever run across the name of David Coughlin of South Shore Fishing? Chars asked and looked closely for some visible reaction.

There was only confusion.

"No, I don't think so," said Mr. Smalley.

Chars believed he probably did not have any idea about anything that went on around here, much less why some poor fisherman lost his chance to receive a license to fish. Smalley picked thru a pile of paper clipped bunches of papers as if searching for the answer.

"Well, I don't see anything here. Let me check the files of patrons who filed negative feedback reports."

He opened a file cabinet behind him and pulled out a hanging folder. Chars saw that the file in fact had a tab that was labeled, Negative Feedback Reports.

"This file contains the complaints filed," Mr. Smalley said as he straightened up in his chair.

He flipped through a very thin file.

Smalley smiled almost triumphantly, "You can see that we have not had many complaints!"

Placing the folder on his desk he flipped thru the paper clipped papers.

Chars said, "Looks like you are very well organized, Mr. Smalley."

Smalley looked up with an earnest smile.

"Have to be, Mr. Charles. Have to be. But Mr. Charles, if that is what you came to find out, let me just ask my right hand man. We will get to the bottom of this."

Smalley leaned over to what must have been an intercom system that had just been installed. He pushed a large button in the middle of the console, but spoke hesitantly.

He said, "Mr. Jones, could you come in here for a moment?" The door next to Chars opened almost instantaneously. It was so abrupt that Chars was startled, sat straight up and then relaxed with a sigh.

"Oh there you are Mr. Jones. You have met Mr. Charles, right?" Smalley asked perfunctorily.

Mr. Jones lifted an eyebrow at the mistaken name, but nodded with an affirmative.

Mr. Smalley continued, "Good, good. Do you know or does the name David..." he paused and looked for help from Chars.

Chars filled in, "Coughlin."

"Yes, Coughlin. Does that name mean anything to you?"

Chars noticed that Mr. Jones stiffened a little as if being challenged.

Jones said, "I am not familiar with every person that comes in here, but I do seem to recall the name. Perhaps you could refresh my memory."

Chars said, "He owns a company called, South Shore; runs a boat called the Wampus Cat."

Mr. Jones turned his head slightly to the left trying to place the name.

"I do remember something about a boat with that name. I think he failed to get his request in on time or was lacking an inspection or something to that effect. I would need to search for the file to be sure."

Mr. Smalley turned back to Chars and said, "Is this what you are inquiring about?"

Chars' demeanor changed. He was finally getting somewhere.

He scooted up on his seat, sat up to his full height and said "Yes, I believe it is."

"Mr. Smith, I was not aware that we had to turn anyone down for a license." Mr. Smalley had a puzzled look on his face.

Jones was confused also having been called Smith. Chars' eyes were watering from trying not to laugh. This poor man must mix everyone's name up.

Realizing that he was encroaching on Mr. Jones' (aka Mr. Smith) normal duties, Smalley softened a bit.

"Do you recall, the reasons, this…" again he turned to Chars.

Chars cued him with "David Coughlin."

Smalley continued, "Yes, Mr. Coughlin was denied a license?"

Chars noticed that Mr. Jones bristled ever so slightly, but Chars was not sure if it was Jones' relationship with his boss or the topic at hand. Mr. Jones was clearly not comfortable with being questioned by his boss, but he seemed to weather the insult of having to explain the situation.

Jones said, "I would have to check his file, but I seem to recall it was not so much that we denied him a license, but more that he failed to get his paperwork completed."

Chars started to ask a question, but Mr. Smalley interjected, "Yes, yes, I am recalling something about this now. But does he have his paperwork completed now?"

Chars briefly had a vision of Colonel Klink in Hogan's Heroes. The man had no clue.

"Yes, he completed the inspection, provided proof of insurance and has submitted the application for approval." Mr. Jones gave the same thin smile that Chars had seen earlier.

"Good, good," said Mr. Smalley, "so that's settled."

Chars was slowly shaking his head somewhat confused.

Chars said, "I am under the impression that Mr. Coughlin is not getting his license."

Mr. Smalley snapped to, as if awakened from a nice day dream. His eyes moved side to side and he shook head as if clearing his mind.

"But Mr. Jones, you said..."

Jones struggled to maintain his decorum and interrupted, "I said," pausing for Mr. Smalley to stop talking, "that he had his paperwork complete. He has turned it in, but it was after all the allotted licenses were issued."

Chars decided to cut out the middle man in this conversation and go to the real source.

He asked Mr. Jones directly, "So what happens to his application now?"

Mr. Smalley was nodding his head in agreement, "Yes, what happens to his application?"

Mr. Jones' thin smile returned. It was an expression of one trying to be patient with an impertinent customer. Mr. Jones was being polite only because he had to be and wished that these people could understand that he deals with these license issues everyday. Chars was sure that this guy was either some kind of control freak or he had been working under Mr. Gingko Biloba so long, that he was about to bust a gasket.

Jones said, "Mr. Coughlin's application went onto a waiting list. Mr. Coughlin will be eligible as soon as the City Commissioners authorize additional licenses."

Jones' expression hardened and he gave another smile. This one said: There you are and fuck you very much.

Mr. Smalley leaned back in his chair with a very concerned look on his face. His hands were placed on his chest and he appeared lost in thought for a moment. Chars just sat there looking from Smalley to Jones and back. Chars leaned forward with his head cocked to the side in anticipation of Mr. Smalley's pronouncement. It finally came.

"This is very disturbing that one of our locals can't get out there and do his thing," he looked to Chars and then to Jones, "You know... fish."

Jones face showed his impatience with his boss, but he said nothing. He was obviously used to waiting till Mr. Smalley arrived at the same place everyone else had been waiting for some time.

Chars started to speak as did Jones, but Mr. Smalley continued and both Chars and Jones stopped mid-word.

"Mr. Jones, I would like to see that file. And Mr. Charles," he paused to look over at Chars and gestured with an open hand.

Chars turned his head slightly to the left and smiled.

"I personally will see to it that Mr.," he paused.

Chars head leaned in and tried to assist, "Coughlin."

Smalley gave several affirming nods, "Yes, Mr. Coughlin gets heard on this matter." Again he paused searching for the right word.

Jones finished his sentence, "Oversight."

Smalley looked to Jones and extended his open hand to his worker. "I think you are exactly right, Mr. Jones. This must have been an oversight and can surely be corrected. I will call the Mayor on this...."

Jones stiffened and Chars saw a slight panic in Jones' eyes. Jones quickly regained his composure. Chars looked very curiously at Jones thinking, what was this?

Jones said carefully, "Mr. Smalley, would it be better if I check to see when we can expect the additional licenses to be authorized. Maybe I could secure an exception for Mr. Coughlin."

Mr. Smalley considered that and looked over to Chars. Chars knew something was up, but was not sure that this was the best time to grill Mr. Jones. Chars main mission was after all to get Dave his license, thus make Debra happy and possibly reap the rewards. His mind started to think about the reward, but he quickly refocused.

"So the Wampus Cat can get the license? When will that happen?" Chars deliberately looked at Smalley for the commitment. Smalley started to speak but only took in the breath. Smalley looked over to Jones for the answer.

Jones said in a very conciliatory tone, "I will have an answer by then end of the week."

Chars was not going to let him off that easy. He knew that this guy would avoid his calls as long as he could and then simply say that the additional licenses were forthcoming at some later date. That would not help Dave. Smalley was nodding that he thought that was reasonable. Chars was not agreeing.

"Mr. Jones, you are saying that you will check. I need something more concrete. Otherwise, I think the story that runs in the Miami Express is going to paint a very unfavorable picture of this office."

Offended by the implied threat, Mr. Smalley sat up straight in his chair. "Mr. Charles, I am disappointed that you are taking that tact. We are trying to resolve an oversight. There is no need for a defamatory story to sully the reputation of public servants."

Chars figured that this guy has practiced this speech so often he has it down pat. Chars' lip tightened and pushed out a short breath through his nose. He was used to pushing these bureaucrats into seeing things his way, but he knew that it worked better if you could put this in terms of benefit and cost. Chars looked at Jones with a distrustful look and then back to Smalley with impatience.

He said with a measured tone, "I appreciate the work you do here. I don't think that a legitimate business man should have his livelihood taken away just because of a bureaucratic snafu. Mr. Jones, you are too young for this, but do you know what snafu stands for?"

Jones just stared at Chars with what might be turning from annoyance to visceral dislike. Jones did not answer. In a surprising moment of clarity, Mr. Smalley did know what SNAFU meant.

He said, "Mr. Charles, that kind of talk will not be tolerated in here. We can get this problem settled without the coarseness. Mr. Jones, please look into getting Mr. Coughlin his license. I know you have many things on your to do list, but do it today. Give me an update by tomorrow. Take this man's number and call him by midweek with what you are able to do. Mr. Charles, that is all we can commit to. We are just the infantry, not the generals. Now, if you will excuse me, I have an appointment to keep. Mr. Jones will show you out."

Chars smiled in amusement at this whole conversation, but Mr. Smalley had turned his attention to some papers on his desk. Chars stood and was escorted to the lobby by Mr. Jones. Once outside amongst the line of people, Ray Jones stepped back behind the counter.

Jones held up Chars card, smirked, and said in a dismissive tone. "I have your card."

Jones turned and walked into his office and shut the door, Chars looked at the line of people. Fifteen people in line, still one clerk. *Snafu,* thought Chars.

Chapter Nine

Tampa Bay Port Authority

Jones sat down behind his desk. He felt a dribble of perspiration run from his underarm down his side and his body gave a little shiver. He stood up and then sat down again. He pulled a number from under his desk pad. Jones brought his hand to his mouth while contemplating his situation. He let out a deep sigh and dialed the cell phone number he had been given in case of emergency

"We have a problem here. We need to talk."

The person on the other end said, "I will have to call you back on a different phone."

Ray Jones stood and moved over to the window wall of his office and separated two of the plastic mini-blinds. Hoping the reporter had left, he angled himself to see to see the furthest side of the outer office and then the other. He closed his eyes relieved to see only the schmucks standing in line.

Ray Jones' cell phone rang loudly, startling him. He quickly silenced the volume. He pushed the green accept button. He heard the familiar clicks and tones.

Jimmy Fred's upbeat voice was recognizable, but a little distorted. "Okay. What's up, my man? You got my delivery I hope."

Ignoring the statement, Jones said in a panic, "You remember the fishermen that I had to delay so that your boats received licenses?" Jones was speaking in short bursts and did not wait for a reply.

He continued, "A Miami reporter, named Reynolds, was here, wanting to know why one of the fishermen did not get his license. Smalley got involved. If this Coughlin guy does not get his license, the Miami Express guy is going to run an article about the inefficiency of the Bay Authority. If he keeps digging around, he is going to figure out that Coughlin's was one of those licenses given to your boats."

As if knowing something that Ray did not know, Jimmy Fred answered in a calm tone, "Ray, don't get your knickers in a twist. You can handle this. Our boats are legitimate. They're owned by a company that will hold up."

Jones was incredulous. "You don't think that the shit will hit the fan when people find out it is a gambling boat?"

"Look, The Oasis is a legitimate business. These ships are sailing out of every port along the Atlantic and the Gulf of Mexico. They paid for their license, the other schmuck didn't."

"I think you are underestimating this Reynolds guy. I looked him up. He is a heavy hitter in the news business; some kind of Ralph Nader. This Coughlin guy must be a friend of Reynolds or maybe Reynolds has an interest in the Wampus Cat. He's going to know that I deliberately delayed Coughlin's application."

Jimmy Fred wondered, *what is a Wampus Cat?* He was annoyed by these minor irritations, but could tell that Ray was upset and this could possibly escalate. "So, if he wants a license, find him one. The reporter, you said his name was Reynolds, he will go away."

Jimmy Fred wrote the name Charles Reynolds from Miami Express in the margin of a note pad.

"Yeah, right," Jones said knowing that the seriousness of his situation was not fully appreciated. "That was the problem in the first place. This license quota was not about security. It was about unions and blue crabs and who knows what other bull shit agenda. There are not likely to be anymore for at least a year."

"Look Ray, I don't think this is that big of deal. What about issuing a duplicate license?" Jimmy Fred said while starting a doodle of a sailboat on his notepad.

"I can't just create a license sticker. They are inventoried and numbered, plus, there aren't anymore for that size of boats. Remember? That is why you needed me." Ray was very agitated. "If Smalley sticks his nose into this we could really be in for trouble. He is just likely to go to the press. Then all hell will break loose."

"Ray, calm down. You say you got lots of licenses for the smaller boats. Just fudge a little on the size of this Wampus Cat," Jimmy Fred said as he swirled his bourbon and ice. "If anyone asks, say it was a clerical error. Happens all the time with organizations like yours."

There was a pause while Ray considered that possibility. After thinking thru the possible downfalls, he said, "Well I guess I could do that. They really screwed up when they did the allotment on this deal. They did not know what they were doing. I don't think that the council is going to approve anymore licenses, do you?"

Jimmy Fred blew a smoke ring up in the air. "Ray, Ray, Ray. Don't be so naive. Those boys at city hall and the state boys knew exactly what they were doing. And no, new licenses aren't likely, because they made this out to be a security issue. I think they got wind of some kind of terrorist act in the works. Now they are stuck and can't do a damn thing about it. They already know that we did an end run on them. Now look Ray, you slipped into a nice piece of change for very little effort. You don't want to go messing that up do you?

Jones was biting the end of an eraser. "What about the reporter?"

"Okay, I will see if I can't get this," he checked his notepad, "Mr. Reynolds on to someone else's shit. Ray, next time only call me in an emergency, okay."

Chapter Ten

Washington, D.C.

"Senator Todd's office, this is May speaking."

"May, this is Senator Kaspar. Is Marcus around?"

May Wilson recognized Senator Kaspar's voice and she immediately tensed up. "No, Senator, Senator Todd is in a committee meeting. I think it is your committee."

"Right, right. I have been delayed unexpectedly," Kaspar said, but he had already decided not to attend the meeting.

"Can I direct you to someone else?" May knew that Senator Big Stuff was not going to talk to a lowly staffer, but she asked anyway.

"No I was just conversing with a lady in my office and wondered how I could have missed out on hiring her, a Miss Laura, I think her name was."

There was a pause, but May made the connection. The Senator was inquiring about Lori. May thought, *what a piece of shit Kaspar was. He was a dog looking for the first hole to stick his dick in.* She made a mental note to let Lori know about the reputation of Senator Kaspar as soon as she finished talking to the asshole.

"Senator Todd did hire a new girl named Lori, but I don't think we have a Laura."

Kaspar smiled and said, "You are right, May. It was Lori."

"Do you need to speak with her?" May said feigning sincerity.

"No, no, no," Senator Kaspar said trying to minimize any suspicion. "I just had not met her before and was curious if she was part of your office staff."

Wishing he had not called, Kaspar realized now that his reasoning was superficial and would probably cause some gossip. That was alright he thought; keep them guessing was his motto.

"Thanks, May. There won't be anything else."

May's face grimaced at the insult of being dismissed by someone who was not even her boss. She tried to not let it show that she was offended.

She simply said, "Yes sir, let us know if there is anything else. Good bye." She placed the phone in the cradle and said audibly, "What a piece of shit."

She stood up from her chair and walked back to a small office that housed Lori Tucker. Lori had been hired just a week ago and May thought that Lori did not deserve to be assaulted by the sleaze, Senator Wayman Kaspar

"Hey Lori, how's everything?" asked May.

"Great May. Thanks," Lori said with a genuine smile.

May wanted to seem casual about bringing up Senator Kaspar, but instead went for the direct approach.

"Say Lori, did you meet a Senator Kaspar?"

Lori looked a bit taken off guard, thinking that there must be surveillance cameras in the offices or something. Seeing no harm in admitting that she had in fact met the Senator, she nodded a confirmation.

She let out a slow, "Yes."

She had a questioning look on her face and May picked up on that. May let out a little breath of exasperation and leaned in so no one else would overhear the conversation. Her voice was low and secretive.

"You just need to watch yourself around him."

Lori raised her eyebrows in surprise. May nodded sadly in a knowing sort of way. She was giving this poor girl some much needed, inside information that would save her some real heartache.

"He is a whore dog," May said in a confidential tone.

Lori's face showed surprise and she asked, "Really?"

Her tone conveyed a slight disbelief that a Senator could be anything less than forthright and honest. She did not want to seem eager and she did not want to do anything that she could not cover up for later. She in fact, wanted to get to close to Senator Wayman Kaspar. Very close.

Lori waited till May had returned to the front reception area before she made her call. She pulled out a secure cell phone and called her real office. Lori listened to the usual clicks and tones and then the phone was answered. It was a male's voice that simply said, "Hello."

Lori said, "Hey Honey, I found the pasta we're looking for. It was where you said it would be." She listened and then said, "Yes, it was in the same aisle as the anchovies." Again she listened. "Absolutely, I am looking forward to sharing it with you. Do you want to take care of setting the table and getting the wine?" Lori Spradling a.k.a. Lori Tucker, Special Agent for Federal Bureau of Investigation said, "Love you too," and ended the call.

At 601 4th Street in Washington D.C., Garrett Loose placed a call to his director. "Lori made contact and says that Senator Kaspar met with Jimmy Fred." He listened for a moment. "Okay, call me when we have the authorization for the tap and we will get it into place."

As soon as he finished the call, Garrett placed another call. "I am going to need a line tap and a bug crew. We are waiting on an authorization that will likely happen today. I want it done tonight. You will have to come up with a cover." Garrett listened for a moment then said, "Russell Senate Building."

Chapter Eleven

Ft. Lauderdale, Florida

Agios Nikos "Nikki" Nikolaos finished up a Super Long Lucky Stripe cigarette and squashed it into the cheap tin ashtray sitting on the edge of the cheap mahogany table. Nikki however was not sitting on anything cheap. He was aboard a 116 foot, Benetti tri-deck motor yacht in Coral Bay in Ft. Lauderdale, Florida. Nikki had just concluded business that would finally allow him to relax without worry of ever running out of money. He had just met with two investors that were going to pay him 41 million dollars. His pizza franchises were strung up and down the Florida coastline, both east and west. Nikki was still recovering from the sting of a Federal Investigation into his Oasis gambling boats. Because of a minor felony charge, Nikki was ordered to sell his gambling business. He had fought it in court and lost. He almost landed in jail, because during the FBI interrogation, Nikki was so agitated, he leapt over the table and attacked an agent with a stapler. Nikki did sell to some corporate conglomerate for about half of what the business was worth. He was bent over by the Feds and Miramar Industries was right there to stick it to him.

Nikki adjusted his trousers, ran his hands through his graying blonde hair and twisted his neck around causing a popping sound. He took the stairs up to the yacht's upper deck. He gave a little wave to the captain and stepped across to the dock. Nikki dug in his pocket for his keys and pressed the control on the automobile remote control. He heard the familiar beep, beep, beep from his white 760 Li BMW. He opened the door, slid in and took the wheel.

The engine ran so quietly, most people wondered if the engine was even on. A perfect combination thought Nikki, *stealth and power*. Nikki slowly accelerated down the private drive. He could feel the road but still felt like he was driving luxury. Nikki appreciated the finer things in life. He knew that you only obtained those things by working hard and holding others accountable. He knew that people naturally slacked off if they could, particularly when it came to making him money. Nikki picked up his cell phone and punched in the number of his lawyer. He gave a half-hearted wave to an armed security guard that he did not recognize. Nikki thought the neighborhood association seemed to go through a lot of guards. The guard returned Nikki's wave and pushed the button to raise the barrier. The guard also pushed a speed dial button on his cell phone. When the call connected he pressed ### and pressed end call. Then he erased the speed dial number from his phone and stepped out for a quick smoke.

The guard's phone call sent a "go" code. It was received by the "control man" who was squeezed into the passenger side of a rented, Chrysler 300. The rental was parked down the street from where Nikki would be turning. The "control man," nicknamed "The Scorpion" measured a full six three and weighed 280 pounds. He nimbly pressed the walkie-talkie function button on his Nextel i580 phone.

He said in a barely audible voice, "The lamb is moving."

Nikki turned left out of his private residential neighborhood and headed south on Seminole. He was speaking to his lawyer, Johnny Brebowski. As usual there were a number of issues to be discussed. Over the years Johnny had become more than a lawyer, he was a trusted friend of Nikki. Nikki did not like having to keep him on retainer, but that was the cost of doing business in today's litigious society. Johnny had covered Nikki's ass several times over the past 12 years and he was going to make things right with the Feds this time. Nikki had been screwed by Justice, but this time he had some information that was going to get him a permanent "get out of jail free pass".

"Johnny, did you check with the Feds?" Nikki asked.

He listened intently. While Nikki was on his way to East Sunrise, three other vehicles moved discreetly onto the road. Nikki did not notice partly because he was stealing a look in the mirror to make sure that his hair was perfectly quaffed. He was also listening to what his lawyer was telling him. Satisfied with his hair, he turned his attention to driving and began to accelerate.

"You know," Nikki said to Johnny, "I knew that Jimmy Fred was a slimy son of a bitch. I never thought he would be in bed with them. So, when did you set up the meeting?"

Nikki paused and listened to his lawyer for a moment.

"Hey, but if they don't want to give me something out of this, tell them to go to hell."

Nikki checked his rear view mirror. This time he did notice a gray Chrysler 300 in his rear view mirror. He frowned having noticed that the trailing vehicle was up so close on his bumper, but move his attention to the traffic ahead and his conversation with Johnny.

"Sure I am going to tell them. If that gets the FBI off my ass and the assault charge to disappear. I will tell them everything I know about this Miramar Productions. But Johnny, Jimmy Fred lied to me and Justice screwed me. So I am expecting a little more than just a pat on the back. Plus these people that are involved in this aren't even Americans, isn't that against the law? I should not have had to sell my boats anyway, that was a bunch of crap. Plus, only to have them bought by...."

Interrupting his thought, a delivery truck nosed out of a luxury villa complex causing an obstruction.

"Hey, look, traffic's a bitch. I am headed to the office now. I will talk to you when I get there. Okay, see you in a minute." Nikki abruptly pressed the end call button and tossed the phone into the passenger seat.

As Nikki's car approached the merging truck he let loose a string of expletives. Nikki downshifted and started to switch over into the oncoming lane, but at the last second slammed on his brakes. There was already some one pulling through his blind spot and directly beside him. It was the 300 and Nikki had no choice but to slow down and let the car pass. But the Chrysler did not pass. It simply traveled along side the BMW matching its speed. Nikki came to a complete stop in front of the Giovanni Vegetable Truck.

Nikki slammed his hand down on the steering wheel and yelled, "Damn Florida drivers." The tinted window of the 300 lowered and out poked a Beretta 93R.

Nikki now realized that he had driven into a trap. He slammed the gear into reverse and leaned over toward the passenger seat. He punched the accelerator pedal, and the front wheels spun causing a spiral of smoke and rubber. But Nikki's automobile did not travel but three feet before it slammed into a second large delivery truck that had pulled in close behind Nikki's BMW.

A flash of automatic gunfire could be seen and heard coming from the 300. In little less than 5 seconds, 20 rounds of 9mm ammunition had been pumped into the BMW from the bottom of the driver's door to the top. Shards of glass exploded on top of Nikki, but it did not really matter. He was dead, killed by the first three shot burst of automatic gunfire. The extra rounds that poured through the vehicle were superfluous, but "The Scorpion" was known for his thoroughness.

When the gunfire ceased, the vegetable truck pulled the rest of the way onto the street and headed on its way. The 300 pulled slowly away and the delivery truck that took the hit from the BMW backed up and headed up the street. The BMW was left a porous shell. The street was typically vacant of people. Today was no different, just as the killers had planned. No one actually saw the attack, but the noise drew the attention of an elderly man who was just walking out of a nearby town home. But, the deed was done and all he saw was the bullet-riddled BMW sitting idle at the edge of the street. Looking around, he saw a delivery truck turn the corner, but did not get a good look at it. Two stories above, a lady turned down the television volume and looked out of her high rise apartment window. She gasped at the site of a white automobile that looked like Swiss cheese. She dialed 911. It would take just five minutes for the police to arrive, but the culprits were long gone. Nikki Nikolaos, Long Island born and raised; a son of an immigrant from the island of Cypress that had risen to height of multi-millionaire, had just been assassinated.

Chapter Twelve

Tampa, Florida

Chars decided that he would head back to the Grand Hyatt Hotel of Tampa. The hotel was situated on a 35 acre, wildlife preserve on the Tampa Bay beach. He loved the fact that upon arrival the desk personnel greeted him by name. Chars took pleasure looking outside his balcony at the view of the bay. Chars selected the Grand Club Double room which was $228. It was well worth the price, especially when it was courtesy of the Miami Express News.

Each room, a spacious 350 square feet, was accented by a large work area and a luxurious marble bath. Chars opened the bottle of chilled champagne. It was a bottle of Joseph Perrier Josephine from 1990. Chars figured that the bottle of champagne alone was at least $100. He cut up a piece of Gouda cheese and placed it on a rosemary and olive oil wheat cracker. The champagne was perfectly chilled, not too dry and not too sweet. He pulled out a note pad from the desk. He wanted to make a note of the brand and year. He turned the bottle in his hand. The vintage delicacy was a pinot and chardonnay blend.

He would call Deb and see if she would be interested in joining him in his suite tonight. Since he was in the Grand Club room he had access to the VIP suite.

Free drinks and appetizers were plentiful and there was sure to be some of the more well-healed Tampa socialites in attendance. Later on, well, that would certainly be worth looking forward to as well. Chars smiled at the thought of rekindling that romance.

He called Deb's cell phone. She answered on the first ring. Chars felt that she was probably anticipating his call. He would play it cool. "Hey Deb, it's Chars."

"Chars, I am so glad you called. I talked to Dave. He called me after you two met. Have you found out anything?"

"I did find out some things that may be interesting. I think that here is a good chance that Dave will get his license. But how quick is the question. Hey, I'm staying at the Grand Hyatt and I can make reservations at Armani's. Would you like to meet for dinner and discuss the details?"

Confidently, Chars smiled at his very tempting proposal.

"That sounds great Chars. I would love to see you again. It will give me the chance to introduce you to my fiancé," Deb said enthusiastically.

Chars' head dropped and he was speechless. She had never said anything about getting married.

Deb continued, "I have told him so much about you. He is really looking forward to meeting you."

Chars managed to recover. "I hope you did not tell him everything," he said, faking chivalry.

Deb laughed and said, "Of course Chars, I had to tell him about us."

Much cooler to the idea of dinner, Chars had to extricate himself from this mess. Chars said, "All right, let me check if there is an opening at Armani's. If not, maybe we can get together for lunch tomorrow before I head back for Miami…"

Interrupting enthusiastically, Deb said, "Oh Chars, I will call Armani's, I know the Head Waiter really well. I know he can get us a reservation. Let's say 8:00 p.m." Changing the subject she said, "Chars, thank you so much for helping out with Dave's problem. Say listen, I have got to go. See you at eight."

And she was gone. Chars stood their in stunned silence. He did not remember Deb talking so fast. Chars sighed and shook his head in disgust with his bad luck.

He yelled out, "Crap! Crap! Crap!"

Chars remembered he needed to check for messages with the Tampa office. He called in to his voice mail. There was a message from the office bitch. "Mr. Reynolds, Mr. Stanton wants you to check in with him today. He is not sure where you are. And, oh by the way, just a reminder, you received a memo last month reminding you that the Express will not reimburse any hotel charges that are not booked through the corporate travel department. Have a nice day."

Chars hit the delete button emphatically and said, "Bitch."

Chars was suffering through dinner with Deb and her fiancé. The Italian cuisine from Armani's was out of this world, but Deb and Roger wanted to give every detail of their meeting. Then as sort of the final twist of the sword, both insisted that he come to the wedding. Chars was immediately thinking about what excuse he would use. A death in the family always trumped a wedding. Chars thought about who would have to die.

After eating, the happy couple wanted to dance while listening to the piano man. Chars watched the couple dance for a little while. When they returned, Chars politely declined a dance and another drink. He said convincingly, that he was beat and really needed some sleep. Deb and Roger probably were happy to see Chars retire; after all, the night was still young.

Chapter Thirteen

Tampa, Florida

Chars awoke with the satisfying feeling of having had sex. Then he remembered that he had only dreamed about it. He thought about the previous evening that held so much promise earlier in the day, only to have his fantasy squashed. He frowned and swung out of bed. He showered, slipped on pair of Hathaway trousers and a Florida appropriate, flowered print shirt.

Downstairs, inside Petey Brown's, Chars sat at the breakfast table with a notepad, plotting his to-do list for the day. His breakfast had arrived along with a steaming refill of his Bavarian Cream coffee. Even though his trip had not included the intimate rendezvous that he had hoped for, he was still determined to see the story through. Something was up with those two idiots at the Bay Authority. He could start the background information for his story now, but he was going to need to call a friend of his on the Mayor's staff. He needed to know who was behind the license. That might clue him in on why Dave's license had been denied.

Chars considered the possibility that the problem was just an oversight. But, Smalley and Jones were truly unique. The old man was oblivious to everything and the young man was obviously in need of a career change.

Chars' phone vibrated. He checked to make sure it was not the office bitch and recognized that it was Dave Coughlin. "Hey Dave, how's everything?"

Excitedly, Dave said, "Chars, you are incredible! I don't know what you did or who you talked to, but it's incredible!"

"What's incredible Dave?"

"I got a call this morning from TBPA. They have my license ready. All I have to do is pick it up." David was effusive.

Chars' brow furrowed and his face scrunched up in confusion. "Really?"

David said emphatically. "Yes! They called this morning, first thing."

"Dave, I would go over there right now before they change their mind."

"Already ahead of you, bro. I am getting in the car as we speak. I just wanted to say thanks. I just figured I was screwed," Dave said with sincerity.

Still with the quick change of events swirling in his mind, Chars asked, "Dave, who called you?"

"I don't know. He did not leave a name that I remember."

Chars asked, "Do you remember who you talked to over at the office that turned you down each time?"

"Well I guess it was the office manager. I think his name was Jones. But Chars, it does not matter any more. They are going to give it to me this morning."

Shaking his head in wonderment, Chars said, "Dave, I am glad it worked out for you."

Chars was really puzzled now. How could Jones have picked up an extra license that fast? If he could have done it this easily, why put up such a fight? Unless, thought Chars, there is something going on much bigger than a measly fishing license. Chars stirred his coffee, but did not drink. He turned the cup in circles. What could possibly have been the reason for denying Dave and two others their licenses? He was really curious now. He called the Mayor's office and asked for the Chief of Staff, Darryl Johnson. "It is Charles Reynolds."

Darryl Johnson was getting ready to read the Tampa Morning Gazette, with his usual attentiveness. It was neatly folded on the corner of his desk. He needed to ferret out any potential problems for the Mayor. His phone line buzzed and the intercom came to life. "Mr. Johnson, a Mr. Reynolds is on one."

Darryl smiled and said, "I will take it, Margaret, thanks."

"Chars you old scurvy dog. I have not heard from you in over a year!" Darryl said enthusiastically.

He and Chars had gone to high school and college together. They worked on the high school yearbook together and then the college newspaper.

"Good to talk to you too, Darryl. It has been too long. I am here on a story, but I needed some background information."

Darryl said, "You are in Tampa? We have to get together."

Chars said, "I would like that. Maybe for dinner tonight. I will have to see if I need to head back to Miami or not. I need some information."

"If I have it, it is yours," Darryl said quickly.

"I am working on a story that involves the Tampa Bay Port Authority. I am trying to find out who pushed for the license change for the Bay?" Chars asked.

There was a pause.

"Interesting, interesting. Chars, what have you found out?" asked Darryl.

Chars stopped to consider how much he should pass along, but dismissed a sense that this was a touchy topic. "I am looking into the story from a security perspective."

"Security?" Darryl's brow wrinkled somewhat amused. "Did someone tell you it was about security?"

Chars raised his eyebrows and tried to recall where he first received that obviously erroneous information.

Chars said, "I guess when I talked to the head of the TBPA."

Darryl broke up laughing. When he got himself somewhat under control, he asked, "Did you get to talk with Milton Smalley?"

Chars was getting the picture now. Darryl knew all about Mr. Smalley.

"Yes. Quite enlightening about the professionalism that you are able to employ here in Tampa," Chars said.

Darryl had regained his composure and relaxed. "Smalley is all right. He has been around for ever and is about to retire. The Mayor is going to let him finish out his last few months and then start the job search for a new TBPA head. Are you interested?"

That thought caused Chars to miss his mouth while sipping his coffee. He tried to catch the liquid before it stained his shirt.

Darryl started laughing again, "Chars, I am just joking. We have several people lined up for that job. What did Smalley tell you?"

Chars was smiling now too at irony. He was amused at the thought of working for the government instead of trying to expose corruption.

"Not anything really. These candidates that you have, is a Mr. Jones in the running?"

"Probably thinks he should be. He's a real prick. He will last about fifteen minutes when we get somebody new in there. He's a senior clerk because he has been at the TBPA for 2 years. He acts like he's in charge. I don't know how he even got the job. He must have known someone, somewhere. I think he knows once Smalley is gone, he won't be far behind," Darryl said with a little bit of satisfaction.

Darryl unfolded the Tampa Gazette. In a headline story it read, "NIKKI NIKOLAOS KILLED IN AMBUSH" the byline said, "Mob Connections Questioned."

Darryl held the phone in place between his shoulder and ear. He began to fish through his desk for his personal phone book.

"So who is behind the new requirements?" Chars asked, cutting back to the chase.

There was a pause and when Darryl spoke again it was clear that his demeanor had changed. "Excuse me, I am sorry, Chars. What did you ask?"

Chars thought he needed to clarify and said, "I am just trying to figure out who's idea this new fishing license was and I thought you would know."

"Well that is a bit more complicated than a phone call. Can we just say that it had several proponents?" Darryl was obviously choosing his words carefully.

"Come on Darryl. Was it the defense department or mothers against drunk boating or who?" Chars asked.

"The problem is, Chars, that I know that this is probably going to end up in your column and I would need an asbestos suit if it was connected to me," Darryl said very softly.

It was obvious to Chars that he was worried that someone might overhear his conversation. Chars was confused by this abrupt change in tone. Perhaps someone had come into his office.

Chars paused and asked. "Could you talk more freely out of the office?"

"I don't think you understand. This is not something I can talk about at all." He rephrased, "Or want to talk about at all. This is something that I would advise you to just to take a pass on."

"Darryl, I am sorry. This must be a touchy subject around your office. Maybe we should leave this conversation for dinner," Chars tried to backtrack. He was astonished at Darryl's change of demeanor.

"Chars, I can't really help you on this one. Sorry to cut you off but I am heading into a meeting, and I have to go. Give me a call the next time you are in town." The line went dead.

Chars' face crinkled and he thought, *what in the hell was that? What happened that caused that? I have known Darryl a long time and that was not like him at all.*

Chars was still trying to figure out why Darryl's demeanor had changed so abruptly. He gathered up a newspaper that had been left at the table next to him. As Chars looked at the front page, he saw the headline about a Miami restaurant owner that had been gunned down in Ft. Lauderdale. Now it was his turn for an emotional shock. Not for the same reason as Darryl, but nevertheless, Chars knew the man. He had interviewed and knocked around with him. They were not close friends, but Chars considered him a friend nonetheless. Chars' heart sank as he read on.

The article detailed how Nik the Quick (as he was referred to by close friends), was in the process of negotiating a deal for his restaurants. He recently sold the rights to a floating casino company out of the Tampa Bay and Ft. Lauderdale areas. The article also included a short biographical history of the man and his story of rags to riches. No arrests had been made and the police were inferring the murder was a professional hit.

Chars skimmed the article for pertinent details: The FBI was involved, but very few clues had been left; The murder weapon was a semi-automatic pistol; The slugs were being tested, but nothing of consequence had been gleaned from the evidence; The only real clue was that the assassins drove a Chrysler 300; His cell phone was recovered at the scene; Nikki evidently was talking to his lawyer right before the hit, so the Feds were following up with him.

The article said that Nikki had been on his yacht meeting with some potential partners. Chars remembered being on that vessel. It was nice, but clearly not as luxurious as some out there. Chars had traveled on the gambling boats as well. They were not very luxurious either. Chars figured the 150 foot cash cows were kept very

Spartan to save on costs. People went on these little trips to gamble on a budget. Nikki always seemed to understand who his customer was. Chars remembered thinking that Nikki was enjoying 'The Life''. But now that someone had whacked Nikki, maybe Chars' life was not so bad after all. Chars read on. The hit occurred just outside his residential area while he was driving. Witnesses had been few, but two people did fill in the blanks with some decent information.

Chars had little wonder about who made the hit. Nikki was always bucking the system, but he had pissed off the mob. Chars thought this was a classic mob hit. They had to have killed him. They must have been upset about a union issue or the gambling issue. Chars thought that maybe Nikki had promised his gambling boats to someone and then sold out to someone else.

Chars had followed the story about Nikki and the Justice Department in the paper, but decided to stay out of that scrap because he genuinely liked the man. Nikolaos had put together an impressive group of restaurants. Starting with nothing he built his empire. His mistake, which he would even acknowledge, was that he got greedy. He decided to get in to the gambling ship business. He bought two boats that sailed out of Tampa, and one out of Ft. Lauderdale. Chars had been on The Galleon, once. It sailed out of Ft. Lauderdale, made a huge loop in the Atlantic Ocean and then returned home. The trip was okay, but Chars had not been that impressed. The gambling boat was fixed up, but it was hard to match a real casino. Chars' mind returned to Nikki's murder and his stomach felt nauseous. He swallowed the last bit of coffee in his cup and went to the counter for a refill when his cell phone vibrated.

"Hey Chars," the caller said in a deep scratchy Brooklyn accent.

Chars smiled because the caller ID had already alerted him to the fact that call was coming from the Miami Police Department. Sergeant Jerry Collins had been Chars' friend for almost seven years. Jerry was a stout man, not quite six feet, with the gray encroaching on the bottom half of his head. Chars thought him to be a slight look alike for Fred Flintstone. He usually looked a bit disheveled, but not sloppy. Jerry looked every bit the part of a cop; square jaw and barrel chest. He walked on his toes like he was always ready to tip over. He constantly had to tuck in his shirt to compensate for his lapping belly. His voice still had the roughness of a former cigarette smoker. He reminded Chars a little bit of a lighter version of the late Chris Farley of Saturday Night Live.

The fact that police officers and reporters were seldom friends was not lost on Chars. The two of them however had become friends over the years after Chars assisted in solving a murder-suicide case that Jerry was investigating. The two just seemed to hit it off.

The relationship had grown and their families had enjoyed cookouts and other outings together. Jerry's gruff exterior masked his sense of humor and good nature. Chars was just the person that could cause Jerry to double over with laughter. When Chars' wife died in an automobile accident a few years back, Jerry was there for support.

Still a bit solemn from the news about Nikki, Chars asked, "What's up Jerry? How's the family?"

"Good, good," said Jerry.

Jerry did not volunteer any further details. Chars was genuinely interested but realized that if Jerry was calling him during the day, that this was a business call and something was up.

Jerry did not waste a lot of time getting to the point of his call. "Have you read the papers? Did you hear about the hit over in Ft. Lauderdale?" asked Jerry. Chars moved back over to the table and creased the paper over to the story about Nikki.

"Actually, I was just reading about it. I know he could be a pain in the ass for a lot of people, but I really liked him."

Jerry thought about that and said philosophically, "Yeah, I never met him, but he seemed to be a pretty good guy. I guess if you piss in enough canteens, eventually someone is going to shit on you.

"What's the talk?" asked Chars.

"Has mob written all over it, but we can't say that," Jerry said.

"I thought it might because of the union deal. You know, Nikki never gave in to hiring union workers," Chars said.

"Except that he sold his gambling boats. Why hit him after he already sold?"

"Maybe the family did not like who he sold it to," Chars responded.

"Maybe. Anyway, that's the direction we are going. We have picked up a couple thick necks that really fell into our lap," Jerry said in a matter of fact tone.

That got Chars attention. He sat down readying himself for the next bit of information.

"Really? In Miami?" asked Chars.

Without pause, Jerry continued, "Miami Dade patrol pinged a car on a traffic stop. They rolled a stop sign or something like that. When they did a license search, the car was registered to Thomas Topolo."

Chars thought that name meant something and then remembered where he had heard the name. "As in "The Hammer" Topolo?"

Jerry said, "That's the one."

"I have heard of him, but who is he again."

"Topolo is the reputed Chicago mafia boss that oversees the Miami organization. He spends a good bit of time down here. At least enough time to need a car on call."

Chars reached for his coffee and the last bite of a wayward sausage link. He sipped and chewed while trying to put this story in context. He knew there was a mafia, but did not think about the mafia in Miami.

"In Miami?" Chars asked somewhat disbelieving.

"Hey we have them and about half dozen other groups that we are constantly trying to shut down: the Mexican Mafia, the Cuban Mafia, the Chicago Mafia, the Russian Mafia."

"You are joking?" asked Chars

"You live a very sheltered life, my friend."

"I am a reporter, so why wouldn't I know about all of these?"

"Because if you knew about them, you would not be with us anymore."

Jerry continued, "Evidently the car that they normally drove was in the shop and Thomas lent the boys a car to drive. One of the cops remembered the guy getting nabbed years earlier in a larceny case."

Chars asked, "If Miami Dade cops recognized them, does that mean they were local?"

"I don't think so. Those guys get around, Chicago, Miami, Las Vegas. They have got to check on all their business enterprises," Jerry said wryly.

"Did they find anything else, say like a Chrysler 300?"

Jerry laughed a little and said, "No, but since that car was reported in the paper, I expect the Lauderdale police will be answering leads on suspicious 300's for the next few days. I would not want to be driving one. Nikki was a popular guy in Ft. Lauderdale. I can see someone doing something stupid if someone driving a 300 looked suspicious."

"What about the car in the shop?"

"We thought about that; not a Chrysler either."

"So there is nothing to tie these two guys to a hit in Ft. Lauderdale."

"No, but, they were carrying $45,000 in cash."

Chars whistled and said "Really?"

Jerry continued, "Well anyway, the cops called in some back up and hauled them all in for questioning. One of the thugs had a license to carry that probably should have been denied when the background check was done."

Chars interjected sarcastically with, "You mean a criminal record would not have made the guy a good candidate to have a legal weapon?"

Jerry said, "Exactly."

Chars said, "And let me guess, the gun has been tied to the hit."

Jerry said, "Actually no, but the boys in Organized Crime were able to detain them until they could get a search warrant for the trunk and their hotel room."

"And what did they find?" asked Chars.

There was a pause and Jerry said, "Nothing incriminating. They found a piece of paper from a spiral notebook." There was another pause.

"Let me guess," Chars said angrily, "it had the address of Nikki Nikolaos."

"No, the note had the initials C.R. on it."

Chars thought about that for a second and furrowed his eyebrows and giving a disbelieving smile. "That could be anything. They may have been supposed to pick up a bottle of Crown Royal." Chars said.

"It also had the initials M.E." Jerry said and let the comment hang there.

Chars thought about the coincidence of his initials and Miami Express' initials being on the same page. Jerry waited for a response, but Chars was silently considering the possible ties.

Jerry finally said referring to the Organized Crime Unit, "The boys in O.C. brought it up to my office when they could not figure out what it might refer to."

Again, Jerry paused. Chars was trying to make the connection. He could not.

He said to Jerry, "It had been over a year since Nikki and I talked about anything or spent any time together. That was before the FBI and Justice Department made him sell the Oasis gambling boats.

"Chars, this is an awful big coincidence. And the two of them were in Miami. If the mob has you on their list you ought to leave town," Jerry said.

"I am already out of town."

Jerry said, "Good. Stay there."

"But now I am thinking I need to get back quick." Chars said.

"Oh yeah, that's exactly what I would do. Come back to Miami, so they can measure you for your own pair of concrete sneakers," Jerry said with dripping sarcasm.

He was speaking as a friend, even though it came off as a little condescending. Deciding that he had probably gotten his point across, he continued.

"Is there anything else that you are working on that would piss off the mob?" asked Jerry.

Chars was silent.

Trying to jog Chars' memory Jerry asked, "What about any stories on gambling or the restaurant industry that Nikki may have owned or a business that he may have had a financial interest in?"

Chars still said nothing, because he could not think of a common thread. Chars continued to search his memory, but nothing came to mind.

"No, I really can't think of anything," Chars said.

Jerry said, "Well, give it some thought. I have not told the OC boys about my little intuition. I did not want to set them on you without at least talking to you first. It may just be a complete coincidence."

Chars said reflectively, "Yeah, a coincidence. I will do some thinking, but I can't think of anything."

Jerry said, "Just thought you would want to know that the F.B.I. is now showing some interest in these boys as well."

Chars said, "The F.B.I.?"

Jerry said, "I only know what I hear, but if you say you don't know anything, then I guess it is all just a coincidence. But, give it some thought and let's meet for drinks later in the week. In the mean time, I would stay out of town if I were you. They turned them loose this morning."

"So they are still in Miami?" asked Chars.

"Yeah they are in Miami, The O.C. boys said they will call me with anything else they uncover on this."

Chars said, "Thanks Jerry and give Melody my best."

Chapter Fourteen

Salt Flats Housing Project – South Border of the Lazy C Ranch

Two days after the football game ended abruptly, Stevie Small Feather and his group of friends went out the door of Stevie's cinder block house. They headed towards the plateau in a casual stroll. On the other side of a court yard stood Mark and his group. Stevie look straight at the group and showed no fear.

Mark said, "Where you going, Stevie?"

His tone was one of contempt. Stevie was wearing the faded red shirt that he had been wearing during the football game. It had been mended, but did not quite fit right around the shoulders.

"None of your business, juedo," Stevie said knowing that Mark would take offense to the term.

Mark turned a fighting red and said, "Small Feather, should be changed to Small Dick."

Mark's entourage laughed in unison. Stevie was embarrassed, but would not let anyone else see it. He felt the need for a real insult.

Stevie said, "Your mother didn't complain last night."

Mark took a step forward and said. "You're a yellow, ball kicker."

Stevie said, "I'd rather be a ball kicker, than a ball licker."

Mark let out a growl and charged Stevie. Stevie stepped to the side and let loose another front kick, which once again was on target. Mark doubled over and fell to the ground holding his crotch for the second time. He began to wail. Mark's friend thought about rushing Small Feather, but when Stevie crouched down ready to unleash another mighty strike, they thought better of it. They began a verbal barrage that would embarrass a sailor.

Stevie simply stood up straight and said, "Any of you pukes want your nuts in your mouth, just come on."

No one moved and the groups separated. Stevie's friends just moved away toward their original destination. Stevie looked over his shoulder and saw Mark being helped up by his friends. He was still holding his crotch and crying.

Creating a little misdirection, they walked parallel to the tree line. Lil' Mike said, "You got to show me that kick man, it's nasty good."

Looking behind to make sure no one was following and no one could see the three boys double back after ducking into the forest. Stevie, Sean and Lil' Mike were following a trail that led up a slight incline. They moved along at a determined pace toward the plateau. It was a trip that they had taken several times during the beginning of the summer months. It took them almost twenty minutes to arrive at the crest. They proceeded thru a greenbelt until it ended at a large stand of trees that bordered a huge lake. The water looked inviting and they sat down on a fallen tree. Each of the three kicked off their shoes and stripped off their shirts and slipped off their shorts. Sean uncoiled a rope left from a previous trip, and threw it over a branch of a large oak tree that hung over the lake. He tied a slip knot and pulled it tight.

Stevie approved and said, "This is going to be great."

Sean tested the line with a big pull and gave a big smile. He wrapped the rope around his arm and took several steps back on the bank. He leaned forward and broke into a sprint. His momentum carried him out a good twelve feet over the serene lake. He let go of the rope, flew several more feet and dropped into the cool, blue green water. When the rope returned, Small Feather reached out over the water and retrieved it. He took several steps back and ran as fast as he could. He reached the peak of his swing and did a flip, landing a perfect entry into the water. Sean was the next one to go and from there on, it would be a solid hour of swinging and splashing. The pure joy of uninterrupted boyhood continued until the three boys were worn out. They finally took a break and were lying on the bank enjoying a mixture of shade and bright sunshine. An occasional breeze caused goose bumps to form on their brown bodies. They talked about their school, their football games, their parents and their neighborhood. They talked about their plans for life, their dreams, and of course, girls. They told stories, jokes and lies.

Stevie was telling a story about his cousin Ricky, when the sound of a motor stopped him in mid-sentence. It was coming from the other side of the lake and was growing more audible. They froze and thought about whether they should retrieve their clothes. Their position would be comprised if they tried to recover their clothes. Instead, the three of them quickly moved into a crouch behind a nearby tree. They were still small enough to fit undetected. They remained motionless as the late model vehicle pulled toward the water's edge on the far side of the lake. The car sat idling for what seemed to be an eternity to the boys, but in fact was just a few minutes. It was impossible to make out details within the car, but a driver's silhouette could be seen. The door finally opened and a man dressed in a suit and sunglasses emerged with a cell phone to his ear. Stevie signaled to the other two boys to move into a better place to observe and not to be observed. They moved silently around a bend under the cover of the trees and undergrowth to take up a position where they had a clear view of the car. The man appeared agitated as he talked on his cell phone. They could hear his voice, but were too far away to be able to discern what exactly he was saying. While he faced away, they continued to creep closer and almost covered the entire end of the lake. As he predictably turned in their direction, the boys dropped to the ground and the cover of high grass.

"I want to hear what he is saying," said Stevie.

Both, Lil' Mike and Sean were shaking their heads no, but each time Stevie moved closer, they were right with him. Curiosity was overcoming their fear and within a few moments, the three of them were within earshot of the man's conversation.

They could hear him say, "Yes, I am here, but how in the hell am I supposed to know where to look. This is a huge lake."

He paused for a moment, obviously listening to the person at the other end of the conversation.

"Screw you. You tell me to take care of it, but how am I supposed to do that, when I don't know where to look.

The water is not exactly clear enough to just see to the bottom, you dick."

He began to swear in a foreign language that the boys could not understand. The boys had advanced around the lake and were now laying belly down under one of the many low lying branches that laced the edge of the water. They did not dare to move. Carefully the boys watched this strange man and tried to figure out what the interloper was saying and why he had invaded their private lake. Again they were on the move around the edge of the water and found a good viewing point. The tall grass would conceal their presence. They were close enough to throw a rock and hit the tires of the vehicle. The man on the phone was pacing up and down the bank of the lake. He was heavy set, about five foot seven with black hair and an olive complexion. Stevie could see that he was not Indian, but was not sure what nationality he was. Sean caught a glimpse of the man as he turned around and saw a hand gun strapped to his side.

Sean whispered quietly, "He's got a gun." Stevie quickly brought his finger to his lips to signal, be quiet.

Sean whispered, "I got to pee."

Stevie gave him a glare that said, shut up. Sean gave a pitiful look that said what am I supposed to do? Lil' Mike rolled his eyes. Sean quietly rolled to his side, facing the lake and began to pee down the bank. Ten seconds later, he was finished and shook himself. He gave a little smile and they all returned their attention to the man. But the man had disappeared. The three of them were scanning the banks and the trees, but the man had disappeared.

From the side of a tree, off to their left, they heard a rustling sound and the man said, "What in the hell are you little queers doing?"

It was a rigid statement with a funny accent, but all three of the boys jumped to their feet in absolute fright. The man was standing within five feet of them with his gun pulled.

"You little shits were spying on me and I am going to cut your dicks off and feed them to the turtles!"

The man moved toward Lil'Mike and grabbed his arm.

Sean let out a slow, "Mister, we did not see anything."

Stevie did not wait for this situation to get worse. He stepped forward and let loose a kick that caught the man right between the legs. The man released his grip on Lil' Mike and let out an animal yelp. He doubled over and instinctively grabbed his crotch. The ball kicker had struck again. The boys scrambled away in to the underbrush and ran for their lives. Through blurred vision, the man saw three naked bottoms sprinting toward a stand of trees.

Sean turned to see the man as he dropped to his knees and heard him moan and say, "Oh my God!"

Charlie "The Shark" Fratelli took off his sunglasses and wiped his eyes. He tried to regain focus. The three devil children had skedaddled by the time Charlie had brought himself upright. The pain was agonizing but his anger was building. If he only had time he would track those insolent shits down and cut off their scrawny little balls. He pushed the Sig Sauer P229 into his waist and reached for his cell phone. It was not in his pocket. Charlie felt panicked for a moment, but he saw that the phone was in the grass next to his foot. Despite the pain, he sighed in relief, picked up the phone, composed himself with deep breaths and hit redial.

Still wiping tears from his eyes, he returned his sunglasses to his face and said, "One of the little shits kicked me in the nuts and they took off running."

Charlie could hear Luigi laughing and telling the others.

"Hey Luigi, fuck you; this should have been you and Little Don doing this not me."

"You know we had something detain us in Miami, Charlie or we would have been there," Luigi said.

"Okay, tell me again where it is?" asked Charlie

He listened. "Okay, I see the tree and it is opposite of the tree. That is where I was just looking you asshole. I did not see any markers!" Charlie the Shark said, looking down the bank.

He then looked in the direction that the boys had run away. He was still in too much pain to smile, but the thought that he might actually get his hands on those three was a pleasant thought. At that moment he saw movement off his sightline. It was a red shirt being pulled on by an Indian boy less than 50 yards away. Charlie started moving that way, while trying to listen to person at the other end of the call. The boy looked back over his shoulder through two trees. The Italian and the Indian made eye contact and they both froze in time. Small Feather smiled, gave Charlie the Shark the finger, and bolted away. That really pissed Charlie the Shark off, but he would never the catch the fleet footed Indian boy. Not today.

He began venting his anger on Luigi by yelling into the phone, "There is not supposed to be anyone here!"

He listened. "But there was! Do you hear me? What if they have seen something that they are not supposed to have seen?"

Again, he listened. "No!" he said emphatically. "They did not see me do anything, because, I have not done anything. I cannot find the marker."

Charlie walked around to the spot where the boys had redressed. He was looking around back toward the greenbelt and then back into the water. He continued walking and listening.

Charlie the Shark looked around and then, in Italian, "Questo sembra una distanza molto lunga trascinare un corpo. Potrebbe essere che vado la sbagliata indicazione intorno il lago?"

The caller evidently acknowledged that possibility of the wrong location because Charlie the Shark was nodding as if I told you so, you stupid idiot. He would have to come back later with Little Don Fratelli, Charlie's brother.

Charlie the Shark looked around one more time and said, "I don't see no fucking blue marker." He ended the call and walked back toward where the boys had been dressing in hopes of seeing where there ran off to. He saw the rope hanging from the tree and all the foot prints the boys had made. He looked toward the direction they had run, but could only see trees. He was not going to traipse through the woods right now.

Charlie did not find the blue marker, but he did find something that made him smile. He found a boy's athletic shoe.

He picked it up and felt that it was still damp. Inside the shoe, written on the tongue in permanent ink, was the name Sean.

"Just like Cinderella." He said with a smile, "You are going to regret kicking Charlie the Shark in the nuts."

Back at the housing project the boys were still shaken, but had recovered enough to be breathing normally. They had gathered in Stevie's small bedroom. Stevie was lying on his bed staring up at the ceiling. Lil' Mike was lying on the plank wood floor staring out the window. Sean was curled up in the corner of the room with his legs tucked under him.

"But why would he have had that gun?" Lil' Mike asked. Stevie had wondered the same thing.

Lil' Mike, called that because his dad had been Mike, said, "We need to forget we saw the man, and hope we never see him again."

Stevie had considered that as well.

Sean asked, "Who owns that land anyway? I bet it was not that guy. He looked lost."

Stevie said, "He wasn't lost. He was looking for something and did not know where to look."

Sean said, "I don't care what he was looking for. I just want my shoe back. My mom is going to kill me when she finds out. I can't even think of a good story to tell her."

Sean sounded as if he were going to cry.

Sean, I have an extra pair that you can take. Just tell her that you got yours muddy and I loaned these to you," Lil' Mike said.

"Thanks, Lil' Mike," Sean said, "I think we should tell Amos."

Amos was Sean's uncle and the Sergeant in the Tribal Police.

Small Feather thought about that and said, "If we tell him about the man, we have to tell him we were at the lake."

Sean said "And then Uncle Amos tells my mom that we were off wandering around where we weren't supposed to be and then...," for effect, Sean brought his open hand down on the wood floor.

It made a huge pop. The other two boys jumped at the noise and then glowered at Sean who was oblivious to their looks.

Sean continued, "Whack, my fucking butt gets the switch!"

Prior to going to bed, Stevie decided he was going back to the lake first thing in the morning. He wanted to find what that man was looking for. He would get up early to investigate. He would recover Sean's shoe and maybe even a treasure chest of money.

Chapter Fifteen

Salt Flats Indian Reservation

Early the next morning Stevie woke without an alarm. It was Saturday and his mother would be sleeping in. She always worked late on Friday, sometimes very late. At the restaurant where she waited tables, it was not uncommon for the townspeople to gather late on Friday at the diner. Stevie thought he could be up and gone, way before she woke up. Maybe even return before she woke up. He slipped out of bed and into his red t-shirt. He pulled on a pair of boxers, then his gray gym trunks. On his way thru the kitchen, Stevie opened the refrigerator door, and pulled out a quart of milk. He took two swigs of milk from the carton before returning the plastic container to the shelf. He exited toward the back yard and silently closed the screen door on his way out.

Stevie breathed in the morning air and smelled the scent of the coming rain. The valley needed rain, but Small Feather wanted it to hold off until he had his mission accomplished. It seemed like a short trip out the back of the Salt Flats Housing Unit and across the fields of scrub grass, cactus and briar. Stevie "Small Feather" was used to dodging various plants and things that could inflict serious pain. The stickers alone could cause some painful pricks by themselves, but the wound could also get infected. Stevie's mom used to swab a bit of Campho-Phenique on his bug bites and cuts. But she had not seemed so worried about those things anymore. When his Dad left, (his parents were never married), Small Feather was only seven. His mom seemed much more attentive to his needs back then. But now, she had to go to work. Stevie guessed that before Dad left, she could focus more on him since that was her job. Marta, Stevie's mother, told her son that his father had joined the American Army. Stevie had remembered feeling proud of his father. It was not until later that he heard his mother talking to Stevie's grandmother, that he realized that his dad was not coming back. Since then it was just the two of them.

He tried to ask what happened to his father, but his mother just said, "Your father is not coming back." The look she gave him warned him not to say anything else, nor ask again. He also tried to ask some of his relatives secretively. They always just said, 'You will need to ask your mother about that.' Small Feather just settled on the story that his father was killed in the American Army, but he resolved to find his father one day. One day, he came home to find his mother crying. A friend of Marta's wrote that Stevie's father had been killed trying to rob a convenience store in Texas. The owner shot and killed him so that was that. Stevie decided to stick with the Army story. It sounded better.

Small Feather climbed the last incline just before the plateau that was the home of Respite Lake. There was an increasing cloud cover and Small Feather felt a gentle breeze. Even with the wind it was already in the middle 80's. The rain would cool off the area when it came. Small

Feather turned his face into the breeze from the west and again smelled the rain coming.

During the really hot months, morning was one of the best times to go swimming. The water was so cool from the evening temperatures and the sun was perfect for sunning. Today, he would not have time for swimming or for that matter, sun for tanning. Stevie was much more cautious this time as he came upon the stand of trees leading up to Respite Lake. He quickly maneuvered through the stand of trees. When he reached the southerly tree line, he crouched down behind a tree and peered out. As usual, no one was there. It was as quiet as it has always been. The surface of Respite Lake was placid except for the occasional splash of a fish coming to the surface to snag an insect.

Stevie and his friends had been coming up to Respite Lake all summer long. Lil' Mike and Stevie had discovered the oasis one late afternoon on an exploratory hike. It was easy enough to get thru barbed wire fence if you knew where to look. The boys really did not take the faded No Trespassing sign very seriously since there did not appear that anyone was around that cared.

Small Feather and Lil' Mike let Sean in on their find, but otherwise had managed to keep the secret. Small Feather did not know for sure, but he believed the property had been uninhabited for quite some time. And it was a shame to have a lake that nice and no one to use it. Stevie thought to himself, *I wonder what is on the rest of the ranch. There has got to be more than just this lake. I bet there is a house or barn or something. Maybe next time I will explore the rest of the property.*

Small Feather reached the furthest edge of trees where they would normally strip and stash their clothes. He again checked to see if anyone was looking. There was not. The rope hung lifelessly; Stevie draped it up on a branch where it normally rested. Stevie replayed the events of the other day in his mind. He remembered that the dark complexioned man was looking for something on the other side of the lake. Stevie slowly walked around the lake, looking deeply into the water. It was clear water, but still it was hard to see down for more than a foot or two. Since Stevie did not know what he was looking for, it was a bit tedious.

He thought, *if I had one of those diving masks I could swim around and I bet I could see everything.*

But he did not have a mask and would just have to make the best of the situation. He slowly walked around about a third of the lake. He had seen some fish and even a turtle, but nothing that seemed unusual. A small groundhog darted from behind a tree causing a startled Stevie to jump six inches in the air. A tin can at the bottom of the lake caught his eye. Stevie pulled a stick from one of the areas that had undergrowth and poked at the can. It was nothing, but Stevie decided to keep the stick for future use. He moved around the periphery, but with no success in finding the buried treasure or whatever that man was looking for. Stevie continued to peer deep into the water, but after almost and hour of walking, he had found nothing. He finally reached where the man had first pulled up with his vehicle and the boys first saw him looking into the water.

Stevie thought, *surely a man, knowing what he was looking for would have seen it had it been where he was looking. Maybe the guy couldn't see so good. Maybe it was just a little too deep. Maybe if I get in there and swim down to the bottom I will be able to see what he could not.*

Small Feather climbed up to the ridge above the lake and checked to make sure that no one was coming. There was not. The lake was truly deserted. He looked around one last time and listened. No one was around and Stevie chided himself for being a pussy. He started to wade in but stopped. If his mother even suspected that he was up this morning swimming, she would switch him for sure. He pulled his shirt off and then his shorts. He gave a second thought about his boxers, but decided he could always leave them behind.

Stevie thought, n*o, what if the man comes back and finds my underwear?*

He would have to take them with him, wet or dry. Finally he decided. He slipped off his boxers and laid all of his clothes behind a rock. One more glance around and he began wading into the water. Stevie gasped at the change of temperature. It was as cool as the evening and when the water reached his waist, he took a deep breath and pushed off into the water. It was colder than he thought it would be and he felt a shiver run throughout his body. It was not long though, before his body temperature began to adjust Soon it would seem colder outside of the lake water than in it. Stevie needed a plan because the lake was too big to just haphazardly swim around willy-nilly. His feet squished into the sediment and lake moss each time he stepped. He felt the mud squeeze between his toes. He figured that anything that was sunk would have to be within ten feet of the shore. Each step that he took left an underground tornado of swirling sand and silt. He felt his feet sink and he had to pull them back out. He felt the suction that was created as

100

his foot sank into the ooze. He needed a plan for sure. If he swam out ten feet and then swam back at an angle he could probably cover most of this side. He did just that and used his hand to reach down to the bottom while trying to keep his eyes open.

Despite the disturbance that he was causing, the water really was very clear. However, opening his eyes up to see was not very comfortable. He had trouble seeing more on his way back to the shore because he had stirred up the bottom silt and sand. But he could still make out the bottom and there was nothing. On his third trip he was getting a little tired and he actually had to make an unscheduled trip to the top to get air. He used this time to check for any interlopers, there were none. He ducked back down and noticed a significant drop off. He would have to go back to the shore, get a deep breath and then return. He swam back to the side of the bank where he could stand. As the sun came from behind a cloud, Stevie peered down into the lake. After the drop off, he saw a glimmer of a blue light or metallic piece of ribbon. He took a deep breath and headed back towards the drop off. There was a significant amount of lake grass more that a foot high at the bottom of the ravine. He could not see the blue object, but realized the sun had moved behind a cloud up above. He was also having trouble seeing because every where he went, he kicked up sand and silt. He ran out of breath and returned to the top.

Wait! There it was again, a blue flash that marked his treasure. It was off to the left a little bit. Big breath, okay let's go.

Stevie thrust himself down as far as he could and made it all the way to the bottom. He could just see the metallic object. It was a tag or something. He could just barely reach it. He grabbed it and tried to pull it. It was stuck on something. With both hands he gave it a tug. The force brought up a section of grass and sticks. One more pull....the corpse of Raleigh Allen was floating toward a horrified Small Feather. With hollowed out eyes and flesh that had been nibbled at by various lake inhabitants, the decomposing body floated up at Stevie. He screamed, causing him to take in a gulp of water. He tried pushing the body away from him frantically. But his movement seemed to just bring the corpse closer. Stevie was panicking, trying to get the corpse away from him. Stevie pushed himself away by kicking the corpse in the mid region. Stevie felt his foot enter the dead body. He panicked and took in another mouthful of water. Gasping and desperately trying to get free, he planted his foot in the body's bony pelvis and grabbed for the water above.

The body, which was tethered to an improvised anchor, slowly fell back to the bottom of Respite Lake. Stevie swam toward the shore, but momentarily was blinded by all the particles that had been disturbed. His stomach raked over a heavy branch on his way back to safety. The pain caused Stevie to flinch, but he was determined to survive. When Stevie reached the surface, he was panicked and nearly drowned. He broke the surface and gasped for air while simultaneously throwing up. The milk that he drank earlier came up with the added lake water. The vomit burned his throat and Stevie was sobbing as reached the bank of the lake. He was crying, coughing and gagging while he pulled himself up onto land. Looking down to reconcile a sharp burn, Stevie noticed a three inch laceration on his lower abdomen. The blood was not obvious because the lake water was still washing it away. However, now that he realized that he was injured, even the adrenaline could not mask the pain of his injury. The cut began to burn worse and the tears of fright became tears from pain.

Still coughing up lake water, he tried to compose himself. Stevie was still in shock, but he began to pull himself up. He managed to get over to the rock and gathered up his clothes. A combination of the change in temperature and fear caused him to shake uncontrollably. He looked around and still no one was there. He began what seemed to be a very long trip around the lake. He was still crying but had managed to stifle it to a sniffle. He finally made it to the tree stand and sat on an old stump that was still in the sun. He pressed his boxers to his cut to try to stem the bleeding, and it seemed to be helping. He would have to wash them out in the lake water or throw them away. His mother would not overlook the blood and she probably would notice that a pair of his underwear was missing. When your wardrobe was as limited as that of Stevie, it was not hard to notice when something was missing.

Stevie somewhat regained his composure, but still shivered. He thought of the corpse's empty eye sockets and threw up again. This time there was nothing left and he dry heaved. Wincing at the pain, he lay down in a patch of tall grass. A moment later, he looked around to see that no one was in the vicinity and headed back to his home. He was completely repulsed when his foot penetrated the body. He would take a shower when he got home. And then, Stevie stopped in his march back home, and another thought made him sick to his stomach. He was going to have to tell someone about the body. Tears welled up in his eyes at the thought of the dead body, but Stevie wiped them away with his arm and continued on to his home. He would make it back home before his mom awoke after all.

Chapter Sixteen

Respite Lake, Lazy C Ranch

A dark blue Lincoln traveled on East Shea Boulevard toward Respite Lake. Little Don Fratelli was the passenger and his younger brother the driver. Both were tired from flying in late the night before, but pressed on with their mission. The morning sky revealed the fact that a storm was brewing and the brothers were trying to make their early morning recovery and avoid the inevitable downpour.

"Okay, I know that we have to move the body, but why does it have to be done right now?" Charlie asked.

"I told yuz. The owner of the Lazy C is coming in tomorrow. We mayz not be able to get backs on the property. If somebody finds da body, wez going to have some shit hitz the fan. Capisce?" Little Don said with a patience that was required when dealing with a small child.

They pulled off the main highway and traveled down a dirt road. Pulling through the gate and over a cattle guard, Charlie slowed down once on the property. He wanted to keep the dust down and not attract any undue attention. They drove past a barn, onward to the fork. Taking the right fork, the car slowly ambled toward Respite Lake. Another 100 yards and they had arrived. Charlie swung the car around so they could back up to the lake.

"We needz to hustle befores that rainz getz herez," Little Don said.

"Okay, I want to see you find this marker," Charlie said.

"I don'ts knows hows yuz could miss it. Did yuz bring the fish hook?" Little Don asked.

"Yeah, yeah, I got the hook. I had the hook the last time," Charlie said with a bit of an attitude.

The two men, one very large, Little Don and one medium, Little Don's younger brother Charlie, exited the car.

"Come right over here," Little Don said.

He moved around to the left of the car and down to the edge of the water. He was careful not to get is Armani leather shoes wet.

Charlie moved over to where Don was moving. "I was right there. Right there," said Charlie defensively.

Little Don said, "I'm no Injun, but looks like therz been someones else here. Look at that. Were the boys that you saw over here?"

"No, said Charlie, they were around that way and over by the trees." Charlie was looking at the tracks trying to figure out some logical explanation.

Little Don said, "Looks like a liddle person laid down here and walks up to the ridge, then back down. Was this wherez those little bambinos was?"

Charlie was feeling a little spooky now and with irritation said, "No, they were over there," pointing toward the end of the lake. "Then they were over by those trees, Little Don. Just like I said. Let's just find this guy and get the hell out of here before some Indian spook comes down here. I've seen those movies and how's the Indians don't like people messing with their burying grounds."

"Shut up Charlie, this ain't their burial ground, it is ours. Nowz shut up and get over here. Little Don said, "I marked the body with a metal strip from his license plate, because the water is so deep here and the body tends to sink into the bottom. He's probably fish food by now, but we can't really take noze chances with the Kiwi coming in."

"Why would you use his license plate?

"Wez had to gets rid of the plates, you know. So we shred it up and threw it in the desert. Luigi missed a piece so I decided to tie it to the body to help us find it iffin we had to find it. Turwns out we duz."

Don moved down a few more feet and said, "Look about ten feet out. There. Seez it?"

Charley looked down and said, "Where? I don't see it. Where?"

Little Don looked at Charley with disbelief and said, "Charley, are you color blind or something? It is right therez."

Charley looked up at Little Don and wondered if this was some kind of test or maybe a trick. He decided to ask, "Little Don, is this some kind of trick?"

"Look right there yuz stupid blind fuck," Don said and pointed into the water. Charlie lifted his sunglasses and looked hard in the water.

There it was. A bright flashing blue metallic tag about 10 feet out and 6 feet down. Just like "Little Don" said. "Why couldn't I see it before?" Charlie said aloud.

Little Don said, "Let me see those sunglasses, you dick."

He put Charlie's glasses up to his face and looked at the marker. It disappeared. He lowered the glasses and the blue marker reappeared.

"You stupid shit. Your sunglasses, would they be Blue Blocker sunglasses?"

The Shark thought about that and said with enthusiasm,

"Yeah, Blue Blockers. They are."

Little slapped Charlie on the back of the head.

"Hey what did you do that for?" Charlie protested.

Shaking his head in disgust, Little Don said, "Go get the hook and the plastic, Charlie."

Lil' Don opened his cell phone and placed a call.

"Yeah, we got it," Little Don said.

"Okay, hurry up and get that taken care of. It was supposed to be taken care of last weekend."

"There waz some confuzion over wherez da body was sunk."

"I figured that out. Now get rid of it somewhere it won't be found and get to Tampa," Tommy Topolo said and ended the call.

Charlie had successfully hooked the body with a large hook attached to an extendable pole. He dragged the body on shore and rolled it onto the plastic. The two men rolled the body up and lifted it into the trunk.

"Let's get the hell out of here. We gotz to go to Tampa," said Lil' Don as he slammed the trunk lid, "and find that reporter.

Chapter Seventeen

Phoenix, Az.

Hamish Cain arrived from Los Angeles by way of Tahiti and Hawaii. Hamish was having problems keeping his elbows on the seat rest while the plane was landing at Sky Harbor International Airport. After the white-knuckle landing, the small Canadair jet maneuvered to the gate adeptly. Hamish deplaned and made his way through to the internationals arrival area. Hamish removed his visa and passport from his jacket pocket, and presented it to the officer. With nothing to declare, Hamish went through customs with surprising ease. He claimed his available luggage and went straight away to the Rental Car desk. Hamish was not able to claim one personal piece of luggage. Due to a scheduling problem with the airline, that particular package left a full day and one half later than Hamish. He would have to make a return trip to the airport tomorrow.

"How may I help you?" asked a mid twenty, clean cut young man.

In his heavy New Zealand accent, Hamish said, "I am looking to rent a car. Could you direct me to the carpark?"

The man was obviously not used to dealing with foreigners, but was only stumped for a moment. He smiled and said, "I can help you and then I will direct you to the parking lot."

Hamish rented a Jeep Wrangler. He liked the bright yellow color and thought this would be a good tryout vehicle. He planned to buy an automobile after he was in the U.S. and became situated.

He took the keys and began pulling out. He saw a car that was headed directly for him. He swerved out of the way of the oncoming car into the right lane. The oncoming car momentarily slammed on the brakes, causing the front end of the car to dip. It was then Hamish remembered that in the Americas, people drove on the wrong side of the road. Hamish continued on into the right lane and headed toward the exit. The driver of the other car gave Hamish a nasty stare, but nothing else. Hamish noticed the fuel gage was practically on empty and thought that the rental agency had made a mistake.

As he approached the exit and the attendant, he lowered the window and said, "Sorry to trouble you mate, is the vehicle supposed to be so low on petrol?"

"Yes sir, you are to fill up the tank and bring the car back as empty as possible."

Hamish's face showed his surprise. He looked strangely at the young man and said, "Get off the grass!"

The boy just stared at the Kiwi, not knowing what to say. Finally the boy cocked his head to the right, and asking for a clarification, he said, "I'm sorry."

Hamish thought the boy was apologizing for his mistake and said, "That's okay mate. It could happen to the best of us. I am sure I can fill up somewhere near here."

The boy could only smile, because he understood very little of what the man was saying. Remembering to stay on the right, Hamish did find a petrol station without incident. He did a quick calculation to figure what the price would have been in New Zealand dollars, before handing over his newly acquired U.S. currency. He decided that the U.S. gas price was about twice what he would have paid at home. He was able, with the help of an employee of the gas station, to determine which direction the ranch was located.

He took Highway 202 toward the Lazy C. After traveling about 20 minutes, he pulled into the Hampton Inn on Shea Street that seemed to be convenient. Again, communication was more challenging than Hamish would have imagined, but he was able to secure a room. He was given a map, since the desk clerk was from Pakistan or India or somewhere. He noticed a small grocery store across the street. Hamish would buy some basic necessities and maybe a stubbie or two.

Hamish decided to wait until tomorrow to go to the ranch. He had checked into his room without any trouble and sat slumped in a comfortable side chair. He was well impressed with his accommodations. Below his second floor room was a swimming pool. People of all sizes were enjoying the cool water that helped dissipate the late afternoon heat.

He pulled out a tablet and pen from the middle drawer of the desk and began a list of tasks he needed to accomplish. He would assess the living possibilities at Lazy C and then decide how long he would need to stay in the hotel. He would have to find a place to eat tonight, but for now he was content to take a nap. He laid down on the king size bed and was asleep in moments.

After a short nap Hamish awoke, he felt refreshed enough to go exploring. He went downstairs and out the front of the hotel. He crossed the road and entered the store named Salt Flats Easy Stop.

It appeared that there no customers and the only other person in the store was the one behind the counter. She did not acknowledge Hamish went he entered. Hamish thought that she might actually be sleeping. He picked up some basic staple items and looked in the huge refrigerator full of various drinks. Unfortunately the store only stocked canned beer, but Hamish spotted a row of Fosters. He pulled out four cans and placed them in his cart. He decided that he would get a fizzie too, as he was moving to the front of the store to check out.

The lady behind the counter looked like she might be the original owner of this place that could have been unchanged since the middle of last century. She was definitely a native Indian. Hamish made a quick calculation in his head and decided the lady must be in her seventies. She had a weathered face and was wearing a homemade necklace of blue stones. Hamish approached the counter with his intended purchases. She remained seated, staring directly at Hamish. She said nothing. Hamish finally broke the silence. "Can I pay you for these?"

The Indian smiled a huge smile and said, "You are the Crenshaw boy." It was a statement, not a question.

Hamish smiled back wondering about this old turnip.

"Yes, I am. How could you possibly know that?" Hamish said with a puzzled look in his face.

"There is not much that does not come thru this store. People love to talk. Your parents died and left you the Lazy C. I knew you were from New Zealand and as soon as you opened your mouth, well, that was that. I am Mavis."

Hamish was still smiling. Maybe this place was more like his native home that he thought. If something happened in his town, everyone would know about it as well.

"You are exactly right. I am Hamish. I am going to the Lazy C to find out where exactly the place stands."

"Are you planning on living there?" Mavis asked while she was sacking his groceries and beer.

She was not being nosey, just genuinely interested, thought Hamish. She was the real deal, short, squat and tough as leather.

"I will have to see what is there. Maybe you know," Hamish suggested.

"Did you ever meet your former tenants?" Mavis asked in a casual manner.

She was slowly sacking the remaining items, and clearly in no hurry. Maybe she was taking even a little extra time in hopes of picking up some valuable gossip. Hamish was amused by this woman and did not mind being the object of her intrigue.

"Can't say that I have. That was all handled by our real estate man. Their lease was up, so we informed them a few months ago that they would need to vacate. Were you familiar with them?"

Hamish assumed that there was a reason behind her question. Hamish thought that perhaps they had left an unpaid bill. Looking at Hamish for confirmation Mavis had a pleased expression on her face. Again she had information that was germane to the conversation.

She asked, "Was the agent John Edwards?" but she already knew the answer to her own question,

Hamish again smiled. The lady certainly was a great store of information.

"Yes, John Edwards. I don't know him or his location. Maybe you could be of some assistance."

Now Mavis was feeling good about this conversation. Since Hamish did not know the people that were renting from him these last two years, she was in a position of serious superior knowledge. Just the way she liked it.

"John Edwards is a sack of bear shit. He rented your place to a bunch of thugs and hit men."

Hamish's eyes widened with his eyebrows high. He did not say anything, nor did he need to. Mavis was more than capable of carrying on a conversation all by herself.

"Dark cars coming round all times of the day and night. I think they were running drugs out of there if you ask me."

Hamish did not ask her, but he continued following her conversation by having a face that was appropriate for shock and dismay or disapproval, whichever was fitting. Mavis had evidently not spoken to the police, but clearly had discussed her suspicions with everyone that would listen. Hamish thought she had finally finished. He was mistaken. Mavis continued on giving Hamish the "shortened version" of the history of the area as well as the Lazy C.

"Just make sure that all those criminals have evacuated before you spend the night. The old house that is on the property has not been painted in more than two decades, I can recommend a painter if you need one."

"Criminals?"

"They weren't from around here. They only came in the store once, but I saw them when they drove by. Always at odd hours. Late at night or even in the morning hours. They looked like Tony Soprano's group. You know the T.V. show?"

Hamish moved his head slightly side to side indicating that he didn't. The only television that Hamish watched in his home town was at the local sports bar. He and his buddies might stop in if the New Zealand Black were playing away. The bar owner did not actually receive his own signal, but jerry rigged from the neighbors satellite. If the neighbor's wife, Henrietta suddenly switched over to a soap opera, the whole bar crowd would let out a groan. Hamish thought that Henrietta knew exactly what she was doing. Someone would have to go next door, beer in hand to ask Henrietta to forego her show. Usually she would comply with the beer as a bribe. Her favorite was Foster's of course and she liked it real cold.

Mavis continued, "I always thought they were dressed a little too nice, drove new cars and were on the shady side. So when you go out there just be real careful."

Mavis continued on with precise details about the Lazy C and all the various locations. After quite a lengthy lecture and not knowing what to think about this little lady, Hamish simply nodded and said "Mavis I cannot thank you enough. You have been a wealth of information."

He stopped for a moment before exiting the store and asked back over his shoulder, "Mavis, where is a good place to stop for brekkie in the morning?"

Mavis was momentarily befuddled. Hamish made an eating motion with his hand.

"Oh, the diner up the road fixes a breakfast that will last you all day at not much pay," she said and gave him a winning smile.

Hamish had taken care of many of the details prior to coming to the states. He had switched over the utilities to his name and various other tedious items. He thanked Mavis for all her help and promised he would be a frequent customer. He would need to see about the housing prospects, but for now he would stay at the hotel. After checking his map and having Mavis give him directions, Hamish started back out on the highway. It was a short eight and one half minutes before he pulled onto the Lazy C, through the gate and over the cattle guard. The road was still damp from the previous day's hard rain, but the road was packed down enough to remain intact. He passed the barn and made a left at the fork just as Mavis had told him. Not more than a hundred yards up on the left hand side just north of the pinions, was a single story house with a porch. He stopped the car in front of the horse tethering station. Hamish exited the Jeep, pulled a bedroll and his bag from the rear compartment. He turned and took in the view of the ranch from the front porch. It was bigger than he had imagined, but every bit as beautiful. He took a deep breath and headed inside.

Chapter Eighteen

Salt Flats Indian Reservation

The local authority in the Salt Flats Indian Reservation was the Tribal Police Sheriff. Each reservation was its own country, if you wanted to be plain spoken about it. It was a world within a world, with its own traditions and customs. Small Feather had finally gathered his courage and was headed to see Sherriff Amos "Black Sand". He had his story rehearsed and ready to give the account. He was careful not to include the part about the other boys. He would just have to leave out the part about Lil' Mike and Sean. Sean especially needed to be excluded from the story since Amos was his uncle.

When Stevie opened the huge wooden door, leading into the office, it made an eerie creek. Stevie had to lean into the door just get it to budge. Stevie thought the door alone was probably enough trouble to dissuade many complaints. He walked on in the large room. While the activity was minimal, having a small boy enter evidently was no big deal, because no one as much as glanced over to Stevie. Stevie wiped his palm on his shorts and then ran his hand through his jet black collar length hair.

Not knowing what else to do, Stevie just headed toward what looked to be the largest office. He was correct, inside sat Sherriff Amos. He appeared to be resting, but when Stevie cleared his throat, it was evident to Stevie that

117

the Sheriff was simply looking down at some important papers.

He deliberately took in the sight of Stevie and then broke into a warm smile. "Small Feather, I am pleased to see you," Amos said while he stood behind his desk with his hand extended.

Stevie was intimidated at first seeing how large the man was. Stevie thought that while the man was sitting, he could look him in the eye. Stevie shook his hand as strongly as he could while struggling to maintain his composure. Stevie had met the man once or twice before, but never at the police office. While Stevie tried to think of what to say, his eye moved down the big man's body to the weapon holstered at Amos' hip. Stevie wondered if Amos had ever had to shoot someone. He thought about asking him, but decided that it might be better to wait.

"You can call me Stevie," he said, then quickly added, "if you want to, sir." He quickly followed it up with "Please."

"Of course, Stevie, of course. And you can call me, Amos. What can I do for you Stevie?"

Following Stevie's altered version of the discovery of the body in Respite Lake, he rode in the front seat of the police version of a four door Ford Explorer. He marveled at all the technology that was crammed into the front seat area. He also noticed that the front compartment was separated from the rear by a heavy metal cage divider. Stevie knew from watching television that was to keep the bad guys from attacking the officers. Stevie did not realize that every police car had its own laptop computer.

He asked, "Do you ever play video games on that computer?"

Amos let out a hefty laugh and said that once during an 18 hour stake-out, he did in fact play a game called Hearts. Of course Amos was more interested in hearing about this body that Small Feather had come across. Stevie thought the questions would never stop. What were you doing there? What part of the lake was it? Who was with you? Did you see anyone else? Was the body that of a man or woman? Was the deceased black, white or Indian? Stevie was trying so hard to keep his story intact. He did not want to draw in Sean and Lil' Mike. So he had to remember every detail and give his account the same each time. It was difficult to lie, Stevie thought. His mother had told him that very thing. The truth was a lot easier to keep straight because when you told the truth everything fit into place. Lies had to keep changing to fit the new facts as they were revealed. Stevie was glad his mother was not with him while he told his story because she was always able to tell when he was not telling the truth. Amos of course did not believe that Small Feather had been alone, but he did not see any purpose in contesting that fact until the body had been located and identified. He assumed that this little boy had nothing to do with any death, but he might have to push the child a little to get every detail. Amos had already noticed a couple flaws in the boy's story, and he made a mental note to revisit those details. His best guess was that his nephew Sean had plenty to do with this.

The Explorer left the highway and entered the Lazy C entry gate. Amos drove slowly, to allow his eyes to take everything in. One hundred yards in was a small barn that needed a good coat of paint. Since they were not on the reservation any more, Amos wanted to be careful. He decided not to notify the county sheriff until the body was

119

actually located. If this was a mistake, he did not want to sound the alarm.

"Why aren't you driving on the trail?" asked Stevie. He was sitting up on the edge of his seat. He thought he knew the answer to the question but just wanted to confirm his instinct.

"I don't want mess up any tracks that might be needed later," Amos said. "The rain yesterday probably took care of that, but no sense in being careless."

Stevie was confused about where the lake was. The ranch looked differently coming in from the highway side. A fork in the road was ahead. Amos, however, did not hesitate.

"How do you know which way to go?" asked Stevie.

"I know the general direction of the reservation by where the mountains are, and the direction of the lake is easy," Amos said.

He slowed down the car to a crawl and lowered his window. Leaning out of the car he looked down at a set of tire tracks.

"Stevie, you said it was a car, correct?"

Stevie nodded yes. Amos continued speaking while looking over the edge of his door.

"There is a set going in, but I don't see any going out. These don't look like car tires, more of a truck tire. The rain must have washed the other tracks away. Bad luck," Amos commented to no one in particular.

The lake was just over the horizon, and Amos looped off to the right and park about twenty yards away.

"Stevie, we will walk from here. Let's try to disturb as little as possible."

Amos was looking for any tracks while advancing toward the lake. He said nothing while taking steps in a crossover fashion. Every once in a while, he would lean down and look closely. Then he would start walking again.

"I will show you the body," Stevie said as he sat on a large rock protruding from the ridge above the waterline. He began pulling off his shoes.

Amos stopped him. "Let's see what we can find without getting wet." Amos looked around the area and began with the questions again.

"This is where the man was parked?" Amos asked while looking to Stevie for confirmation. Small Feather nodded that it was.

"And he was driving a new dark blue or black four door?"

Again, Stevie indicated yes with a slight nod.

Amos studied the landscape and all the various tracks that the rain had muted but not destroyed entirely.

"Okay, Stevie show me where you saw the body."

Stevie first moved up to the ridge and peered down into the water. He looked up at the sky checking for clouds. He saw a couple clouds, but none that were keeping him from seeing the blue marker. Stevie peered into the depth of the water with complete concentration. He could see nothing.

"Maybe the blue marker came loose," Stevie said, peering into the water's edge.

"Can you see it?" Amos asked. He too, was leaning and looking.

A voice behind Amos and Small Feather caused both of them to jump.

"Good day, gentlemen."

Small Feather was ready to run. Amos was embarrassed that he had not heard the man coming up behind them, but they were concentrating so hard on trying to see the body. For a moment the three of them just stood there staring at each other. Hamish was not trying to embarrass them, but truly curious about what was going on. They certainly did not fit Mavis' description as bad guys, so they were probably just looking for a place to fish or something. That would be fine with Hamish.

"Sorry mates, did not mean to put a scare into you. I heard your vehicle go down the fork. I am expecting the real estate agent and so I thought he must have taken the wrong fork in the road." Hamish continued, "Can I help you find something?"

Amos was trying to figure out who this guy was and how much to tell him. Amos was tempted to unsnap his holster, but thought that might be a bit to overt.

Amos finally said, "Well sir, are you the owner of this property?"

Hamish stepped forward. "Hamish Cain."

He extended his hand and Amos cautiously shook. Small Feather turned his attention back to the lake and his effort to locate the body. He quickly slipped off his shirt and shoes while Amos and Hamish finished introductions.

Amos said, "I heard that a family member was headed back from New Zealand."

Stevie slipped into the water just as Amos turned back to bring the boy into the conversation.

"Stevie, don't…" but it was too late. The little boy was already underwater diving to the underwater ravine. Amos was again embarrassed. He turned back with his hands extended and open.

"The boy came to me this morning claiming that he saw a body in the water."

"A body!?" Hamish said rightfully horrified.

Stevie was under water for almost 30 seconds. He was frantically moving the lake grass around with his hands. The lake water began to burn the cut on his lower stomach. He was running out of breath. The dread of seeing the awful corpse again was replaced by panic. The body had been here, but now it was not. He returned to the surface for another breath. He did not even wait for Amos to say anything. Back under he went. This time he went further down the ravine. Stevie thought the body may have moved further down after he loosened it up. The body was gone.

Stevie swam toward the edge. He was breathing hard from being under water for so long. Amos had a stern look on his face. Stevie had a look of defeat on his face.

Forgetting to address the officer formally, Stevie said, "Amos, it was here. It must have moved with the rain or by somebody."

Stevie looked suspiciously at Hamish. Amos had his eyes closed and was slowing shaking his head. Small Feather couldn't tell if he was upset. He did know that his story would be dismissed as the imagination of a twelve year old boy.

Hamish was still sorting all this out and suggested, "Could it have just been a log or dead animal?"

Feeling challenged, Stevie curtly replied, "It was no fucking log or animal. It was a dead body."

"Small Feather! Don't talk to this man that way. You need to watch your mouth, not to mention that we are on his property."

Hamish was not sure how to react. "No, no. You have nothing to apologize for. I had an active imagination when I was this bloak's age."

Stevie mumbled, "Wasn't my imagination Crocodile Hunter."

Stevie bent over to put on shoes. He was successful but winced at the pain.

Ignoring Stevie's disparaging remark, Hamish noticed the blood.

"Hey, you've taken on a nasty cut. I have a first aid kit at the shack up the road. Let's go up there and get you patched up."

Stevie looked like a rattlesnake coiling to strike.

"Well at least let me take a look at it," Hamish said and moved toward Stevie.

Stevie took a half step back. Stevie flashed an angry look and began to unleash his mighty weapon.

"I wouldn't let you patch me up if ..." Amos stepped in quickly and Stevie's kick never landed.

"Whoa, whoa, Stevie, stop that! What in the hell is wrong with you!?" Amos wrapped the boy up in his arms and laughed out of embarrassment. "The boy is a bit high strung. We will be leaving now."

As Amos was practically dragging Stevie toward the car, Stevie stepped on something metallic. It sliced his foot and he came up lame quickly. He let out a painful yell. Amos thought that Stevie was just resisting and did not realize the boy had actually hurt himself. Amos picked up the wet boy, slung him roughly over his shoulder and carried him toward the police car. Stevie looked back to see what had cut his foot. It was the blue metal tag.

"Amos, there's the blue tag! Stop, there is the body tag!"

Instead of stopping, Amos swung Stevie up and around over his other shoulder. He strode purposely toward his car, opened the rear passenger door and unceremoniously dumped the boy in the back seat like a sack of cattle feed. Amos slammed the door and strode around to the driver's side. Stevie tried to open the rear door of the police car to no avail because the police vehicle did not allow for an unassisted exit from the back.

Hamish was left shaking his head in amusement. He noticed the boy had dropped his red shirt in the melee. As Hamish reached down to pick up the shirt, a blue glint flashed. He dug the 6" metal strip out of the dirt. It was a thin aluminum tag of some sort with two ragged edges. Or at least it was a part of a tag. Blue on one side and silver on the other side, the metal strip now had a small amount of blood covered in sand. There was a small elongated hole at both ends. He paused while looking at the curious find and then taking a look back at the lake, headed up to the ranch house.

Chapter Nineteen

Tampa, Florida

Chars figured there was little else he could accomplish in Tampa. He checked the paper for the funeral home that was handling Nikki's funeral. He would want to attend. Since his death was the focus of a murder investigation, the service may not happen for a few days. But if he went to Ft. Lauderdale now, he might be able to get some information about who had killed him. The fishing license story may have to be put on hold. He could go home for a couple days and catch up on paperwork. Jerry had warned him away from Miami, although Chars thought that risk minimal. Having thought it through, he decided that Ft. Lauderdale was the prudent choice.

Thinking about tying up one more loose end before leaving, Chars called David. "How did the trip to the license office turn out?"

David was still pumped up at the change of events. "Smooth as silk bro, smooth as silk. I still can't believe it."

"David, I need you to do some investigative work for me. I am trying to find out why this happened in the first place. Could you find out who received the licenses originally?"

"Hey, I appreciate what you did, but I am not sure that I want to rock the boat," Dave said and then laughed at the appropriateness of his metaphor.

"Well, I think there may be a story here. You were being given the shaft and when I starting asking questions, somebody jumped," Chars said.

"They sure did." David effused, "I could not have done it without you. If you say you need some information then I will do my best."

Chars was not real good at playing the hero part. He exhaled and said, "Dave, you don't owe me anything and more importantly, if asking questions is going to cause problems for you then I can figure something else out. I just think that if I knew who else received licenses then I can figure out who was behind this mess."

"Okay Chars, I will do some checking and get back to you."

Chars hung up with a bad feeling. He did not want to screw up what he had already accomplished. Dave had his license and he did not think that anyone would renege on that.

He packed up his stuff and went downstairs to check out. As he left, Chars turned back to the young lady working the counter and asked, "Marcy, could you call ahead to your location in Ft. Lauderdale for a reservation for three nights?"

"Absolutely, Mr. Reynolds, I highly recommend the Hyatt Regency at Pier 66," said the nicely proportioned young woman. Chars caught a whiff of her perfume. It was nice and she was very attractive. Chars momentarily thought about asking Marcy for her number. His little fantasy was interrupted when Marcy asked, "Shall I use the credit card that is on file, the Miami Express, Amex?"

Momentarily lost in thought, he did not respond immediately. He realized the question was his to answer and said with an appreciating smile, "Yes, thank you so much."

He really enjoyed having a company credit card and thought: *Stick it up your ass Stanton and Patti. Let them track all the costs they wanted. He was not going to be intimidated by a putz like Stanton.*

His moment of reverie was halted as his cell phone vibrated. It was the office. *The bitch must have my mind tapped, he thought to himself.*

He put on a fake smile and answered, "Charles Reynolds."

"Chars, this is Thom. Where are you?"

Ignoring the direct question, Chars said, "I am heading for Ft. Lauderdale to investigate the Nikolaos murder."

"Good, I was just calling to suggest that you do that very thing. Can you run by here before you leave? I want to go over an angle on this that may not be so obvious," Stanton said in his nice voice.

The voice that Chars had learned meant that Stanton was about to pull a fast one. Chars was immediately suspicious. The last time his editor had requested his presence, the Miami Police were there to question him about his whereabouts during a homicide. Chars started to ask him if the Miami P.D. was in his office, but decided against it.

"Oh, Thom, I can't. I am already on my way. I was finishing up background on another story that involves the TBPA controversy. What angle are you thinking?"

Stanton said, "Oh it will keep until you come in. Think we can see you tomorrow?"

Chars brow furrowed, his face showed contempt. "More likely, it will be toward the end of the week. I am planning to attend Nikolaos' funeral."

Stanton said, "I did not know you were a friend of his."

Again Chars' brow furrowed. "Just a peripheral friend, but I knew him."

Chars was becoming indignant but knew that Stanton was his boss whether he liked it or not.

Stanton said, "Okay, good. And send me the article on the TBPA, I want it before we go to the crush meeting at 4:00."

Stanton hung up the phone. He looked to the two F.B.I. agents and said, "He's been in Tampa and is headed to Ft. Lauderdale."

Chapter Twenty

Washington D.C.

Garrett Loose asked, "What have you got, Mike?"

Loose had just finished a conversation with the Deputy Assistant Director of the F.B.I. It was not a happy conversation. The hit on Nikki ignited a fury of activity and the big dogs wanted to know what happened.

Michael McLemore was sitting in an unmarked Federal sedan overlooking the boulevard where Nikki had been murdered. The seven year veteran of the F.B.I. checked his notes before responding.

"We've nothing down here. We don't know why Nikki got whacked or who did it. Miami P.D. picked up two thick-necks yesterday that would be good candidates. They were part of the Topolo Crime Family out of Chicago. I would say that they were high on the potential perp list, but we really can't place them at the scene. The only witnesses saw the vehicles but since no one got out, they could not identify them. All that they could say was that they looked Italian."

"If they did not see anything, how can they say they were Italian. They were probably watching reruns of the Sopranos," Loose said, shaking his head.

"I don't know. They think they saw the shooter and he was dark complexioned," McLemore interjected.

"Great. So Nikki makes contact with Justice and within 48 hours he gets hit. Sounds like we may have a problem," Garrett said with regret. "I always figured Nikki had mob ties, but why would they whack him?"

McLemore said, "We don't know but, it may have to do with the restaurant sale or maybe the gambling boat sale. Nikki was making noise that he had been cheated out of some of the money for his restaurants. Maybe The Hammer and the boys just got tired of his beefing."

"The common denominator for both was Jimmy Fred," said Garrett, "and that always makes things sketchy. I would love to fit that son of a bitch with concrete shoes and drop him in the Potomac. Okay, what time do you meet with the lawyer?"

"I have an appointment with Johnny Brebowski at 1:00 p.m.," McLemore said.

"Good. See what he will tell you. Probably nothing. He was a real dick when we were dealing with him in Nikolaos' last go round. Anything on the car that was involved?" Loose asked.

Michael sighed but sounded hopeful, "The locals are dragging a nearby inlet. Some young man driving by thought he saw the air release of a car being sunk, but nothing yet."

"What about the lead on the reporter?"

Michael smiled and said, "I sent Ron Eads over to the Miami Express. It was just a hunch, but it turns out Reynolds knew Nikki, so it makes the connection more likely. His boss is named Thom Stanton. He was very cooperative, but Reynolds was a no show at work today. Stanton was able to reach him on Reynolds' cell phone, but he seemed evasive."

Loose liked the sound of that information and said, "Sounds like he may be in hiding."

"Could be, but Stanton said that Reynolds is a Prima Donna. Showing up for work is optional for him."

"Any chance he is involved?" Garrett asked.

"Not likely, unless it is on the exposing end. He is fairly well known for his reports on corruption. He's kind of a smart ass from what his boss says," McLemore stated matter of factly.

"Can we get our hands on him?" Garrett questioned.

"Fairbanks and Terrell are going up to Ft. Lauderdale to intercept him there," McLemore said.

"Good, let's see if we can put the squeeze on this Reynolds guy. Sounds like a real flake."

Chapter Twenty One

North Servery Cafeteria, Dirkson Senate Office Building
Washington D.C.

Munching on the best chocolate chip cookies on the Hill, Jimmy Fred and Senator Wayman Kaspar were talking in a confidential tone. Kaspar had his elbows on the table and his chin rested on his interlocked fists. Normally a cool customer, Kaspar looked pale. His eyes shifted from the front of the restaurant to the back. A small bead of sweat had appeared on his forehead

Jimmy Fred was leaning back in his chair with two of the four legs in the air. He said in a low tone, "I know this thing could go south. But the worst thing we can do is panic."

Kaspar said quietly with mild irritation, "I am not panicking. I just don't see why it was necessary to eliminate Nikolaos. He already sold out of the casinos. What was done, was done."

Jimmy Fred returned his chair to the normal position with all four legs resting on the floor. He leaned in close now conscious that others might overhear their conversation.

"I don't know who hit Nikki," Jimmy Fred lied, "But somebody did us a favor. He was a threat because he just could not let things go."

Jimmy Fred took a bite of his cookie. Glanced around once and then gave the Senator a reassuring smile. The smile did nothing to assure Kaspar.

"This was no favor," Kaspar said with emotion, "it is just going to cause people to look at the deal. Your Miramar Productions is going to get a proctologic exam and all the shit is going to be visible."

"You have nothing to do with Miramar, that's a Florida deal," Jimmy Fred said in a nonchalant manner.

Jimmy Fred stacked three sugar packets together, tore off the top and dumped them into his coffee. Both lifted their mugs at the same time and took a sip. Senator Kaspar looked around nervously, but as discreetly as possible.

"This is way too public of a place for us to meet," Kaspar said as he avoided eye contact with the Junior Senator from Wyoming. "People remember meetings like this. We need to go into a prevent defense," Kaspar said using his college football playing experience as a metaphor.

"I am already on it. I have some friends checking to make sure everything is copasetic," Jimmy Fred said then took another sip of the coffee.

He grimaced and then grabbed another two packs of sugar for his coffee. The cookies may be top drawer but the coffee could use some work. Kaspar was losing his patience now. He leaned in with his face turning a crimson color. Barely audible, Jimmy Fred said in a frustrated tone, "You are messing with my trifecta."

In a hushed anger, he said, "Trifecta, trifecta! Try fucked up. You have no fucking clue about this Jimmy Fred. I do." The Senator paused to gather his self-control. He continued quietly, "This going to turn into a political

134

explosion. The two disappearances in Scottsdale were bad enough and you said that was it. Once you, or whoever it was killed someone as visible as Nikki Nikolaos...who by the way was already on the Fed's radar, bumps the whole case to the front of the line. All I needed was the labor vote in the last election..."

"Which you got," Jimmy Fred interrupted still unruffled.

"Yes, I got..." Kaspar said, but he was cut off again.

"And you also received some major funding for your campaign," stated Jimmy Fred as if reading down a checklist.

"Yes, I did," Kaspar said and gave a deep guilty sigh. Once again, he leaned in for privacy, but this time his anger was in check. "You are dealing with some people that are like..." He searched for a good description.

Jimmy Fred helped him out, "Like bulls in a china shop; ruthless; unforgiving."

"Yes." Kaspar said with satisfaction at having made his point. He scooted back in his chair and adjusted his shirt sleeves, took a bite of his chocolate chip cookie.

Jimmy Fred continued quietly, "The Hammer is not subtle. And Senator, you need to remember that."

Kaspar stopped in the middle of his chewing. His stare bore into Jimmy Fred. Jimmy Fred raised his eyebrows and opened up both hands as if saying, you knew what you were getting into.

Kaspar swallowed his bite prematurely and it caught in his throat. He began coughing and reached for a glass of water. People around the Senator glanced over at the choking Senator. After a minute he recovered and people returned to their respective conversations. Kaspar took a drink and wiped his mouth and then his brow.

Kaspar's vision was still a bit blurred from his coughing fit but he leaned in and said in a quiet angry tone, "Look you piece of crap. I was in a close race and if I didn't get elected, your friends don't get their damn casino."

He pointed his finger at Jimmy Fred, then began driving it into the table. Jimmy Fred's expression remained unchanged, but not his emotion. Kaspar looked away in time to see a young staffer watching and quickly avert his eyes. He stopped pointing and clasped his hands on the table.

"Sounds like we were good for each other and things worked out the way we planned," Jimmy Fred said just before another sip of coffee.

The two were locked in a glare. Jimmy Fred was annoyed, but Kaspar's look was full of animosity. Jimmy Fred finally broke the standoff by offering up a concession.

"Look, Senator, I know that we have reason to be concerned. I am doing everything I can. Your name can stay out of this if we maintain our control."

Jimmy Fred was now speaking in a calming tone.

Kaspar looked directly at Jimmy Fred. He was thinking, *you are going to destroy my career. I knew I should not have ever let you in my door. You are going to ruin me.*

Resigned to his fate, under control and ready to stack sandbags in preparation for the oncoming flood, Kaspar said, "What are you going to do next?"

Jimmy Fred allowed himself a slight smile feeling that Kaspar had decided to get on board with "whatever needed to be done".

"I am going to Florida to Nikki's funeral. After all, he was a friend. My question is: What are you going to do?"

Kaspar pushed back from the table, wiped his mouth and his hands with his napkin. "This needs to be the last time that we meet."

Once again concerned, Jimmy Fred said, "I am sorry you feel that way Senator, and I am not sure that I can make that promise."

Both men stood and gave an unenthusiastic handshake. Kaspar headed for the door, while Jimmy Fred went to the restroom.

Toward the end of the order line, there was a nicely dressed young man in a dark suit and red paisley tie. He was not unlike the other patrons in the Servery. The only difference was that the rest of the lunch crowd did not have a micro-camera hidden in their lapel pin. He watched as Jimmy Fred emerged from the restroom and exited the same door as the Senator. The young F.B.I. agent returned his menu to the counter, as it was no longer necessary to order.

Chapter Twenty Two

Scottsdale, Arizona

"Mavis, what do you think this is?" Hamish was holding out the blue metallic piece that he recovered along with Small Feather's red shirt.

Mavis took the piece in her hand. Turning it over and holding it up to the light, she said, "Looks like a strip of a license tag. Look here, this could be a letter or a number and this is where the screws go. It has the blue and down here you can just make out the mountains. On the back it has no color, just corrugated silver."

She handed it back to him. Hamish considered the license idea. It seemed plausible. "Do people usually cut up there license plates? It is sharp. Bugger would cut your hand if you weren't careful."

"I don't know of anyone who cuts up license plates. Where did you find it, Hamish?" Mavis gave his name a heavy H sound instead of keeping the H silent.

Hamish smiled at the curious pronunciation of his name and said, "Over by Respite Lake. There were a couple criminals there, just like you said."

Mavis looked at him keenly, "You don't say?"

Unable to control a mischievous smile, he said, "Some guy named Amos and a particularly little nasty called, Stevie Small Feather."

Mavis looked concerned, not yet catching his subtle humor. Then she broke into a laugh. "Hamish, you are a tricky one, you are!"

Then she said in a very serious tone, "Oh no, I hope that you did not get cross ways with Amos. He's with the Indian Police."

No, if we had more time we would have hit it off like two bugalugs, but the little one had a bit of a wobbly," Hamish said.

"What's wobbly?" Mavis asked.

Hamish thought about the word, "You know, spit the dummy, hissy fit." When Hamish saw that she understood, he said, "No worries, he was just a sprog."

Mavis closed her eyes and shook her head from side to side. She laughed and sighed at the same time. "You are sure something, Hamish. What were the boy and Amos doing on your land?"

"Looking for a body, they said."

Mavis exclaimed, "I knew it! I knew it! It was those wise guys wasn't it?"

"I don't know. The anklebiter could not locate the body. Accused me of being in on the caper. I was sort of wondering if this sort of thing happens around here all the time," said Hamish.

Mavis looked thoughtfully and said, "No, not all the time, but when it does happen, it is not always something that makes the news. People tend to mind their own business around here."

"I certainly believe in that. But it sort of is my business if someone carked it on my land. Sort of involves me in the caper, you know?"

Mavis said, "Hamish, I think this is one that you leave alone. Those men that were here are of a nasty sort. No conscience, you know what I mean? You are here now and they are gone. Let the police handle the … carking."

"One more thing, Mavis. I want to return the boy's shirt to him. Can anyone go on the reservation? Or do you need a, he paused, reservation?" Hamish said and then wondered if he had used the wrong word.

Chapter Twenty Three

Ft. Lauderdale, Florida

Chars arrived at the Hyatt Resort, Pier 66 reception area and began the check-in procedure. The long reception desk was tastefully decorated with wrought iron lamps, evenly distributed along the counter. He was signing the register when his cell phone vibrated. He indicated to the clerk that he would need to take this call.

"Hey Jerry, what's up?"

"Not much, Charles. Where are you?" Jerry said in his usual raspy voice.

Chars smiled. Jerry did not usually beat around the bush, but this was a little terse, even for him.

"What, no small talk. No 'how are you doing?'" Chars was kidding, but tried to sound offended.

Then he realized that Jerry called him Charles. Something was up or more likely, someone was listening.

"Charles, things are heating up around here. Are you in town?"

"Say Jerry, this connection is bad. I am going to need to call you back." Chars said and pressed the end button.

Chars finished checking in, glanced out at the magnificent swimming pool and cascading waterfall and before taking the elevator up to his room. He decided to hold off on unpacking until he talked with Jerry again.

Upon finishing his call with Chars, Jerry leaned back in his chair and said, "He is going to have to call me back. The connection was not very clear."

Agent Ron Eads, an F.B.I. agent looking unconvinced, said, "We know he is headed to Ft. Lauderdale. When he calls back, it would be helpful to know where he is staying."

"Agent Eads, what do you want Charles Reynolds for? He barely even knew Nikolaos. If you want to talk to him, just call him," Jerry said and took a gulp from his water bottle.

Chars told Jerry that if he drank eight bottles of water a day, he would lose ten pounds. Jerry figured it couldn't hurt. But, the frequent bathroom trips were a real pain.

"Look if there is nothing else, I need to take a piss," Jerry said dismissively.

Special Agent Ron Eads leaned up against the door frame. His sizable frame was enough to cover most of the door. He held a contentious look on his face.

"There is something going on with Mr. Reynolds and this hit on Nikki Nikolaos. Why else would he have a hunting party of wise guys after him?"

Jerry thought, *these guys have no clue and they are just fishing.*

"Look, if you are trying to protect him it is one thing. But have you considered that by searching him out the way you are, might just make him a priority for someone, like say the mob?"

"Sergeant, there are a couple things that we need to clear up. One, Reynolds was on their list before we even knew who he was. Two, it is obvious to me that you are not being completely forthright about Mr. Reynolds' whereabouts. That I cannot possibly understand, after all, you are in law enforcement. If he is your friend, as we know him to be, it would seem to me that we might be able to save the man's life if we can find him," Eads said.

"Very cavalier, Agent, but I don't buy it. You think that he has some insight about the murder and you want to get to him before the mob does. What is it that you think he knows?"

"Regardless of our motivation, I don't see it as within your purview to withhold information about Reynolds' whereabouts." Eads said.

His face was becoming a slightly maroon shade. His arms were crossed and his look was a glare.

Jerry thought to himself, *screw you and the horse you rode in on, bucko."* But instead said, "Agent Eads, I believe that our conversation here is over, unless you tell me how you think Charles Reynolds fits into this. I mean surely the F.B.I.," he said with exaggerated emphasis, "has a theory."

"We might form a theory if we could actually talk to Mr. Reynolds. Do you have some reason for protecting this guy? Is that why you are stalling us?"

Eads stepped in a step in closer to Jerry, which was a mistake. Jerry reacted by stepping toward the agent. Eads had a good foot of height over Sergeant Collins. Jerry did not seem to be intimidated even in the slightest amount.

"Tell you what, Agent Eads, if you leave my office right now, then I won't need to embarrass you by throwing your size 42 suit out. If I get any information about the whereabouts of Mr. Reynolds that I think will be in the best interest of Mr. Reynolds, then you will be the first to know. Now, good bye."

Jerry bumped the agent as he reached for the door. He opened it and Agent Eads walked briskly out.

Jerry hurried to the restroom and then back to his desk to call Chars. Chars answered on the first ring. "Okay Chars, what in the hell is going on?"

Chapter Twenty Four

Washington D.C.

Jimmy Fred pulled his newly acquired cell phone out of his pocket to answer a call that he had been expecting most of the day.

"Hey, I just got in," Jimmy Fred said.

"Can we talk on this phone?" asked Tommy Topolo in a very perturbed voice.

Jimmy Fred heard the impatience in his voice and grimaced at the thought of this man getting upset. Tommy was upset and he was going to take a bite out of Jimmy Fred's ass. Tommy sat up in his chair, moving his substantial girth forward to prepare for the verbal assault that he was planning to deliver. Tommy Topolo had just finished a meal of veal and fettuccini with red sauce at his Chicago restaurant. He called Jimmy Fred even though he knew talking to Jimmy Fred, was likely to give him some indigestion.

"Yeah this phone is clean. I just bought it," Jimmy Fred said, hoping that it was true. He was confident that his previous phone had not been compromised, but he liked to be careful.

He continued, "It was the flight from hell. We had a mechanical in Atlanta. Two hours later I am sitting next to a snot-nosed baby who wants to chew on my reading glasses. Can't get the little shit to leave me alone. The mother thought it was a joke," Jimmy Fred said.

It was not exactly a lie, he did have the experience on his flight, but that was two days ago. He also left out any mention of his meeting with the Senator Kaspar.

"I don't want to hear about your fucking flight problems. What in the hell is going on? I have the papers saying that we whacked Nikki. I got this guy that disappears in Arizona with too much knowledge for his own good. My man in the Tampa Mayor's office is telling me I have some reporter investigating my boats. I did not get my boats on the Atlantic and I am not sure that I am good on Salt Flats. I have some kid witness that can make one of my guys pulling a body out of the lake. And I have the Feebees trying to give me the rubber glove treatment. None of this is supposed to be happening and I ain't too happy about all this. And, most of it is because I listened to you."

Jimmy Fred said in a deferential but firm manner. "I know the Atlantic deal did not work the way we planned, but you did get the Tampa boats. That was a good deal for both you and your union buddies." He started to go on but Topolo interrupted.

"And now we had some damn Miami reporter poking around. Just this morning his fishing buddy started nosing around. I had to pick him up just to get him out of the way. The dude at the Bay authority called me ready to piss his pants."

Jimmy Fred was confused. "Who called?"

"Well, he called one of the local guys and they called me. You don't need to know his name," Tommy said pleased that he had a card up his sleeve that Jimmy Fred had no clue about. Jimmy Fred thought he was such a wheeler dealer and Tommy was pleased to make Jimmy Fred a little uneasy.

Jimmy Fred was confused, *why would Ray Jones be talking to Chicago?* He was afraid to ask, but did anyway.

"And this was the guy that was helping out on the license?" Jimmy Fred said carefully, trying to avoid another verbal barrage.

"He was the one helping the union out. Your guy was just a low-level person that made sure the licenses were available." Topolo said. "What? You did not think that I had the head of the Tampa Bay Authority in my pocket. You underestimate me, Jimmy Fred."

Tommy was pleased with his little enlightenment. Wiped his mouth with his napkin and pushed away from the table.

"You need to be more careful, my friend," Tommy said, but the words "my friend" had an ominous tone to it.

Jimmy Fred was not sure if that friend was the friend that he wanted to be with Tommy Topolo.

Tommy continued, "You made a lot of money on your boat deal and the casino deal. I have been paying both sides to make sure you couldn't fuck it up. Somehow it still got fucked up," Tommy said as he waved to one of his guys to take his empty plate away.

It was then that Jimmy Fred realized that Milton Smalley was Tommy's man. The old guy that seemed oblivious to everything was faking ineptness. Jimmy Fred made a mental note to put this bit of information away for future use.

"Look, the deal in Arizona is done. Granted it was a little messy, but the fact that dude stumbled on the deal, was just bad luck," Jimmy Fred said.

He was now feeling the pressure of the conversation, sensing that it was headed in a bad direction. Tommy the Hammer was not someone to be messed with.

"Yeah, messy describes it. I am still figuring out what to do with all the shit. Every time you call up here, you are needing someone else dropped. We can't just be punching tickets all the time. We still don't know where the snitch took off to."

"He'll turn up." Jimmy Fred said, but he really was not sure of that at all. It was just as likely that the man was sitting in some Federal office somewhere spilling everything he knew. Jimmy Fred knew that this could be disastrous, but said nothing else.

Tommy shook his head in disgust and made a mental note to check on the status of the fugitive from his justice. He went on to the next problem.

"Is the Senator still cooperating?"

Jimmy Fred's twitch under his left eye began to act up.

"He was a bit spooked when Nikki got hit."

"Pass along my best to the Senator and tell him for me personally, that if he has a problem with our arrangement, that I will personally come see him. My sources tell me that he has Feds trailing him."

This sent a chill up Jimmy Fred's spine. If that were true, Jimmy Fred may have been compromised.

"He will be fine. He knows what's at stake."

"I am tired of this crap, Jimmy Fred," Topolo said. He leaned back in a wicker chair, and fiddled with his Hyde Park Macanudo cigar.

"I understand," Jimmy Fred said and took a swig of his Maker's Mark bourbon, summoning the courage to speak again. "I will talk to the Senator again. Why do you think the reporter could be a problem? The one in Arizona was not a problem."

"Look clown, you know I can't just go around whacking people all the time." Tommy swilled his Chianti and took a healthy swig and lit the cigar.

Jimmy Fred thought better of saying that it seems like you go around whacking people all the time. Again he paused for a long time, gathering his composure. Sounding much more reasonable, Tommy finally broke the silence.

"Look, the reporter is evidently a well-connected guy. The other one was a nobody. This one could bring some heat, so if and when we whack him it is going to need to be a little cleaner than most. First things first, what about the Senator? Is he a problem or not?" asked Tommy. He blew a large plume of smoke toward the ceiling.

"No he is not going to be a problem. The up side is that you got the legislation out of him, and I think we can work that on him. He won't want that to come out," Jimmy Fred said.

But Tommy did not respond. There was only silence.

Uncomfortable with the silence, Jimmy Fred sought to reassure Tommy. "He will be fine," he said trying to sound more confident than he actually felt. "He's going home to Akron next week and will have a chance to calm down," Jimmy Fred said and immediately wished he hadn't.

Topolo sat up straight and barked, "So he's upset. I knew it. That was the word that I heard on the streets. I think the little prick is going to squeal."

"He can't afford to say anything to anybody. He is in too deep. I really don't think we have to worry about Wayman."

"Don't use his name, you meat head."

Jimmy Fred cringed at the rebuke but did not think there was any chance of someone listening to there conversation.

Jimmy Fred continued, "He is headed back to Ohio. He'll have some time to chill. The reporter is the one I am worried about. He is some sort of celebrity in Miami."

"I had two of my men looking for him in Miami after we talked last time. They got picked up for questioning. I guess the F.B.I. was trying to tie them to the hit on our friend. They had to let them go because of course, they weren't even around when the hit occurred."

Jimmy Fred carefully said, "So it wasn't them?"

"Hey, numb nuts, I just said that it wasn't them." Tommy said through a burst of smoke. "I will have someone look into the reporter again. You stay tight with the Senator. I want to know if he is getting Pepto on us. I got two working on the ragazzo; giovane istigatore. Il ragazzo che ha calciato Charlie nelle noci."

Jimmy Fred sighed because he knew zero Italian. He did not know whether to ask or not. He could hear a couple of them laughing in the background. One of Topolo's men while laughing said, "Calciatore di noce."

They all started laughing; Tommy too. Jimmy Fred was happy they were laughing, but hoped that it was not bad news for him.

"What is Pepto?" Jimmy Fred asked.

"You are so stupid. Upset stomach," Tommy chided

When they finally stopped laughing, Tommy got serious again with much effort.

"We will take care of the Senator. What else needs to happen?"

Jimmy Fred massaged his temples and began to develop a plan. He wondered how could he have anticipated all this? He needed to buy some time on several fronts.

"I need the fisherman to stop asking questions," Jimmy Fred managed to say.

"I can't just go around whacking everybody," Tommy said gruffly.

"Okay, can you just detain him a little while?" asked Jimmy Fred.

"Okay, but Jimmy Fred, this better start smelling better real quick." Tommy slammed down the phone to end the call.

Chapter Twenty Five

Ft. Lauderdale, Florida

Puzzled by Jerry's obvious anger, Chars said, "I am in Ft. Lauderdale."

He could not figure out why Jerry would be mad at him. He told him not to come home, but did not say anything about going other places.

"Chars, the F.B.I. was in here. First O.C. comes in and now the F.B.I. What in the hell are you in to?" Jerry moved around his desk and shut the door the remaining bit.

"What did the F.B.I. want?" Chars was very confused.

"They obviously want to talk to you very much. They already knew you were going to be in Ft. Lauderdale." Jerry said and took another swig from his water bottle.

"How would they know that I was going to Ft. Lauderdale and secondly, why would they even care?" asked Chars.

"They think you have some information about the Nikolaos hit."

Chars thought a moment and said, "It was news to me. Like everybody else, I figure it was a mob hit. But it is not like I have any secret information."

"They want to talk to you any way," Jerry said shortly.

"Fine, who do I call?" asked Chars in a tone of resignation.

"Let me rephrase that. They want to pick you up and then talk to you," growled Jerry.

Chars was shaking his head. "Do you have a phone number for any of them?"

Jerry reached for a card that Agent Ron Eads had presented to Jerry upon arrival. He gave Chars the number and said, "Watch your back, Chars. Having the F.B.I. after you can be worse than having the mob after you."

"Thanks Jerry, but I don't even know what I am supposed to know. I have to find out what I am supposed to know."

"Just be careful and watch your back, I will see what I can do on this end."

Chars ended his conversation. He opened his laptop and connected to the hotel internet service. Checking his e-mail he remembered he needed to make a follow up call before he could submit his story.

He called Dave Coughlin in Tampa. The phone was answered, but not by Dave.

"Hello," A man with a heavy Chicago accent said.

Chars frowned and offered, "Hello. I am sorry, I must have dialed the wrong number." Even though he was sure he didn't.

"Whoz were you trying to reach?" The man asked in a friendly tone.

Chars stuttered for a moment, but managed, "I...I must have dialed the..." he was interrupted by the man.

"Arz youz looking for Dave, cauz I'm taking his callz for him. Can Iz tell him whoz callin?"

Chars now was very concerned, "Can I speak to David?"

"David's busy. But if you give me your name, I willz pass it on."

There was a hard knock on Chars' hotel room door. Chars moved toward the door to look in the peep hole.

Another knock was followed by a loud voice, "Mr. Reynolds?"

Chars covered the receiver, but too late. Amused with his continued good fortune, Little Don said with a chuckle, "Soundz like you has someone at your doors, Mr. Reynolds. Let's see, 786 area code, must be Miami? "

Chars was trying to think quick and started to respond to the phone call. There was another bang, bang, bang on the door.

"Mr. Reynolds, it's the F.B.I." the voice from hallway boomed.

Little Don said, "Sounds likes youz better answer that Mr. Reynolds, it's the F.B.I." He then ended the call.

Chars yelled in frustration and concern, "Damn it." He moved to the door and unlocked the deadbolt. Upon opening it he saw a well dressed man and a sharp looking woman.

"Charles Reynolds, I am Special Agent Fairbanks and this is Agent Terrell of the F.B.I.

He showed his badge, the lady agent did not even bother showing her identification.

"We need you to come with us."

Chars started to shut the door, but thought better of it. He said," I don't know anything about Nikki's murder. I am here for the funeral and I have no intention of going anywhere with you."

Fairbanks started to protest, but Chars cut him off holding up a hand.

"If you would like to talk here and save some time, that would be fine," volunteered Chars to head off a potential showdown.

Fairbanks smiled thinly at the contemptuous statement.

"Mr. Reynolds, may we come in?"

Without speaking Chars opened the door wide and opened up his hand in a short sweeping motion toward the sitting area. The two agents moved inside the spacious room. Agents Fairbanks momentarily stopped to look 16 stories below, out the balcony sliding glass door. Chars' room had a panoramic view of the water way and hundreds of sailboats docked below. Thinking about the unfairness of the world, Fairbanks looked straight down at the Pier 66 terrace off the main dining room. He took a seat at a desk in the corner of the room. Chars moved past Terrell who took a seat on the edge of a decorative sweater box at the end of a plush king sized bed.

Agent Terrell broke the silence, "Nice room, Mr. Reynolds."

Chars initially ignored the statement, but decided that these two were just doing there job. He might be better off just answering their questions and sending them on their way.

"Thanks."

"The newspaper business is doing well," Fairbanks said with a touch of sarcasm.

"Would either of you two like something to drink?" Chars asked in an obligatory tone.

"I would take some water if you have it," Terrell said pleasantly.

Chars went to the chill box and pulled out a water bottle. He started to wipe off the condensation with a napkin, but Agent Terrell stopped him with. "Oh, here I will do that." She took the napkin with one hand and the bottle by the cap with the other. She set down the napkin on the coffee table and then placed the bottle on top. Chars noticed that she did not open it.

"Mr. Reynolds, you have come to our attention because of the murder of Nikki Nikolaos. We know that the two of you were friends," Fairbanks said as a statement of fact.

Of course he only suspected that Nikolaos and Reynolds may have known each other, but usually a person will correct an obvious misstatement quickly. Reynolds did not object. Terrell was intently staring at Chars while Fairbanks was speaking.

Fairbanks continued, "Maybe you could tell us the last time that you saw Mr. Nikolaos alive?"

"I would be guessing, but I believe it would have to have been over a year ago." Chars said with mild irritation, but determined to get this group off his back.

Terrell decided to interject, establishing her value to the investigation, "Mr. Reynolds, would you say that you were good friends with Mr. Nikolaos?"

Chars let out a sigh, "I met him a few times. I liked him as a person. He invited me out on his gambling boat once, and I was on his boat The Galleon, docked here in Ft. Lauderdale, once or twice. I would not be on his A-list of friends, but I knew him and we were occasional friends."

Fairbanks continued while Terrell looked for any signs of dishonesty, "I need to ask you, in confidence of course, what stories you are currently working on."

Chars' eyes narrowed and he said in a calm voice, "I don't believe that anything that I am working on has any relevance to the Nikolaos murder. I am planning on doing a piece on Nikki following the funeral, but I don't have any big revelation. It will be a soft piece. He was a unique guy."

Fairbanks seemed to measure Chars' response before going on.

"Do you know anything about the charter boat sale?"

Chars figured this was what this whole thing was about. "I only know what was in the paper. He was forced to sell by you guys..."

Terrell corrected Chars, "Actually it was the Justice Department that required him to sell."

Chars agreed as if saying that is what he meant. "Well, you guys are all part of the same team."

Both Terrell and Fairbanks adjusted in their seats uneasily in response to that statement, but said nothing. Chars smiled inwardly knowing that he had landed a dig with that generalization.

Terrell asked, "Do you have any information that would lead you to believe that someone might have been unhappy with the transaction?"

Chars responded, "I read in the paper that Nikki was not happy having to sell. Nikki thought he was having to sell way below the market price, because people knew that he had to sell."

"We understand that. But what I meant, was there anyone that might have wanted to buy the business that was frozen out?" Terrell clarified her question.

"I don't know of anyone, but it sounds like a possible motive, except for the fact that the business was offered to the public," Chars said.

Fairbanks leaned in a little bit and said, "But if someone found out that Nikolaos deliberately excluded a bid, that would make for a good story wouldn't it?"

Chars sighed and raised his eyebrows as if to say, that goes without saying. He let out a breath that signaled he was getting impatient with this line of questioning.

Chars said, "If, that led to his murder."

"Right. So what did you find out that someone might not want to come out?" Fairbanks asked, abandoning the more artful approach for the direct frontal attack.

It was not asked in a way that might lead one to guess whether these two thought it may or may not have happened. They were already convinced that Chars was sitting on some crucial bit of evidence.

"You are saying that I know something that I do not have any knowledge about at all," Chars said with his hands opened up wide.

Terrell said, "Mr. Reynolds, I know you are a talented reporter. I also know you are a willing to pursue the tough stories. I respect that, but I don't think you realize that you have some very nasty people on your trail. You are in danger and need to give us everything that you have on this hit."

"I can't give you something that I do not have," Chars said in a pleading fashion.

Feeling a lack of progress, Fairbanks decided to try the more aggressive approach, "Where have you been for the last three days?"

Chars noticed the change in demeanor of his inquisition and sat up in his chair. "I have been working on stories."

"Before you go any further, Mr. Reynolds," Terrell said, "we have talked with your boss, Mr. Stanton. He said he did not know where you were for the last three days."

Chars laughed with contempt and thought: *It figures that Stanton had something to do with this. The piece of shit.*

"That does not surprise me. I try to tell him as little as possible."

"Mr. Reynolds, if you feel pressure to withhold information, we can protect you. We can take you into protective custody and put you somewhere the Topolo family can't find you." Terrell said, letting the name purposely slip to register Chars' reaction.

Chars' reaction was one of surprise. He thought, *they had finally shown their hand.*

"The Topolo family has no reason to want me. I have nothing that they would want. Don't you think that I would know if I had something that was important to them? Nothing that I have done or am doing even remotely involves the mob."

Then Chars' mind stopped abruptly. He thought about Dave. In the confusion over these guys busting in, he had forgotten poor David. He knew for certain that the man that answered Dave's phone was someone from the mob. Chars got up from his chair to buy some time. He walked across the room. He reached in the chill box to grab a Coke.

With his back to the two agents he placed some ice in a glass and poured. He needed a way to get out of this meeting and call David back. But it was already too late. Chars had sent him asking questions and the result was that he was probably dead.

Fairbanks was losing patience. "Mr. Reynolds, we cannot help you if you are not going to cooperate."

Chars turned around and said with more confidence than he felt, "I have told you everything I know. If you have a card, I will contact you if I think of something else."

Unwilling to arrest Chars at this point, both agents stood. Terrell picked up her water bottle by the cap leaving Chars' fingerprints in tact, just in case. The agents moved toward the door. Fairbanks handed Chars his card.

"You are playing a very dangerous game Mr. Reynolds. Your life may be the price you pay," Fairbanks said, then paused before closing the door. "Or someone else's life."

Chars looked at the card thinking, *I hope you are not right*. Chars dialed in Debra Coughlin's number.

Chapter Twenty Six

Conway, Arkansas

Scott Tivy sat in the corner booth of a truck stop. He had used the last of his cash to buy lunch, a greasy, chicken fried steak and some pasty mashed potatoes. He located a day old, USA Today resting on the seat of the booth. Flipping thru the paper, the story about Nikki Nikolaos caught his eye. As he read, he stopped when he came to the part about a possible mob connection. The name Topolo sent a chill thru his veins. Next to the AP story was an article, on the slain man Nikki Nikolaos, by Charles Reynolds of the Miami Express. It was a nice piece on the life of the Nikolaos and his rise from poverty to wealth. Reynolds' name was familiar to Tivy. Scott remembered that Reynolds had won some award for uncovering a bribery scandal or something in the Florida. Being in city government, Scott paid attention to those stories, even if they were across the country.

Tivy felt like he had made a clean escape from Scottsdale. Unfortunately, Raleigh Allen had not. In an internet café, Tivy read about the disappearance of the reporter on the Scottsdale News website. Two days later, he also read about his own disappearance in a much smaller article. Tivy was amused that no one noticed his absence for a whole two days.

Scott had holed up in Houston for two days, but got restless and decided to hit the road again. But now, Scott was out of money and had grown tired of running. Scott was not broke, but he could not access his money without possibly alerting someone where he was. He was trying to decide whether to risk using his computer to transfer some his money to a place he could access it. He then decided that he would be detected no matter what he did. An ATM would only provide $400 maximum and he would have to keep making withdrawals. That would leave a nice easy trail to his whereabouts. If he wired money to himself to some bank, he would still have to go in to pick it up. Scott berated himself for not planning better.

There seemed to be no easy escape. He did not like being a rat, but that decision was forced upon him. The only possible solution to his problem was that this story had to be exposed by someone, and he could not be the one that was the identifiable source.

He pulled out his cell phone and called information for the number of the Miami Express. Reynolds was on assignment, and Scott was fed into his voice mail. "Mr. Reynolds, I have some very important information for you." He left his cell number, but did not leave his name.

He left the diner and opened his car door. As he was sliding in the door, his phone chirped. He had changed his ring tone from "The Sting" ditty, after the debacle in Scottsdale. He wanted as little attention as possible.

It was a Miami area code and Scott answered on the second chirp with a simple, "Yes," then quickly said, "Hold on," Scott put on his seat belt and started his car. The GPS lady came on with the greeting, "Hello Scott you are at

162

Interstate Highway 40 and U.S. Highway 64. Where would you like to go?"

Scott covered the phone's receiver and said, "Damn it!" He had forgotten about the damn GPS again. Scott had tried turning the damn machine off, but had finally given up. The instruction manual was still in his apartment in Scottsdale. His expeditious exit had not allowed for any planning, much less packing. He left town with the clothes he was wearing. Since the GPS system was integrated with his system at the factory, if he wanted the greeting to be eliminated, he would have to go to a dealer. In the meantime, he would have to remember not to be talking on the phone when he started his car.

Scott hoped that the caller was not paying attention to the GPS, but Chars had already reached for his pad of paper and wrote down Hwy 40 and 64. Chars had no idea where Highway 40 and 64 met, but he could always look it up later if he needed to. He did not hear the name, but the intersection came through loud and clear.

A questioning "Hello?" could be heard from the phone. "This is Charles Reynolds, who am I speaking with?"

Scott felt better that Reynolds was asking his name. Maybe he did not hear the GPS after all.

Ignoring the question, Scott said cautiously, "I am the one who called. I have some information on the Topolo family that you may be able to use." Scott's car remained idling in the parking lot. Scott locked the doors and performed a quick 360 look-about.

Chars was dubious about the veracity of the caller. After Dave Coughlin's disappearance, a call from the blue could be legitimate or a trap. This guy did not sound like a mafia guy, after all he allowed his GPS to give away his location. Chars moved over to his laptop and typed in the area code of the number he called. It returned a Phoenix area code.

"Okay, but I am not currently doing a story on the Topolo crime family." Chars was hoping that if this was a trap, they might decide to give him a pass if he was not writing a story about the family.

"They are only part of the story. They have already killed a reporter and they are after me," Scott said nervously. Each time he thought about that fact, his voice quivered.

Chars typed in Hwy 40 and Hwy 64. It gave him a location in the middle of Arkansas of all places. Chars stood up from his chair, realizing that this was likely a real call. This guy was way too nervous not to be real, and a mafia guy was not likely to be calling from Arkansas. Chars could feel the man's anxiety thru the connection. He needed to find out who this guy was and arrange a meeting. Chars still felt responsible for Dave's disappearance, if this was a legitimate call this man's life was in danger. Chars decided he should advise caution rather than take a chance with this man's life.

"You need to go to the F.B.I. or the Justice Department or your local Organized Crime Unit."

There was silence that made Chars uncomfortable. Evidently the man was considering whether going to the F.B.I was a possibility. Chars hoped that he would get his story first, but he was willing to let the man determine his own fate. Chars was not ready for any more guilt than he already had.

"Of course I am interested, but if you're dead, the story becomes more difficult to prove," Chars offered.

"Look, it is more complicated than just calling the police and the Feds. I need you to find out about a guy named Jimmy Fred. He was friends with Nikki Nikolaos," Scott was speaking in almost a whisper while he quickly made a mental note of the cars parked around him. Scott felt he needed to be moving again.

"How do you know Nikki?" Chars asked.

"I don't, but Jimmy Fred does," Scott said with frustration.

He thought to himself, *why can't this guy just take the information and do his job?* Chars thought, *this guy was not making sense.*

"Jimmy Fred, as in his last name is Fred?" Chars questioned.

"I don't know any more than Jimmy Fred, but he is also connected to Topolo. They are the ones that are involved in your Florida deal, right?" asked Scott somewhat rhetorically.

He checked his rear and side view mirrors. He put the car into drive, checked traffic and advanced onto the access road.

"If you are talking about the Nikolaos murder, it looks like a mob hit, but the jury is still out," Chars said, trying to plan which way to take this conversation.

"Look, I need you to focus on the Arizona deal for right now. The Arizona deal will help you with the Florida deal, I promise. I can tell you that the Topolo family paid off someone to sneak thru legislation that allowed them a part ownership in a new casino in Arizona. It was some bill that allowed financing to go through third party. It was a hush, hush deal."

Scott was trying his best to keep his information in a logical context, but his mind was scrambled. Chars, on the other hand was doing his best to sort through the barrage of information, trying to make connections. Scott accelerated onto the freeway headed west.

Looking into his rear view mirror he checked for anyone following. He saw no other cars and returned his attention to his conversation.

"I know this is a lot of information, and it is coming out a little mixed up, but I am trying to lead you in the right direction."

"Okay, maybe it would be possible for us to sit down and discuss this. I might be able to make more sense of it if we were face to face," Chars said.

"I am not exactly free to just drop in anywhere. Look, are you taking notes?"

"Yes, I am. But quite frankly I really don't know what I have."

"Okay, look. There was some Senator from Ohio involved. I did not find out which one. There was this Jimmy Fred that was the broker of the deal. Then the Mariposa Indians had someone inside working as well. The deal allowed partial ownership of a string of casinos that allowed the Topolo family to have its hand in the till."

This was good information, and Chars was taking notes furiously, but the man's story was so disjointed that it was difficult to follow. He wished he had his micro recorder instead of pen and paper.

Trying to catch up his notes to the conversation, Chars asked, "I thought only the Indian Tribes were allowed to have those casinos on reservation land?"

"I do not have time to explain all of this, but the Senator buried some amendment on some omnibus spending bill. The only hold up turned out to be a certain city councilman. But then he got a slice and everything was in place. I can't tell you why I got involved, but I started asking questions. I was going to tell a reporter named Allen about the deal," Scott said.

"The Arizona legislature did not have a say about that?" Chars skeptically asked.

Scott was losing patience. Checking the rear view mirror, he noticed a Dodge sedan following him.

"I am going to have to make this quick, Mr. Reynolds. The legislation had something to do with Federal lands. I don't know how it made it through, but there must have been some palm greasing along the way. Look, I have to go."

"Wait, what happened to the story?" Chars asked, still trying to piece this together.

"Like I said, the reporter is dead. I was supposed to meet him. They killed him," Scott said in a quiet but hurried tone.

Chars asked, "The Topolo family killed the reporter. Why didn't they kill you?" Scott exited the highway traffic headed east on an intersecting road. Scott watched in his mirror the Dodge exit the freeway.

"They would if they knew where I was. I made it out of town before they could get me. I have been on the run, but they may have found me now. I have got to go."

"How do I find this Jimmy Fred?" Chars asked.

He continued taking notes and scratching questions down while the man spoke.

"You're the award winning investigative reporter. I am just a low level bureaucrat. You will have to find him on your own. I will call you in couple days to check your progress, but that is all I can tell you now."

Scott ended the call, pulled into an Exxon gas station. He pulled up next to the unleaded pump and parked. A moment later, the Dodge Charger slowly drove past the station. Scott let out a long sigh of relief when he saw two children in the back seat of the car. The Dodge pulled into a McDonalds across the street.

Back in Ft. Lauderdale, Chars tried to make more sense of his conversation with the informant. He checked for a message from Deb Coughlin. There was none. He left a message on her voice mail explaining that he was concerned because David did not answer his phone, someone else did. He asked her to please try to contact David and call the police immediately if she could not reach him. Chars did not realize that Deb had left for a four day mini-vacation with Roger and would not be checking in for her messages.

Chars started with a search of Ohio U.S. Senators. Wayman Kaspar's name popped up as a Democrat and Russell Mahue as a Republican. Chars thought he would try the Republican first. He was located in the Hart building. Mahue was listed as serving on the Foreign Relations Committee, Oversight of Government Workforce Committee, Homeland Security Committee, and the Clean Air Environmental Committee. Nothing about Indians. Kaspar was on several committees including Agriculture,

Banking and Finance, Veteran's Affairs and Health Education and Labor. Nothing about the Indians.

Chars figured he would have to call their offices. Or he could search again. He typed in Indian Affairs and Gambling. Then he backed out the gambling and typed casinos. He added Mariposa to his search. He received 9450 hits. He scanned down thru the sites to see if anything with either Senator's name popped up. He then typed in Indian, casino, Kaspar Mahue. Up came the Arizona Area Indian Gaming Commission and the U.S. Senate Committee on Indian Affairs. Wayman Kaspar – Chairman. Chars wondered why that was not included on his website. Chars placed the call.

A nice voice answered, "Senator Wayman Kaspar's office, this is Beverly. How can I direct your call?"

Chars spoke right up, "Hello Beverly, this is Charles Reynolds of the Miami Express."

"Mr. Reynolds, the Senator is in a committee meeting. Is there something that I can help you with?"

"Yes, you might be able to. I am doing a story on the Casino controversy and wanted to get a comment from him," Chars said, making it up as he went.

"I am sorry. I am not familiar with a casino controversy; I can put you thru to his senior advisor's voice mail. Perhaps he could return your call and be of assistance," Beverly said in a professional tone.

She received these types of inquiries all day long and was used to diverting them to the correct office. Senator Kaspar had lots of staff to handle these very types of questions.

"I think that would work. But maybe you could tell me, is there a Jimmy Fred on your staff?"

169

"No we do not have anyone on our staff with that name. I will put you thru to voice mail," Beverly said with irritation.

She did not repeat the odd name or ask for clarification. Chars had been around long enough to know exactly what her statement meant. Her tone said everything Chars needed to know. She knew a Jimmy Fred, but wished she didn't.

Chars said aloud, "Bingo."

A voice came on the phone, "This is the general mailbox for Senator Kaspar's staff. If you would like to leave an inquiry, please do so at the tone." Chars left his name and number, but no message.

Chapter Twenty Seven

Phoenix, Arizona

    Charlie and Luigi took a late afternoon flight from Tampa. International. Tommy had called and dispatched them immediately. He said, "Leave Little Don to take care of the fisherman until Jimmy Fred tells us what needs to be done with him. You two go back out to Salt Flats and handle the munchkin. He's evidently causing quite a bit of unwanted attention. It needs to be done quick, understand?"

    It was a question, but it really needed no answer. Charlie and Luigi understood. Charlie still had the red shoe, but he was not sure if it belonged to the ball buster or not. He planned to shove that up the little snot's ass, right before he dropped him over a cliff.

    Charlie had not decided whether it was necessary to kill all the little peckers or just the one; but definitely the ball buster. Charlie was tired of flying out to Phoenix. And even though Luigi would keep him company, he wanted to take care of this business in one trip and go home. He had experienced the "Animal Treatment" of the airlines once too often. The airline staff would herd them like cattle onto the plane; squeeze them like sardines into seats without enough room; steam the passengers like they were oysters until the flight started; feed them peanuts like elephants; and then freeze them like penguins before it was all over. It was a miserable experience. Charlie had been able to fly first class only when Tommy was in a really good mood. But when things did not go as planned, Charlie knew it was coach class for him. If he didn't take care of the Arizona problem this time, he might be coming back in the cargo area, in a casket. Charlie was not going to let that happen. He looked over at Luigi who was reclined, sleeping with his mouth hanging open. Charlie reached across the aisle and tossed a peanut into Luigi's open mouth then pretended to be asleep. Luigi woke up choking on the peanut. He began coughing violently. Charlie opened his eyes and looked across at Luigi with a genuinely concerned look.

"Oh man, are you okay?" Charlie said and tried not to laugh.

Luigi sat up in his seat, still coughing. He reached for his water glass and took three big gulps. He felt his throat and shook his head.

"Yeah," he coughed again, "I'm okay. I guess I choked or something."

"Got to be more careful there Luigi," Charlie said and reclined his seat and closed his eyes.

Charlie and Luigi arrived in Phoenix and rented a vehicle. This would be a two-day job Charlie figured, and they would need a hotel. The first thing that Luigi wanted to do was get some food. Luigi said he wanted to drive to Scottsdale and eat at Four Peaks. It was on the way so Charlie agreed. Luigi told the story again about the guy whose GPS gave away his name and location. They laughed and agreed that story was a classic. Maybe the guy was eating there again. They might have been further from the truth, but not by much. Scott Tivy was on Interstate Highway 10, cutting across the bottom of Alabama. But he was not alone on the rode. Tommy Topolo had tracked

Scott down and had one of his men tailing Scott. Scott had made the mistake of telling the reporter in Miami where he was.

Tomorrow they would do some leg work. Their contact in the Indian Affairs had given them the location of one Stevie "Small Feather". The little shit had gone to the Tribal Police and reported the body. Fortunately, Charlie and Little Don had recovered it and split before Small Feather could make his claim to ten seconds of fame.

They could check out the place tomorrow during the day and then sneak in at night and swipe the kid. It would definitely look better if it appeared the kid ran away from home.

The crowd at Four Peaks was vibrant as usual. A John Prine song, called "Dear Abby", played on the overhead just barely audible over the crowd. After a long dinner, they headed toward the direction of Salt Flats. Charlie's cell phone vibrated and he moved to the corridor leading to the bathroom in order to hear better. He returned just a moment later.

"This is going to work fine. Our man says that the kid's mom usually works nights. We will find the place in the morning and then go back after dark," Luigi said.

Charlie and Luigi paid their bill, returned to their car and made their way to a hotel near Salt Flats.

About 15 minutes into the trip, Luigi said, "Hey, pull in here, I forgot to take a pee at the restaurant."

"Luigi just hold it till we get to the hotel. This place ain't going to be open at 11:00 at night," Charlie said, but was already slowing down.

Luigi hopped out of the rental and headed for a shadow. The place appeared abandoned and Luigi began to relieve himself by the side of the building. Neither of them noticed the curtain pull back imperceptibly. Behind the window in the upstairs apartment, Mavis peered out to see the Sopranos. One of them was pissing on her wall. By the time she got on her robe and hustled downstairs the two thugs had driven off. She wished she had a number to warn Hamish. She could call the Indian Police, but the ones that worked the late shift were crooked as snakes. She called Amos.

Chapter Twenty Eight

North Scottsdale, Arizona

The sun shown brightly as Hamish Cain drove back over to the airport in Phoenix to claim the luggage that was necessarily delayed. Back in Auckland, when Hamish went to check his favorite canine companion, the airline had filled their limit of transporting of pets. Cowboy, the blue healer, would have to come on a later flight. Hamish started to cancel his flight, but decided the dog would be fine.

He missed having him around and looked forward to Cowboy establishing his territory at his new home, the Lazy C. When Cowboy saw Hamish come thru the claims door he practically knocked over the kennel that served as his home for the past two days. Hamish looked at the animal, his full coat of black, gray and white hair and said, "Sit." Cowboy immediately sat at attention, but a little whimper was audible. Hamish completed the paperwork, opened the kennel, and latched on a dog collar. He then began a vigorous rubbing of Cowboy's head, back and stomach.

"Beautiful dog, sir" the attendant said. "He was growling at me every time I got too close."

Hamish looked at Cowboy and said in a severe voice, "Cowboy, have you been a bad puppy?"

The dog knew he was being admonished. He looked up with sad brown eyes and lay submissively on the ground. When Hamish cracked a smile, Cowboy immediately rolled over exposing his stomach and the happy smile returned to his face.

"Sorry for any trouble mate. I will gladly take him off your hands."

Hamish loaded the dog and headed off to return the shirt to Small Feather. While approaching the turn off, Hamish saw Amos pull out in his patrol car headed toward the Lazy C. Once on the reservation, Hamish saw that most of the houses were made of cinder blocks. Each was of identical size and shape. The only difference was the number of items that littered the yard.

Cowboy was enjoying the ride as usual. Their vehicle passed a couple of emaciated looking dogs scavenging through a small pile of trash. Cowboy now was on full alert and gave his customary throaty growl. Hamish had him leashed in the back cargo area.

"It's okay, boy," Hamish said over his shoulder.

Cowboy moved from side to side, curious about all the new sites. Hamish drove around quite a while before he saw a group of children playing with sticks and a dilapidated soccer ball. He figured that he must be close because he could see the plateau behind some houses where Respite Lake was located.

He stopped and asked the children if they knew Stevie. The whole group laughed at once at the man's funny accent. One boy stepped forward and pointed him in the direction of the homes at the end of the block. One of the children asked loudly, "Can I pet the dog?"

Hamish smiled broadly and said, "On my next trip here you can, but this time I am on business."

A collective show of disappointment rippled thru the crowd of kids. "Ahh" One kid finally, said, "You sure talk funny."

Hamish laughed and pushed the Jeep's stick shift into gear, then peeled out, throwing up a little dust. He could hear the kids hoot and holler. He waved over his shoulder quite amused at himself.

He pulled in front of Stevie's house and parked. He told Cowboy, "Stay." As he approached the Spartan abode, he could hear the television. He knocked, but no one came to the door.

Cowboy was at full attention and gave a slight woof, woof. Hamish turned and there was Small Feather sitting on the front bumper of the Jeep.

"You are very clever, Small Feather," Hamish said while returning to his car.

"Why are you here?" Stevie said with suspicion.

As Hamish got closer Stevie stood and looked like he was about to run away. The boy reminded Hamish of the wild cats that used to live around the barn at his grandmothers' house in Christchurch. They would come around to eat whatever was left out, but you could not get within five feet. Even his grandmother never was able to tame those wild cats.

Stevie's dark eyes were wary. Hamish showed him the red shirt.

"So, you stole my shirt and now you want to return it. Put it right there and I'll pick it up later. Then you can be on your way, Crocodile Hunter," Stevie said as he was moving completely in front of the Jeep.

"How's your stomach?" Hamish asked trying to make progress with this little hooligan. "That was a nasty cut."

Stevie was still slowly moving away and said nothing.

Cowboy sensed the tension and began to growl. That caused Stevie to square up to the dog; which Cowboy interpreted as a challenge. The dog lunged with bare teeth and let out three quick bursts of a ferocious bark.

Stevie was visibly scared and took several steps back. Hamish turned to Cowboy and said, "Cut!" Cowboy stopped barking and sat down.

Small Feather was trying to regain his composure. He was looking from Hamish to the dog and back.

In the heavy New Zealand accent, "No worries mate, his bark is much worse than his bite."

Stevie looked at Hamish and said, "I thought you were from New Zealand, not Australia."

"You can have mates wherever you are from," Hamish said leaning up against the remains of a fence post. Hamish smiled at this very smart little boy. He tossed the shirt over to Small Feather. The boy instinctively caught it with his left hand.

Hamish smiled and said, "You're cackhanded, just like my brother Jon Michael."

Small Feather just looked confused. Hamish motioned throwing with his left hand.

"Stevie, is your mother or father here?"

Stevie said curtly, "You gonna rat on me for swimming in your lake?"

"No, actually, you are welcome to swim up there anytime you like. Seems like a big waste to me if it is not being used. But I would like to talk to your mom or dad if one of them is not busy."

Stevie was still suspicious, but curious at the same time. He said, "Mom's in there asleep. She worked late last night. I am not supposed to wake her up."

"Stevie, about yesterday, I had nothing to do with any body being dead on my place. And if you saw a body, then I will do what needs to be done to help find it," Hamish said adjusting the straw work hat on his head.

Small Feather looked more relaxed and now was leaning against the Jeep. Still, he remained silent, but his suspicion had subsided and his distrust began to dissipate.

"I wanted to discuss hiring you to help me out. You know that I just arrived at the Lazy C Ranch yesterday. I am going to need some help getting things placed in order. I could use some help that I would be willing to pay. I think you would be a good worker and good company for me and Cowboy," Hamish said, looking at the ever attentive canine.

Upon hearing his name, his ears pricked up and he let out a sound exactly like Scooby-Doo used to make, "Ahwoo?"

Stevie looked dubious, but his hesitation showed Hamish that the idea interested him. Earning a little spending money or just doing something different would normally be enticing to a kid, thought Hamish.

Toward the front entry, a dark sedan began to slowly amble down the street. It was way too new to belong to anyone in this neighborhood. A small dust cloud swirled behind the car despite its slow, deliberate pace. It came to a crawl in front of the children playing stick ball. The children stopped their playing again. This time they did not approach the car, possibly sensing imminent danger. When Charlie did not see the right boy, they continued on their way through the reservation.

Cowboy let out a woof, woof. Stevie followed Cowboy's gaze. When he saw the dark sedan, he froze momentarily. Unable to keep his fear in check, Stevie stumbled backward a bit.

He asked, "Did you lead them here?"

"Who's them?" asked Hamish.

"It's him. He's going to cut my balls off and feed them to the turtles," Stevie stuttered from fear and involuntarily moved away from danger.

Cowboy was at full attention, the hair on his back raised. Stevie moved around the Jeep. Hamish was looking confused but alert. He was willing to see what these men wanted. It appeared as if the car was just going to creep on by, slow, like a shark making its first pass.

In truth, Luigi and Charlie had been arguing about what to do. Luigi wanted to leave right then. Charlie was juiced about finding this kid that had kicked him and he wanted revenge, now. His silenced Sig Sauer Mosquito sat on his lap. He thought, *it would be so easy. So what if there was an extra casualty. No one in this sty of a neighborhood was going to say anything.*

"Stevie, who are they?" Hamish asked while quickly assessing what to do. Hamish knew that it was the men that Mavis had spoken of and probably not to be messed with. He was checking the area for possible escape routes, but figured they were not going to do anything to him. Hamish had just arrived in this city and could not possibly have done anything yet. Still he was tensed a bit. He could feel his pulse quicken.

180

"He is the one who was looking for the body," Stevie said looking warily at the passing car.

The car stopped and the automatic window lowered. Charlie "the Shark" was smiling. Luigi was sitting in the passenger seat looking straight ahead.

Luigi said in a quiet but reproving tone, "This is stupid Charlie. Let's just get out of here."

Stevie had moved partially behind Hamish, like a child moving behind a protective mother.

"Is this your boy? Cute kid," Charlie said looking around Hamish, trying to make eye contact with Stevie.

Hamish was of normal stature, but had a confidence about him that allowed him not to be easily intimidated.

Hamish said in a soft voice, so only Stevie could hear, "Go in the house and go out the back to the lake. I will meet you there."

Hamish moved toward the car, Stevie did as he was told, moving toward direction to the house.

Stevie stopped and called to Hamish, "Hey, you will need these." Stevie tossed the rental car keys in the air, gave a quick smile before quickly going inside the house. He quietly moved through the house careful not to disturb his mother and out the back door.

Hamish was momentarily perplexed when the boy had time to steal his keys from the ignition, but could not focus on that right now. He continued walking to the idling, dark sedan. He could not tell if anyone was in the back seat because of heavy tinted windows.

Charlie moved the pistol out of sight as Hamish approached.

"Let's get out of here, Charlie. It is stupid to be letting him see us," Luigi pleaded under his breath.

Hamish asked, "Are you the ones that rented my place, the Lazy C?"

Not answering the question. "Oh you're the owner of the Lazy C," Charlie said cordially.

Cowboy was still emitting a low growl indicating his distrust. Hamish did not bother to correct the Blue Heeler, because after all, he was exactly correct in not trusting these two.

"Not a very friendly dog, is he?" Charlie said.

"Once he gets to know you, he can be quite agreeable."

Hamish noticed another vehicle coming down the dirt road. He recognized the car belonging to Amos. Charlie also noticed the Tribal Police car approaching in his rear view mirror.

"Well, take care," Charlie said, "I am sure we will meet up again."

Charlie did not want to explain his presence to any officers of the law. Plus the silenced weapon could be a bit hard to excuse, so he slowly looped around toward the exit. Hamish watch curiously as one auto left and the other pulled up. Almost like one of the take away restaurants he had heard about.

Amos pulled up to Hamish and stopped. His window was down and he gave Hamish a nod of acknowledgement.

"Trouble?"

"They certainly look like they are up to no good. But no, they did not cause any trouble. The boy said the man was the one he saw looking for the dead body," Hamish said and moved over to the Jeep.

He began petting Cowboy and the dog relaxed somewhat. Cowboy was not smiling and was keeping a wary eye on Amos. Amos flashed a cautious look over at the dog.

Hamish said quietly, "Sit."

Cowboy did as instructed and now his familiar open mouth showed his smile.

Amos watched as the dark sedan finally exited the front of the reservation.

"I figured it had something to do with them. Mavis called. Seems those two came in the middle of the night. I came here to check on Stevie, then went to your place and then back here. Mavis said you might be here returning Stevie's shirt."

"Mavis is a good old Sheila. It was a good thing that you drove up when you did Amos. Those two fuckwits had me thinking about going bush," Hamish said.

Amos, momentarily confused, gave a shake of his head as if that would clear up what the Kiwi had just said. "Is Stevie inside?"

"I am not rightly sure. He said his mother was in there sleeping. What is she a drunk?" Hamish asked sincerely.

Amos laugh a little. "No, she works late nights at the diner. Afraid she has not had much enthusiasm for life once her husband took off, leaving her to fend for herself and the boy," Amos said. His expression had changed from one of mild amusement to one of sadness.

Hamish felt bad for the boy. Stevie had been given the life of an alley cat for sure. The father had left and the mother was emotionally absent. Hamish thought about his own family and how fortunate he was to have all those

183

brothers and sisters. Hamish unleashed Cowboy and said, "Go pee." Cowboy agilely leapt from the Jeep and went off in search of tree that was not in the immediate area.. He finally decided on a wooden telephone pole.

Amos watched curiously, "Nice dog. Blue Heeler?"

Hamish smiled appreciatively and said, "Yes he is. I tell him he's not the sharpest knife in the drawer, but that is just to keep his ego in check."

Amos smiled and then returned to a serious topic, "Mr. Cain, I did not have an opportunity to introduce myself properly at the lake. I was embarrassed having been caught out of my jurisdiction; searching around for what I thought might just be a boy's fantasy. But I did some checking on the people that were leasing your ranch. Did you know them?"

"Not a bit. That was done thru the real estate service," Hamish said.

"It seems that they have connection to a crime family in Chicago." Amos said.

"Chicago. Isn't that a far distance from here?" Hamish asked.

"Yes it is, but we are relatively close to Las Vegas and more importantly, this group seems to be very interested in getting into the gambling business in Arizona."

"I thought that was the Indians' deal; you know running the gambling halls," Hamish said.

Amos' eyes narrowed a bit, but realized that Hamish said exactly what was on his mind. He was not offended by his frank tone once he realized there was no insult in Hamish's words.

"You are right, but a law was passed not too long ago that allows some outside investment in these new casinos opening up. Seems like the Federal Government is tired of losing so much tax revenue. If they allow outside investors, then the profits that flow out of the casinos are taxed as income. The revenue that stays within the Indian nation sponsoring the casino is tax free. Both sides figured it was the best way to attract some heavy development for this area. Newer, bigger casinos draw bigger and better crowds. Of course there were some that did not want this to happen. We call them the CAVE people," Amos said with a serious demeanor.

"CAVE people?"

"Yes, citizens against virtually everything" Amos said and gave a little smile.

The humor was lost on Hamish so Amos continued, "But there are some other well meaning people that were opposed to outside investors because they felt it might encourage a negative element. I guess that group is proving to be correct."

"I see," Hamish said thoughtfully, "I am offering the boy some work. I could use a hand and I can keep an eye on him as well. Do you think the mother will have any problem with that?"

"She won't probably notice. Don't get me wrong, she is plenty strict with the boy, but he is on his own most of the time. A job would be good for him. He's a friend to my nephew. Between the two of them and another boy called Lil' Mike, they are always flirting with trouble," Amos said as he admired Cowboy on his way back to the Jeep.

Hamish reached in his pocket and pulled out a dog treat. Cowboy sat, fidgeted until Hamish finally produced the bone for his taking. Cowboy took the treat and leapt up into the back of the Jeep.

"Anyway, Mr. Cain..." Amos started.

"Call me Hamish," the Kiwi interrupted.

Amos nodded an acknowledgement. "Just keep an eye out. That boy is the only one that has seen a body, if it does exist. I am a little concerned about the other two boys as well, but mostly about Stevie. There may be a personal issue with this man. Stevie saw him looking for the body and ended up in a short confrontation."

"I will keep watch over the sprog for a while," Hamish said while getting into the Jeep. "And thanks for arriving when you did. Cheers!"

Chapter Twenty Nine

Ft. Lauderdale, Florida

Chars spent the next two hours searching for articles that mentioned the mysterious Jimmy Fred to no avail. *Who is this guy?* Chars thought.

It was noon and Chars needed a break. He called room service and ordered up a carafe of orange juice and a cheeseburger.

Chars then turned his attention to the Tampa Bay Port Authority. For the next few hours, only interrupted by room service, he read and tried to understand all the parties involved. When he had pieced it together, it was getting close to dinner time. He needed more food, and did not want room service. The burger was good, but he needed something more. He called Jerry Collins on his cell phone.

Jerry recognized the cell number and answered, "Where are you?"

Chars said dryly, "I am not supposed to answer that."

"Good answer!" Jerry growled.

"Are you on your way home, Sergeant?" Chars continued.

"Yeah, I called it a day, early. I am pulling into my driveway as we speak. Melody is cooking that pot roast that I like."

"I can smell it." Chars said thinking once again about his need for food. He opened his suitcase for a change of clothes. He shook out a pair of khakis and a collared knit shirt. Both would be fine if he hung them in the restroom and let the steam release the wrinkles. He entered the restroom and turned on the water in the shower.

"Do you think your room is bugged?" Jerry said referring to the old turn the shower on trick.

"No, I have been working on the computer all day and have not even showered. I am going out tonight. Any suggestions?" Chars asked.

"I don't know where you are, remember?" Jerry said with a laugh.

Chars could hear Jerry going in the garage door, hitting the close button and the declining door returning to its appointed position.

Jerry kissed Melody on the cheek and said to his wife of 26 years, "It's Chars."

Melody smiled, leaned in toward Jerry's ear and said, "Hi, Chars."

"Pot roast smells great!" Chars said loudly.

Melody smiled while she moved back across the kitchen but still heard his comment. "Thank you, why don't you join us? The kids would love to see you."

Jerry resumed his part of the conversation while heading up the stairs to the master bedroom. "I know I don't want to know where you are, but are you going to the funeral tomorrow?"

By the time he reached the top of the stairs he was breathing hard, but not huffing and puffing. He was glad he did not have to speak immediately, because it would have definitely provoked a derogatory comment from Chars.

"Yes. I am. And, I am likely to be going to your funeral if you don't lose some weight. Even though you are holding the phone away, I can still hear your breathing."

Jerry frowned and said, "Stick to the more immediate issue. Is the F.B.I. still breathing down your neck?"

"Nice segue, Jerry. They paid me a visit. I think I have figured out the deal. I have been working on a Tampa story. The short of it is, there was some sneaky dealing with a fishing license."

"The F.B.I. is after you because of a fishing license?" Jerry said incredulously. Jerry had the phone positioned between his ear and shoulder. He was slipping out of his work trousers in favor of a pair of loose fitting jeans. His breathing had almost returned to normal.

"Well sort of. There evidently were several groups that wanted the traffic in and out of Tampa Bay to be limited or reduced. There was another group that wanted the capture of the Blue Crab stopped." Chars said while moving his pencil down his yellow pad of notes.

Chars noticed that the steam was invading from the shower into the remainder of the hotel room. He moved back into to adjust the water to warm rather than hot.

Jerry said, "Chars, this sounds crazy." He laid the phone on the bed and listened while he changed shirts.

"Stay with me. This wacko environmental group is worried about the premature demise of the Blue Crab. They were convinced that if they limited the number of commercial fisherman, that would solve the problem. They had already tried to get a limit passed and that failed. This was their misguided attempt at saving the Blue Crab."

189

Jerry was headed back toward the stairs, but stopped off at his daughter's room. Chars could hear a soft, "Hi Daddy."

Jerry smiled and winked at his daughter. Softly, he said, "Need to start getting ready for dinner."

"I know," she said obviously involved in her school project.

Jerry bumped down the stairs. "And this fits in how?"

"The Blue Crab group lobbied the city council to issue TBPA licenses on all boats. One of the categories that received a limited number of licenses, was large fishing boats of 100 feet or more," Chars explained.

"I assume that these are traditionally the ones that capture the Blue Crab." Jerry took a drink of ice water.

"I guess," Chars said not really sure. He made a note to himself. He then remembered he needed to call David.

"Isn't that like messing with interstate commerce or something?" Jerry asked.

"The environmentalist wackos don't care about that. In Texas they caused an old-fashion water-war and a whole string of lawsuits just to protect a snail darter," Chars said with a chuckle.

"Chars, where are you going with this?" Jerry asked taking in the aroma of the meal that was about to be delivered.

Chars continued, "Okay, wackos are successful in getting this new license quota on the agenda. In the meantime, Nikki is told that he has to sell his gambling boat operation because of a felony conviction fifteen or twenty years ago."

Chars was still playing the possible sequence of events in his head.

He went over to the refrigerator and pulled a Heineken from the reserve and popped the cap off with an opener. He gave up on the shower for now, returned to the bathroom and turned off the running water.

"A group called Miramar Productions bought the Ft. Lauderdale boat called the Oasis, I think. And another group called First Serve bought the Tampa boat called The Galleon."

Jerry was sitting at the dinner table waiting for the pot roast to be served. "Chars, I don't mean to rush you, but my dinner is about to come and I am going to want to concentrate fully on it. So give me the short version."

Chars laughed and said, "Sadly, this is the short version. I have not pieced it all together, but I think one or both of these two organizations are mobbed up. The city council established a quota of available licenses."

Jerry's family had completely assembled for dinner and the food was being placed before them. He signaled for them to skip the prayer and to start by making a circular motion with his fork. Chars meanwhile took a swig from his beer and continued.

"It was a quota based on the size of the boat. The license was intended to limit traffic in general, but big commercial fisherman specifically."

"Protecting the Blue Crab?" Jerry surmised aloud.

"In the typical bureaucratic FUBAR, it put non-fishing commercial boats in with fishing boats of the same size. That is why Dave was being delayed. By the way, Dave went asking for questions and when I called him someone else answered his phone."

Jerry moved a bite of roast beef to the side of his mouth. He mumbled, "Who's Dave?"

Dave Coughlin, Deb's nephew," Chars said, waiting for an acknowledgement that was not forthcoming.

Jerry said, "I don't know who that is, but go ahead."

"When I went to Tampa to find out why Dave Coughlin could not get a license it must have set off a warning. Bammo, the next day, Dave gets his license. I figure something is up," Chars said and took another gulp of beer.

"So did you call the Tampa Police?"

"No. I called Debra and told her to call the police. I am going to feel responsible if anything happens to him."

"What did you have to do with it? You did not send him fishing for information did you?" Jerry asked. He then took the break in conversation as an opportunity to take a bite.

"Yes," Chars said with sadness.

Chars started pacing up and back within his hotel room. He was placing this puzzle together as he walked. Jerry was used to Chars processing this way. Jerry was actually interested in what Chars was saying, but Jerry was not going to allow this to interfere with his eating. A moment passed with Jerry chewing and Chars berating himself.

Chars continued, "The one connection that I don't get is how a guy named Jimmy Fred fits into all of this."

Through a full mouth, Jerry said, "Who's Jimmy Fred?"

Melody looked at Jerry with a disapproving look. The daughter was giggling that her Dad was being reproached.

Chars said, "I am not sure, but I think he is the key and I am running out of ideas of how to track him down. There is another part of this that is going on in Arizona. I had an anonymous phone call this morning. This guy is on the run and he says that the Topolo family is involved in a casino scandal with the Indians in Arizona."

Jerry took a breath of dismay and said, "Arizona?"

"Hang with me, it all comes back together."

"I am waiting with anticipation," Jerry said and stabbed a piece of potato.

Chars smiled at the obvious complexity and knew that Jerry was losing his patience.

"My caller said that he was in the process of passing the story along to a reporter when someone outed him and the reporter was killed."

Jerry ate the piece of potato and drank a bit of his Columbia Crest 2003 Merlot, his wife's choice of dinner beverage.

Jerry asked, "Did you check with Arizona authorities?"

Chars pivoted and headed back toward the balcony overlooking the ocean. "No, but I looked it up online."

"What is your problem with asking the police?" asked Jerry sounding offended.

"Nothing except when they really could help, they won't. Anyway, the reporter's name was Raleigh Allen. I will call over there after Nikki's funeral. I was just surprised there was not more written about the guy. It seems like his newspaper would have launched a major offensive," Chars said as he reached into the refrigerator for a second Heineken. He tossed his empty into the small metal trash barrel.

Jerry gave a short harrumph, "Newspaper reporters are a dime a dozen, you know that Chars."

Chars ignored the obvious affront.

"Here's what I would suggest." Jerry washed his bite down with a drink of water. "Call the F.B.I. back and give them the information that you have. They will in turn leave you alone and the mob will probably lose interest in you because you have already spilled your guts. If your friend Dave is still alive, that would be his best chance as well."

"I guess so, Look let's meet for lunch tomorrow, say 11:45," Chars suggested.

"Will the funeral be done by then?" Jerry asked.

"Yeah, it should not last past 11:00. You are probably right let's say 12:30. That will give me enough time to drive back to Miami," Chars said.

"Okay, but let's do something near Kennedy Park, like Hungry Bear. I don't have an expense account," Jerry said getting in one last dig.

"Okay, see you then."

Chars checked his note pad, put the time and date on his calendar and transcribed his notes into his Time Text portfolio. When he had finished, he ripped off the pages from the note pad and tossed them toward the trash can. His toss was a little off and the paper rimmed off the can and under the desk. Chars grimaced as he began to bend under the desk to retrieve the errant throw. Chars heard a double knock on the door.

Chars went to the door and looked out the peep hole. Room service had made a mistake. Chars opened the door.

"Hey, I think you guys made a mistake," Chars said to a little man in the hallway standing behind a rolling cart.

The room service cart was filled with several covered dishes, a carafe of iced orange juice. The man had a strong build despite his short height. His dark complexion was emphasized by his white waist coat.

"This is room 328. Are you Mr. Reynolds?"

"Yes and yes, but I did not order room service," Chars said pleasantly.

"Would you mind if I call down stairs to check for the correct room?" the man politely asked.

Chars gave a patient smile and said, "Sure. Help yourself."

The man pushed the cart inside far enough to block the door open and stepped inside the room. He seemed to know where the phone was, no big surprise, and he quickly walked that direction.

Chars' attention was no longer required, so he turned away from the door and moved back toward the bathroom. He remembered that he had not taken a shower. When his back was completely turned, a second man, also dressed in a white server's outfit soundlessly slipped past the cart. From his ring, he removed a small plastic cover that protected a pointed needle.

The first man turned to Chars and in a light accent, he said, "I am sure I can get this corrected. I must apologize for any inconvenience."

Chars would not have an opportunity to accept the apology. The second man stepped closer and Chars never saw it coming; the small needle pierced Chars in the lower neck. It delivered a strong enough dose of Fentanyl that would quickly rendered Chars unconscious.

Chars reacted to the prick by pulling away. "Hey, what did you stick me with?" As Chars began to stumble, the first imposter moved into position and was waiting with open arms.

Chars looked up confused and said to the man with the needle, "Who are you?" and then succumbed to unconsciousness.

Masud Muhammad Al Rashid, also known as the Scorpion, smiled, but said nothing. A third man moved the waiter's cart into the room, placed the do not disturb sign on the handle and closed the door.

Chapter Thirty

Alexandria, Virginia

Jimmy Fred sat in the upstairs dining area of the Grand Carlyle Café, south of Ronald Reagan International, just off of Interstate Highway 395. With the exception of his guest and the waiting staff, the room was empty. It was in fact an hour before the heavy lunch crowd would descend upon the popular eating establishment. Just to assure privacy for this meeting, Jimmy Fred had reserved the entire upper level. And except for the three waiters that had been assigned to this single table, Jimmy Fred and his guest were in fact alone.

Ahmed el Fayed sat across from Jimmy Fred relishing a glass of ice tea, having finished a very delicious Sesame Crusted Seared Rare Tuna Salad and flatbread. The Egyptian-born Islamist could have passed for a well-tanned European businessman. His Armani suit and Podio Italian dress shoes were immaculate.

"Jimmy Fred, I hope you are taking the proper precautions."

Looking around at the empty dining room he said, "Absolutely."

With a penetrating look, Ahmed el Fayed stared at Jimmy Fred trying to determine his veracity. If the mind had been created as an open book, Jimmy Fred would have long ago failed even a cursory examination. Nevertheless el Fayed continued.

"I have authorized the $100,000 that you requested in order to handle the situation in Tampa. You feel that we can still get a boat."

"I think is very possible," Jimmy Fred said enthusiastically.

"And the license won't be a problem?" el Fayed asked.

"This one already has a license. Now, it is going to have to be refurbished in order to be a gambling boat," Jimmy Fred said while trying to read this man's indecipherable face.

"I will deal with that once the boat is in our possession. How much will you need to purchase it?" el Fayed said.

"It is a large commercial fishing boat, around 100 feet. The last price the person was willing to discuss was 1.75 million," lied Jimmy Fred.

El Fayed looked at Jimmy Fred with an unblinking evaluation. He exhaled slightly and said, "When do you need it?"

"This weekend. I am supposed to meet the guy and close the deal," Jimmy Fred said seriously hoping el Fayed would not balk.

"When could we take possession?" el Fayed asked.

"I would think immediately. But it is going to take some heavy negotiations, this deal is not done. But I think when he sees the cash, he will go for it," Jimmy Fred said and leaned back in chair satisfied with his pitch.

He sipped from his water glass, wishing it were bourbon. He dared not drink in front of the very devout

Muslim. Jimmy Fred thought it strange that such a religious man would have interest in owning a gambling ship, but that was his business. Jimmy Fred of course, had no qualms about gambling or anything else for that matter. But the contradiction had puzzled Jimmy Fred. He had asked el Fayed in a round about way one time, and the answer he received was, "Means to an end." Jimmy Fred did not asked for further explanation. He just smiled with his best intent of having a knowing look on his face. Jimmy Fred believed in the proverbial, better to say nothing and have them think you are stupid, than to open your mouth and have them know it for sure.

"Jimmy Fred, I must tell you that we were disappointed that we did not get the original deal for Tampa. Tampa was what we discussed, the Ft. Lauderdale boat was supposed to be in addition to Tampa, not instead. It seems that we paid for something we did not receive," el Fayed said, carefully using his napkin to dab around his perfectly groomed goatee. He did not avert his gaze and Jimmy Fred felt a quiver in his abdomen.

"Yes, well I am sorry that the situation in Tampa did not work out, but it was never a sure thing. Lauderdale was not a cinch either. That deal could not have been put together by just anyone. Tampa was a disappointment, but you are going to get a boat, just a different one."

"For a million five?" el Fayed asked rhetorically. His eyes were like looking into an endless well of the rich crude oil that had made his family a fortune. El Fayed had already reduced the price a quarter of a million dollars to see if Jimmy Fred would correct him.

Jimmy Fred swallowed while trying to smile. "Yes, the original amount that you paid was needed to secure the

Ft. Lauderdale boats. Remember, Nikki was holding out for more?" Jimmy Fred asked. He smiled looking for confirmation.

"Yes, I remember you told me that, and conveniently Nikki is now dead," el Fayed said and signaled the waiter to being the check as he went by. "I read the papers. Who do the authorities think killed Nikki?" el Fayed asked. His left hand stroked his chin.

"Everybody is saying it was the Chicago Mob," Jimmy Fred said while reaching for another drink of water. His mouth seemed unusually dry. He shifted uncomfortably in his chair.

"You knew him well. Whom do you think committed the murder?" el Fayed asked as the waiter approached. He put up his right index finger to signal Jimmy Fred to wait a moment. The waiter delivered the bill and gave a little bow to Ahmed el Fayed as if to say that it was a pleasure to serve. El Fayed placed two $100 bills on the plastic plate and turned the invoice face down to cover the bills.

"Well, we were not close friends. I don't know who it was. I don't really get the lowdown on that sort of thing. But it could have been the mob, it was like a mob hit," Jimmy Fred said while shifting in his chair slightly to his feeling of anxiousness. He nervously fingered a sugar packet while trying to decipher where the Egyptian was going with the conversation.

"I watched your American program "Law and Order" last night. The main character said that there is always a motive for a murder. What could have been the motivation for the mob to have killed Nikki?"

Jimmy Fred shifted in his chair to give himself enough room in front of the table to cross his legs. He brushed some bread crumbs off of his slacks. Meeting el Fayed's eyes, then glancing away, Jimmy Fred gave a little shrug and opened his palms. El Fayed steepled his hands as he continued to evaluate Jimmy Fred.

"Nikki has always had connections to the Mafia. He pissed them off by not hiring their union workers. He probably told them he would sell them all the boats and when he did not, they whacked him," Jimmy Fred said thoughtfully.

El Fayed thought a moment, obviously comfortable with long periods of silence. Jimmy Fred was not; he fiddled with the salt shaker; then his match book. If Jimmy Fred assumed el Fayed accepted his explanation, he was mistaken.

"So, where do you see the situation as it stands?" el Fayed asked.

Relieved for the end of the silence, Jimmy Fred breathed out and said, "You got the Lauderdale operation going full throttle and the money is rolling in. You will get a Tampa Bay boat that can be converted. It is a nice size fishing boat, you could go on a fishing trip," Jimmy Fred said with a smile that was not returned. "The only loose end is the reporter we discussed, that has been nosing around. As I mentioned earlier."

"That problem is being dealt with," Al Fayed said matter of fact.

Jimmy Fred's eyebrows raised and once again he felt out of his league. Jimmy Fred took a quick drink of water trying to buy some time to think about his next response.

He just managed to mutter, "Good," not wanting to know exactly what the Arab meant.

Al Fayed was pleased to see that the thought of someone being dealt with, made Jimmy Fred uncomfortable. He leaned back and placed his napkin beside his plate. El Fayed decided to send another little jolt to this infidel. "How's your Senator friend?"

Jimmy Fred's back straightened and despite his best efforts, his face showed the panic he was feeling. El Fayed could not know about Kaspar. Jimmy Fred considered whether it might just be a bluff. He tried to come up with a good answer, instead he managed, "Which one? I have several friends in office." This was not a complete exaggeration. His mind was racing trying to process all that this might mean and what the Egyptian knew.

Jimmy Fred was clearly unnerved by this revelation; just as el Fayed had planned. "Senator Kaspar of Ohio," El Fayed said and continue to watch Jimmy Fred's face. Unable to meet the Arab's stare, Jimmy Fred looked toward the door as if thinking about making a run for it.

The waiter returned to fill up the water glasses which allowed a moment for Jimmy Fred to regain his composure. He had to find out what el Fayed knew. He could have simply heard about the Senator and done the math.

"Are you friends with the Senator?" Jimmy Fred ventured out the first question.

"It seems that you are friends with him and he seems to have some connections with this organization in Chicago. Is it possible this relationship cost us the boat out of Tampa?" El Fayed asked in an almost casual way.

Jimmy Fred was thinking fast and was trying to come up with a story that would pass muster. Jimmy Fred could feel the cornering questions that were probably not questions at all. He had to remain neutral as long as possible, and give as little information as possible. Again the silence overwhelmed Jimmy Fred.

"Jimmy Fred," el Fayed said in a measured tone, "I want this Tampa boat. I am not going to pay a million and a half dollars for it. I have already paid you. You have also been paid by your friends from Chicago. Get me this boat by tomorrow and I might forget that you have been disingenuous with me," el Fayed said evenly. His eyes showed a fierceness that belied his outward calm.

Gathering all the courage he could muster, "I will leave for Tampa immediately. I will call this afternoon to advise you when the boat is yours," Jimmy Fred said with no emotion. He stood, gave a forced smile and left for the door without any more words.

When Jimmy Fred exited, el Fayed pushed a button on his cell phone. He said softly, "Follow him. When you have possession of the boat, call me."

Chapter Thirty One

Chicago, Illinois

"Where is he?" The question's tone meant so much more than just the words. The question was an indictment that could make even the toughest guy develop a knot in his stomach.

Tommy Topolo did not like the answer: I-don't-know. Little Don knew better than to utter those words. He was supposed to know. The Hammer had killed one of his lieutenants for telling him, I-don't-know. Shot him in the stomach and then asked the guy the same question. When the man said, I-don't-know the second time, Tommy shot him between the eyes. Little Don was not afraid of many people, but that taught him to stay away from, I-don't-know.

"I'm in his room nowz. Someones musta swiped him. They must have taken him out the side doorz," Little Don said uncomfortably.

"Maybe he got spooked and checked out," Tommy suggested.

"Could bez. His stuff is gone. Maybe he will show for da funeral," Little Don said.

Tommy was playing with his unlit Tatiana cigar. He was gripping lightly at one end and then pushing it through his fingers to the other end. He lifted his hand and let the cigar pivot between his forefinger and thumb. Then, the process would begin again.

"Who is with you?" Tommy asked.

Little Don answered, "Nobody, Scotty is in Tampa backs wits the fisherman." Scotty was one of several men Topolo often dispatched to take care of problems.

"How did you find him?"

"I puts out the word that I'm lookin for da reporter in Lauderdale. Shaggy puts out the words to his girls. He called this morning to tellz me Reynolds was in one of his hotelz he collects from. He ax me didz I wants him to do anything. I says just watch him. I drove from Tampa to take care of him myzself. Shaggy sez he ain't left his room all day, so I decides to pay him a visit," Little' Don said.

Tommy was nodding his head and saying, "Yes," with each fact. "And now he's vanished."

"Seems to be," Little Don said disappointedly.

"If the F.B.I. picked him up we could have some problems," Tommy said.

"Da Fed boys don't usually take people outs the back stairs." Jerry was looking out the hotel window. "His stuff is gone, but he did leave a hotel tablet." Little Don smiled at his discovery.

"Check with the Shaggy to see if he checked out. Then make sure we have somebody at Nikki's funeral looking for him," Tommy said.

"Okay," Little Don said with barely a grunt.

"We have a lot of loose ends here that I don't like," said Tommy

"Look, Tommy, Charlie and Luigi will takes cares of the Indian boy. Wez already has the fisher guy under wraps. And it looks like some ones took cares of the reporter for us. What else is therez?"

"What are you going to do with the fisherman?" asked Tommy.

"I'm not sure. I figured you would tell us when yuz was ready. Do you want him to disappears?" Little Don asked.

"No tell Scotty to tie the fisherman up and leave him on the boat. Jimmy Fred is turning a deal. We stand to net a hundred grand if we get off the boat and leave the fisherman there. Jimmy Fred has sold the boat to someone and they are going to get it real quick. If he thinks we can pick up a hundred grand on the deal let's just get the hell out of there. Jimmy Fred can figure out what to do with the fisherman," Tommy said.

"Ands everything's with da Senator is copasetic," Little Don asked.

"Jimmy Fred says the Senator is going to be okay, but I don't trust Jimmy Fred on this. He is full of shit." Tommy said accenting his point by striking a match, biting off the end of the Tatiana and lighting it. "I think Jimmy Fred is careless. I can't handle careless. The Senator knows too much and probably has the Feds up his ass as we speak."

"Tommy, yuz knows what yuz wants to do, but if we start whackin senators, you know the heat's gonna be brutal. Miami is going to seem like a freezer compared to what you are going to have up there," Little Don said in a respectful but forceful tone.

Little Don had seen Tommy get like this before. The guy had some real anger issues and was very impulsive.

"The Senator needs to have an accident," said Tommy. "Natural causes or something like that."

"Tommy yuz can't just whacks this guy. That would be bigger than the F.B.I. agent and maybe even that judge friend of yours," Little Don was speaking as a confidante now, looking out for someone he feared, but for whom he had great respect.

"I will put the Screw on it," Tommy said, referring to Alan "Screw" Luano.

The Screw was known for his adept use of a flat head screwdriver to kill. But he was also very good at disguising a murder if he needed to.

"He's good at natural causes," Tommy thought aloud and then said, "Give me a call when you find out about the reporter."

Little Don Fratello took one final look around the room and just shook his head. A piece of wadded up paper caught his attention under the desk. He struggled to get down on all fours and reached back behind the trash can.

"Everything okay?" Tommy asked when he heard Little Don grunting.

"Yeaz, there's a piece of papers under the desk. It's some notes or somethins."

He uncrumpled the pages and began to read.

"Hey Tommy, I think I knows wherez your Arizona squealer is."

Little Don shook his head amused at his good fortune.

Chapter Thirty Two

North Scottsdale, Arizona

Luigi and Charlie went back to the hotel to lay low. They would have to grab the kid and take him somewhere else. It was decided that they would return to the boy's house in the early morning hours.

Without the use of the ranch, Luigi was concerned about the boy's remains. He could probably be drowned in the lake without much effort, but getting rid of the body created a problem. They were also concerned about getting out of Scottsdale before sunlight. They booked the earliest flight out of Scottsdale. They did not care that the flight was San Antonio bound. They would need to leave quickly before anyone could find the boy's body. The complication of the Kiwi perplexed Charlie. They discussed whether he would be at the boy's home when they moved in to take out the boy. In the end, the two decided that it did not matter. What was one more body in a situation that just kept getting worse?

Charlie and Luigi waited till almost 1:00 in the morning before heading back to the boy's house. Once nearby, Charlie killed the car's headlights and idled up. No one appeared to be out at this time in the morning and the only light visible was from the full moon. No street lights and very few porch lights made for an easy approach. Evidently, crime was not a problem either because the front door of Stevie Small Feather's house was not locked. Not wanting to use a weapon, Charlie had a cloth that would serve as a gag and two short pieces of rope. The only sound that could be heard was the crunch of sand and gravel under the two men's feet as they approach the house. A dog's bark off in the distance caused them to pause for a moment. When there was not an apparent danger they continued on.

With their silenced weapons pulled, both men quietly moved into and through the small house. Luigi moved with his back against the wall, while Charlie looked for the bedrooms. The furniture was sparse and created very few hazards, but Luigi failed to see an electrical cord plugged in near his feet. The heel of his zipper boot caught the chord and a table lamp tipped and fell. Luigi reached out and caught the lamp before it fell to the ground. Both men held steady hoping that no one heard the noise. Light footsteps on wood planks could be heard, and a bedroom door opened.

It was a small figure and Charlie quickly adjusted to get in a position snatch the boy. The lights were flicked on, and the two assailants froze in place. It was not the boy, but the woman, and she raised a single shot, 20 gauge, New England shotgun toward Luigi. Charlie reacted by firing one shot that traveled through the woman's temple, into her skull. Death was instantaneous, and no other shot was necessary. The woman's shotgun clanked to the ground unfired. The woman's blood leaked onto the linoleum filling the room with the copper smell of fresh blood.

The men said nothing and turned to find the boy's room. They opened the door to Stevie's bedroom, walked quietly over to the bed. Aiming his weapon at the head,

Charlie pulled back the covers. The bed was empty, except for the pillow and wadded up blanket that had been used for a previous night's sleep. Charlie silently mouthed the words of a scream, "Damn it!"

Luigi looked around the house for possible hiding places. The closets were empty. The boy was not in the home. The killing of the woman had been pointless. No, it was worse than that, this murder would only serve to intensify the hunt for Luigi and Charlie. It also would eliminate any doubt about the disappearance of the boy. If she had not been killed the authorities might have been satisfied with a possible runaway story.

"Come on," said Luigi, "The Kiwi must have the boy."

As the men carefully avoided touching anything on their way out, Charlie said, "Tommy is not going to be happy about this at all."

Luigi said, "She had a gun. How were we supposed to know that?"

"He is still going to be pissed. A body and no boy," Charlie said, shaking his head.

"Should we take the woman and clean up?" asked Luigi.

"Yeah I guess we better. We will dump her with the boy in the lake. I'll go get the plastic. So many bodies, so little time," Charlie shook his head. Little Don had all the good luck. Things always worked out for his older brother.

"Whose name is the rental car in?" Charlie asked.

"Stolen I.D. and credit card," responded Luigi. "That's good, but this just keeps getting worse. What will we do with the Kiwi?"

They loaded the woman's body into the trunk with little effort and headed out to the Lazy C.

The previous day, Hamish and Stevie had cut wood and cleared brush for the better part of the previous afternoon. To cool off, Stevie, Hamish and Cowboy went swimming. The boys enjoyed it, the Blue Healer did not. Hamish cooked a simple bean and strip steak dinner on the small gas stove and outside grill. By the time everything was cleaned up, Stevie was asleep on a dusty rug in front of the fireplace. Hamish had pulled a blanket out of his travel gear and spread over the top of the sleeping boy. He then made a pallet to sleep on in one of the vacant bedrooms toward the back of the small house. Cowboy slept at the feet of his master.

When Luigi and Charlie arrived, the lights were off at the ranch house. They parked about 25 yards away from the main house. The two men split up, Luigi to the front, and Charlie to the back. As soon as Luigi stepped on the side of the house, Cowboy's left ear pricked up and his eyes opened. He was used to things moving in the night and had learned the frustration of getting up for nothing more than a small varmint moving around. He would wait for another more definitive sound or smell before relinquishing his restful position. The next sound caused him to completely bolt to all fours. It was a creak of the back porch and a minute squeak at the front door.

Hamish also had been alerted by the noise and was up. Cowboy let loose a low growl. Hamish gave a soft "sh" sound and Cowboy became silent. The hair on the dog's back was at full attention. Only a simultaneous entry saved Luigi and Charlie from a full frontal attack by the blue healer. Hamish made a mistake of stepping around the corner too soon. Cowboy let out a low growl. Charlie said, "Okay, come on out where we can see you, and keep that dog back or he will be the first one I shoot."

Hamish reached down and grabbed on to Cowboy's collar and whispered "Down."

Hamish just watched the invaders without speaking. He figured that Luigi evidently did not see Stevie asleep by the fire because he was checking the kitchen and the other bedroom.

From the tiny shadowed space that was created by the hearth of the fireplace Stevie slipped out. From behind he loosed a savage kick between Luigi's legs. It staggered the man and he went to his knees. Luigi gasped for a breath. Stevie raised the small fireplace shovel to whack Luigi on the head. Charlie turned to see the boy spring his trap. Before Stevie was able to deliver the shovel to the head shot, Charlie quickly aimed his pistol, finger on the trigger. Cowboy leapt with considerable speed, hitting Charlie's arm, causing the shot to sail just wide of its target lodging in the hearth of the adobe fireplace just to the right of Stevie's head. The distinctive "thua" sound of the silenced weapon and the impact of the bullet near his head, caused Stevie to duck for cover. Plaster showered down on Stevie as he looked for an escape route.

Charlie tried to defend himself with his forearm against bared teeth and a solid 65 pounds of a flying canine. After crashing to the floor, Charlie took the butt of his weapon and swatted Cowboy across the back of the head, knocking him unconscious. The force of delivering the blow caused Charlie to lose control of his gun and it clanked to the floor. Hamish was able to kick the gun away from the man, but unable to secure it as the two scuffled.

Hamish yelled for Stevie to get out of the house. Stevie started across the floor to the door of freedom. Luigi made a desperate grab at the fleeing boy and at the last possible moment, grabbed the shirt sleeve of Stevie's tattered red shirt. Luigi yanked the boy back and recovered enough balance to land an open handed slap that knocked Stevie off his feet. A small trickle of blood could be seen coming from the corner of Stevie's mouth. Luigi wanted to do a lot more to hurt this kid than just hit him. The pain of his kick still was paralyzing and this boy had to pay for that. Reaching down, Luigi lifted the boy to his feet. With his free hand Luigi delivered a stunning blow across Stevie's face. Again Stevie fell to the ground, but would not give in to the temptation to cry. He just stared up at Luigi with a look of defiance. Blood was coming from a split on his cheekbone.

Considerably younger, Hamish was in excellent physical shape which allowed him to overcome Charlie's weight advantage. Hamish was able to free himself and finally grab the silenced Sig Sauer Mosquito. He moved across the room to help the boy, but was too late. Using an old wooden table as a gun rest, Hamish leveled the weapon just as Luigi yanked the boy in front of himself as his own shield. Charlie struggled to his feet in time to see the stand off: Hamish with his gun pointed at Luigi and Luigi holding the boy around the neck with a gun pointed at the Stevie's head. Charlie stood completely and put his hands up in a sign of truce. Hamish responded with a shot into the floor between Charlie's legs and then returned the aim to Luigi. Charlie jumped back a foot and glared at Luigi for not taking advantage of the opportunity. He realized that Luigi was still recovering from the vicious blow the boy had delivered. Charlie narrowed his eyes, determined to make the boy suffer for the pain he had caused. But now, he turned his attention back to the Kiwi.

Hamish was practiced with rifles, but pistols like this were not part of his expertise. Regardless, Hamish felt confident that he could hit Luigi because Stevie was such a small target.

"Look Mister, this is not your fight," Luigi said. "We can all walk away from this without anyone getting hurt."

Hamish was angling around to the side of a decrepit table. "You already hurt my dog. And he means a lot more to me than either of you two buggers," said Hamish. "In fact," Hamish move the barrel of the gun toward Charlie. "I may take some pleasure putting a hole in you."

Charlie did not move. He just looked at Hamish defiantly. Luigi said quickly, "Look, look," trying to get Hamish to focus on him again. "We have a stand off. Put down the gun and I will let the boy go."

The line of reasoning was so weak, it confounded Hamish for a second. He gave a momentary smile of how stupid do you think I am.

At that moment, Amos stepped into the room, gun drawn. Pointing his weapon at Luigi, Amos said, "I think you should all put down our weapons."

Amos appeared to have a clean shot at Luigi. Luigi released the boy, placed his gun on the floor and raised his hands. Stevie ran to Cowboy who was still lying on the floor. The boy gave the dog a mighty squeeze. Cowboy was breathing was did not immediately respond to the boy.

"I'm glad to see you, Amos," Hamish said.

Amos said to Hamish, "Here, I'll take that before somebody gets hurt," referring to Charlie's weapon in Hamish's hand and handed him a set of handcuffs. Hamish handed him the gun and took the handcuffs. Hamish started over to Charlie to apply the restraints. Charlie was smiling and Hamish thought it was strange.

Once Amos had the weapon, he stepped toward Luigi, but turned Charlie's gun on Hamish. "I am sorry, Hamish, but I gave you those handcuffs for you to put on yourself."

Chapter Thirty Three

Off the coast of Ft. Lauderdale, Florida

Chars was groggy and his head was pounding. He must have had too much to drink last night. His eyes were closed and he felt an uncomfortable pinch around his wrist. His room was unusually dark, as in no light at all. Chars was confused, but then realized that his hands were strapped behind him and he felt a gentle swaying motion. He was on a boat and "ooh" on a nasty floor with his face in something wet. Chars hoped it was his own saliva, but a retched fish smell and a putrid boat odor were now filling his senses.

His feeling in the rest of his body was returning, as well as a pain of some injury to his left ribs and neck. There was something or no, someone that was lying next to him. He could hear the person breathing, deep and slow breaths. It was definitely a man. Chars could smell a musky cologne. He tried to stand and realized that his feet were strapped together as well. He tried to recall his last memory and a vision of the hotel room entered his mind. A man from behind had stuck him with something. It must have been a drug. He could not remember anything after that. But evidently, whoever drugged him threw him on a boat, in a nasty closet on top of some other unfortunate schlub.

Chars' eyes just would not seem to adjust to the complete darkness. It was then he felt the cloth hood over his head. He was able to slouch and then extend his body several times in a row and the hood finally began to slide off his head. When Chars finally was able to remove the hood he could see that his situation was not favorable. He was able to roll over on one side before bumping up against a wall. The room was not much bigger than a closet but much smaller than a room. It must have been some kind of storage area.

He could now see a little bit of light under a door. The body of his companion was leaning up against the door and blocking most of the light. When his captors dumped their bodies, they must have forced the door closed because the other man's body was wedged tightly. Chars pushed off the nearest wall and was almost able to stand to his knees. He lost his balance and fell on the man. The jolt caused the man to stir and Chars tried to quickly right himself before the person regained consciousness.

The man let out a moan and then said, "Hey, get the hell off me."

Chars said, "I am trying to, but we are in a tight space."

"Who the hell are you?" the man asked angrily.

"My name is Charles Reynolds. Who are you?" Chars was now on his knees and by leaning against the wall, he was able to push himself into a standing position.

"The Reporter? Oh, now that is rich," he said quite disgustedly.

Not picking up on the negative tone, "You have heard of me," Chars said with a slight sense of pride.

Ignoring the comment, the man asked, "Do you have a hood on?" He moved back and forth trying to free his hands and feet as well as shake the hood off.

"I already got mine off. If you will hold still, I can probably reach down and get it," Chars said. With his back to the man, he bent his knees and groped for the hood. The man did not remain still; instead thrashed back and forth knocking into Chars. Chars lost his balance and sat squarely on the man's rib cage. The man winced and groaned in pain.

"Oh my God, why did you do that?" he asked contrarily.

"I told you to hold still," Chars came right back at him.

"So you sat on me?! Oh my God, I think you broke my ribs." he asked angrily.

"Just shut up and hold still this time and I will try to get your hood off," Chars said, trying to not lose his temper, but this guy was an idiot. Chars rolled off of the man which caused him to groan again. He repeated the process of standing and once again lowered himself. This time he was successful and the man let out a sigh of relief.

Their eyes had adjusted and Chars looked at the storage room from top to bottom. The boat rocked, causing Chars again to lose his balance, and he fell towards the man. This time the man saw it coming and managed to draw up his knees enough to break Chars' fall.

"Damn it, what is wrong with you?" the man said.

Chars glared at the man, but in the dark the look was wasted. Chars stood much more easily this time from a higher position. He regained his balance and took a moment to compose himself.

"It's a boat, dumb ass. I am not doing it on purpose."

"Just stop falling on me."

Trying to figure out what this was all about, Chars asked, "Do you know who kidnapped us?"

The man made a little laughing sound and snort. "Yeah, but if I tell you, I would have to kill you."

Chars struggled to pull his hands free but the straps were too strong and only caused his wrists to burn due to the irritation.

Chars thought, *what a jerk!* But said, "Okay tough guy, do you have anything we can cut the plastic binders with?"

"No..." he said quickly, but then followed with "wait, yes I do, if they did not check my pants leg. Let me lie down on my back and put my feet in the air."

As the man moved around to his back the light under the door became visible and Chars' ability to see improved tremendously. Now he could make out the man's profile as well as the extension of his legs. Chars was able to push down the man's trouser leg easily, and sure enough a small knife was concealed in a sheath. Working from behind his back was a challenge, but the leather was soft and he was able to lift the knife out. Grasping it in his hands, he used short strokes to sever the plastic leg binder. Despite their close proximity the man was able to stand much more easily this time. The two stood back to back, while Chars manipulated the knife into position. Trying to slice thru the Plasti-Cuffs on the other man, Chars dropped the knife and the process had to begin again.

"Damn it, we need to get out of here," the man said impatiently.

"You do it then," Chars said sharply.

Chars felt like purposely stabbing the guy if he did not lose the attitude. After much effort was spent trying to

219

bend and locate at the same time, the man was able to grasp the knife in his bound hands. He began to slice Chars' restraints. Growing tired and not making progress fast enough, the man began to weave back and forth trying to cut the ties quicker. Chars felt the knife penetrate his back and he jumped, letting out a cry of pain. The quick movement was just what the job required and the plastic cuff fell loose.

"That hurt!" Chars pressed his hand to the small of his back. He felt a warm blood. "Great, you drew blood."

"Uh, sorry," he said unconcerned, "Could you cut me loose?"

"Wait a minute. You owe me some answers," Chars said.

The man's head swung back and forth as if to say, I knew this would happen if he got loose first.

"Look, Huckleberry, I don't need any friends, so let's just get the hell out of here and you can go look for friends somewhere else."

"You are really a prize, you know it. I told you who I am. Who are you?" Chars asked.

The man was silent. He was trying to figure out if there was any advantage of telling this reporter who he was or if there was any threat. He could give a false name, but really, what was the point.

Figuring they were going to die anyway, he finally said, "My name is Jimmy Fred. Now cut me loose."

Chars was shocked, absolutely stunned and speechless. He wanted to say: I have been trying to find out who you are and here you are. Chars' jaw must have dropped a foot, but the darkness allowed Chars to conceal his surprise.

He finally managed to say, "No last name?"

"Look buddy, I told you I don't want to be friends. Cut me loose. We are in a shit load of trouble and the sooner we get out of this..." he struggled for a description, "jail cell, the better chance we have to live," Jimmy Fred said.

Chars cut the plastic cuffs. Jimmy Fred began immediately to feel along the walls for a light switch. He found it and switched it on. He tried it several more times, which irritated Chars. It was obvious there was not a light bulb in the socket.

"Look around for any thing we can use to get out of here," Jimmy Fred said with authority.

Jimmy Fred flipped the light switch a few more times just to make sure it did not work. Chars thought about slapping the back of the Jimmy Fred's head to get him to stop, but thought better of it. There seemed to be nothing in the closet that could even remotely be used for an escape.

With nothing to lose, Chars decided to try a long shot, "Tell me one thing, Jimmy Fred, what happened to Dave Coughlin?"

There was silence. Jimmy Fred's first inclination was to deny knowing who Dave Coughlin was. Jimmy Fred now knew it was a mistake to have told Reynolds who he was. He thought, *I am such a dumb ass. Why in the hell did I tell him or anyone much less a reporter? Damn it, Jimmy Fred, now you are probably going to have to kill this idiot.*

Knowing Jimmy Fred was trying to decide whether to admit knowing David or not, Chars decided to try to prod him along.

"I know you know who he is," Chars prompted.

"You don't know shit. But I can tell you, the last time I saw him, he was sailing his boat," Jimmy Fred answered honestly.

"The last time I called his phone, some mafia goon answered. When did you see him?" asked Chars.

"What makes you think it was mafia?" asked Jimmy Fred.

"Because, the guy sounded like a mobster," Chars said.

"Like a mobster? How does a mobster sound?" Jimmy Fred asked mockingly.

Chars wanted to slap the man, but decided to humor him, "Yuz knows whats Imz goin to duz, I'll tells yuz what Iz going to duz."

Jimmy Fred smiled to himself recognizing the description of Lil' Don, but said nothing. "Well, that is a stereotype and I am surprised that a reporter would stoop so low as to insult Italian Americans."

Chars was unmoved. He asked again, "What happened to David?"

"What is this Jeopardy?" He paused and said, "I saw him yesterday, or at least I think it was yesterday. He sold his boat to the boys upstairs," Jimmy Fred said angrily, "The same ones who stuck you and me down here. Look, we have got to get out of here, so question- answer time is over. Start looking for a way out."

"I think I know why I'm here, but why are you here?" asked Chars.

"Seems they like Tampa better than Ft. Lauderdale," Jimmy Fred said and laughed derisively.

Obviously not making any progress, Chars tried a different line of questioning. "Why did the mob kill Nikki?" Chars asked.

"You know too much. In fact, you know just enough to be dangerous. They didn't kill him. At least I am pretty sure they didn't. Again, I think these Arabs did it. They call us infidels, the fuckers," Jimmy Fred said bitterly. "Look, we're more than likely the next entrée for the sharks, but if we get out of here, just make sure you report that I had nothing to do with these Arabs."

Chars immediately knew that Jimmy Fred was up to his arm pits with the Arabs, but he said nothing. Chars was feeling along the wall and came to a section that was cool to the touch.

"That's odd. This section of wall is cool. Let me see your knife." Chars carefully began to scrape away plaster. "So they're Arabs."

Jimmy Fred ignored the question, but was watching Chars digging into the wall. Growing impatient with Chars' progress, Jimmy Fred said, "Let me see that," repossessing the knife.

He jabbed it into the spot that Chars had been scraping.

Chars protested, "I think we need to take this slow, I don't know what is on the other side."

"That's why you are where you are and why I am where I am. No balls, no glory. Besides we don't have a lot of time to be messing with this."

"It appears we are in the same place," Chars said derisively.

"Shut the hell up," Jimmy Fred said with contempt.

He began digging the knife in. There was a sound of plastic giving way.

"See, progress," Jimmy Fred said.

He pulled on his knife, but it seemed stuck.

Chars deadpanned, "That did not sound good."

Jimmy Fred gave it a big yank. The knife came out. It was followed by a stream of brown water spraying Jimmy Fred in the chest.

"Oh shit!" Jimmy Fred yelled.

Chars stepped back successfully avoiding the spray, but the splash and the smell were not to be avoided.

Jimmy Fred let out, "Oh my God!"

Chars pulled a handkerchief from his back pocket and covered his nose and mouth. The spray of water increased taking a full two inches of plaster away from the wall. Sewage began pouring out the small clearing at the bottom of the door, but the level was slowly rising in the closet. Chars felt the water level climbing up his shoe. The smell was so awful that Chars turned and vomited. Jimmy Fred started stabbing at the plaster surrounding the hole like a man possessed.

The water was running into the next room, and one of the ship personnel entered the room and called out, "Oh shit!" The staff member spoke into his radio, "We are taking on water. Get some people down here!"

The hole in the water pipe actually seemed to be increasing as Jimmy Fred continued to stab away at the wall. He finally cut out a hole big enough that he could grip wallboard with two hands. Chars moved around to help him, and the two of them successfully yanked a gaping hole in the wall. Chars could see light coming through a light socket on the other side. Being careful to avoid studs, he landed a full punch to the opposite wallboard. Chars reflexed with pain in his hand. His hand had broken thru and it was Jimmy Fred's turn. Jimmy Fred stepped into a horizontal punch that extended thru the wall and into the next room. Panicked voices could be heard in mass on the other side of the metal door. They were trying to decide where the water was coming from and what turn off valve would stop it. No one on the staff seemed to have a key to this closet. Chars and Jimmy Fred heard the main thruster engines shut off. Presumably the captain had been notified of some type of breach.

Punching and kicking their way thru to the next room, Chars and Jimmy Fred quickly checked to see who might be about. A door on the other side led out into a hallway. The footsteps of workers could be heard as well as several voices shouting out commands. The water stream was finally shut off or maybe the sewage ran out. Chars and Jimmy Fred slipped out into the hallway just as Masud Muhammad Al Rashid opened the closet door and found his birds had flown the coup.

Just in case The Galleon was, in fact, taking on water, Captain Bill Love radioed a preliminary distress code to the Harbor Master. The signal was also picked up by the U.S. Coast Guard. True to their motto, "Semper Paratus" or Always Ready, the Seventh Coast Guard District's Cutter patrolling out of Miami, changed course. By happenstance the cutter was within three nautical miles and would intercept as a precaution.

Chapter Thirty Four

Lazy C Ranch, Scottsdale Arizona

Stevie jerked around and looked at Amos with a look of disbelief. The betrayal had been revealed and the young boy could not understand.

Amos tried to ignore the boy's stare and spoke to Charlie in an angry voice, "It has been one screw up after another. Do you think you can handle it from here on out?"

"Yeah, Injun Joe, we will handle it from here. All right boys, let's go swimming." Charlie yanked Stevie up from atop Cowboy.

"No you can't use the damn lake," Amos said, disbelieving Charlie's stupidity.

Hamish noticed that Cowboy was slowly regaining consciousness. Hamish took into account the doors and possible escape routes. He also try to assess Stevie's injuries. He appeared to be still full of piss and vinegar.

"Then we have to do it here," Luigi said.

"No not here either! You take them as far away from here as possible. I have already dealt with your blow back," Amos said.

He was clearly irritated at all of this. But it was about to get even more complicated. A police siren could be heard in the distance.

Amos turned and said, "Shit." He quickly looked around and began forming a plan. "Okay Charlie, you will have to take them to the lake now. Just make them disappear till I can get rid of the state guys."

Charlie gave Hamish a push toward the door and gave Stevie a heavy slap to the back of the head. Stevie flinched and gave Charlie a nasty glare.

"Come on, little man. It is nut cutting time and the turtles need feeding."

Stevie turned like a coiling cobra and a look of unabated hatred. Charlie responded with an evil smile and pointed his gun between Stevie's eyes.

"I have been looking forward to this, you little shit," Charlie said and gave Stevie a push out the door causing him to fall on the dirt.

Hamish helped Stevie up and pulled him close. Charlie pointed them in the direction of Respite Lake.

Inside, Amos said, "Luigi, you are going to have to pretend to be Cain. I will try to send these guys somewhere else, but they may to want to check things out. Stay in here and try not to talk."

Amos holstered his weapon and headed out the front door. Out back Charlie herded Hamish and Stevie down a path to the lake.

"Everything is fine," Amos said in a loud voice with his hands up.

He moved out to the arriving state police car. Evidently the officers saw Amos and silenced the siren. The state police cruiser came to a stop, but the lights in the grill were still flashing intermittent red and blue. Amos held up his badge while shielding his eyes from the headlights. Upon seeing the officers, Amos decided on his deception.

He said, "Jon and Greg, how are you doing?"

Both men open the doors and began the process of gearing up. The two officers, Jon Carmel and Greg Lang, were smiling having recognized the tribal law officer.

"Amos, what are you doing up here?" Jon asked.

Greg spoke into his shoulder microphone. "This is unit A1-2-22, we have arrived for the 245-B and we are 10-98."

"10-4, A1-2-22," the voice came back over the speaker. Before leaving the cruiser Greg reached in to turn off the flashing lights and dim the "brights".

Amos had to be careful even though the two officers had obviously relaxed. Everything was being videotaped, so Amos could not make any mistakes.

He waited till they reached him. "Everything is fine. One of the ladies I know that runs a nearby store called me as a friend. She reported someone suspicious hanging out here. I told her not to bother you guys, I could take a look. It was just the new owner, moving some stuff in, that's all."

Greg said, "Are you talking about Mavis?"

Amos cautiously said, "Yeah, Mavis."

Jon said, "That's strange, she is the one that called us."

"She probably got nervous that I was gone so long. I got talking to Mr. Cain, I lost track of time," Amos said.

"Yeah, I can see that," Greg said and gave a smile.

"I can stop back by the store on the way back and put her at ease. Sorry you guys were bothered," Amos said with as little strain as he could manage.

Hearing the conversation outside and eager to play his part, Luigi stepped to the door and waived at the two officers. Amos cussed to himself silently. He was desperately hoping that Luigi would not speak.

Jon said quietly, "That's the guy from New Zealand? He looks like a Chicago mobster. No wonder Mavis was suspicious."

Greg laughed softly and said, "Well, thanks Amos; it looks like everything is fine. If you have everything under control, we do have another stop to make."

Both the officers turned back to the patrol vehicle with Amos moving in step with them. He was feeling like this was going to work out. He just needed them to go on their way.

Turning to Amos, Jon asked, "Whose rental car is that we passed on the way in?"

He leaned into his vehicle and keyed in a few words into the laptop. Amos took in a breath. He had forgotten about the car that was parked up from the ranch house. He tried to think of something quickly but all that came to mind was it was Kiwi's car.

Amos said, "I think it belongs to Mr. Cain."

Puzzled, Jon asked, "This yellow Jeep too?"

Back at the ranch house and having regained full consciousness, Cowboy rose, gave a mighty shake and pushed open the screen door. Luigi turned in time to see the screen door slam back closed. The slamming of the back porch door momentarily broke the conversation of the officers and Amos. The thought had not occurred to them that there might be someone else in the house, and it could have been Luigi, who was no longer on the front porch. Charlie, Hamish and Stevie were within twenty yards of Respite Lake. Racing down the path, Cowboy sprinted to catch up. Hamish was the first to recognize that sound pattern of his dog at full stride and immediately saw this as the chance he and Stevie needed.

Charlie heard the dog approaching a moment later, but not in time. Trying to get off a shot, Charlie stumbled into Hamish knocking him into Stevie. Cowboy left the ground in full stride. He collided with Charlie, knocking the big man to the ground. This time Cowboy latched on to the gun hand forcing Charlie to drop his weapon and cry out in pain.

The officers heard the vicious growl in the distance. Greg cued his shoulder microphone, and the two raced around the ranch house toward Respite Lake. Amos, not knowing how to salvage this situation, followed the officers.

Luigi waited for the officers to leave, then quickly went to the police vehicle. He disabled the radio with a silenced shot. He then sent a shot into the two tires on the driver side. He then went to his own rental car and drove toward the lake, using the moon to light his way.

When the three officers arrived, Hamish was holding the Mosquito. He had called Cowboy off of Charlie, who was holding his bleeding hand. Stevie was standing slightly behind Hamish.

The State Patrol carefully approached shining a flashlight to guide their way. Officer Jon Carmel, weapon drawn, went into a three point stance. He said in a commanding voice, "State Police, drop your weapon, now!"

Officer Greg Lang was again talking into his shoulder microphone, but received no answer. Seeing Amos behind the officer did little to bolster Hamish's confidence in law enforcement in the United States. Cowboy sensing more conflict stood at full height with his neck hair standing at attention. He let out a menacing growl.

"Sir, I need you to drop your weapon and restrain the animal. We will shoot. This can be worked out so no one else gets hurt," Officer Jon Carmel commanded once again.

With the headlights off and hidden behind foliage, Luigi's car came to a stop just 30 yards from the confrontation. He exited the car and moved in closer to the unfolding action. He could make out Charlie lying on the ground, but still alive. He now had to get Charlie, and get the hell out of here. But who to shoot first was a real dilemma. He needed to get closer to hear what was being said. Maybe the cops would kill the Kiwi for him and the Indian cop could lie his way out of the mess. He crept in closer to the action.

"I will put my weapon down, but the man behind you…" Hamish was cut off by Amos who knew his true role was about to be revealed.

"You heard him, put down your weapon and release the boy," Amos said stepping forward with his gun drawn and aimed. Amos' shot was off his target, but still caught Hamish in the upper left arm, causing him to recoil. In one fluid motion, Hamish pushed Stevie down to the ground, kneeled and shot Amos in the chest with the silenced weapon he had recovered from Charlie. Both State officers reacted by going prone, but did not shoot for fear of hitting the boy. Charlie, still holding his injured hand, rolled into the grass and began crawling away.

Hamish knew Stevie was in danger, but his presence was the only thing keeping the officers from shooting. Hamish moved with Stevie into the tall grass and lay down. His arm was bleeding and would soon become a real problem. The pain was unlike any the Kiwi had ever encountered. He needed to buy some time. He was not sure if the police would help them or not. But Hamish sensed that Amos was having to cover his tracks and maybe, these new blokes were potential rescuers.

Luigi was kneeling in the brush watching all the action. No one had noticed his arrival, Charlie included. He saw Charlie over to the side and decided to move any closer would risk being seen by the others.

He called out as softly as he could, "Charlie, come on this way,"

Charlie was not the only one to hear. The voice drew the attention of Cowboy. As Charlie began to move towards Luigi's voice, Cowboy lifted to pursue Charlie. Sensing that Cowboy would be hurt, Stevie grabbed Cowboy's collar. Cowboy dragged Stevie a full two feet before the boy was able to regain control, get his feet underneath, and tackle the dog. Stevie used all his weight to keep the dog from pursuing and possible getting shot in the process.

Officer Lang tracked the fleeing man with his Glock, but did not fire. He was still trying to put everyone in the proper context.

Luigi raised his head enough to see Charlie making his way toward him. He saw Hamish rise up to fire his weapon. Luigi aimed and fired twice in the direction of Hamish. The officer now saw Luigi off to the side. They recognized him as the man in the house claiming to be the Kiwi. But it was obvious from Hamish's accent that there had been a ruse attempted. The truth was starting to be revealed and Officer Carmel was quickly putting the situation together. No longer believing the previous identities and seeing this man firing in the direction of a child, Carmel knew all he needed to know. He fired at Luigi hitting him in the neck, sending the mobster reeling backwards. Simultaneously, Hamish fired at Luigi, but struck Charlie in the upper back as he strayed into the firing path. Charlie managed to crawl to Luigi who was not going to live. He grabbed Luigi's gun then crawled past the body on all fours. Turning, he fired two shots toward Hamish. Charlie made his way to the car and painfully slid into the front seat of the car. Fortunately Luigi had left the keys in the ignition. Charlie started it and threw down the gear into drive.

Greg Lang yelled at Hamish, "Okay, show me your hands and come out."

Jon Carmel quickly checked Amos' pulse and then started up toward the dark sedan. The rental car roared in a circle kicking up a cloud of dust and gravel. Charlie let loose a series of shots that caused Jon to halt his pursuit.

Hamish rolled back over and looked toward Stevie. He was on the ground with Cowboy by his side whimpering. "The boy is hit! The boy is hit!" Hamish yelled. "Call emergency! Oh no! Oh no!"

Chapter Thirty Five

Off the coast of Ft. Lauderdale, Florida

"This is the U.S. Coast Guard's WSES- 2 Sunbird. We are coming up on your port side. We have a visual on you, Galleon. Please state your problem," David Forsyth, the captain of the cutter, said over the radio. The Sunbird was a 109 foot vessel that cruised at 25 knots but could easily reach 30 knots with its two 1800 horsepower diesel engines. This particular vessel included only small arms, but enough to take on all but the most extremely armed smugglers.

Captain Bill Love stated perfunctorily, "I copy you, Sunbird. This is Captain Bill Love of the Galleon. I am told we have everything under control. We were on our return to port when we received a report of water below deck. That is why I sounded a distress call. We had a sewage pipe break in a lower aft compartment. We have sealed off the source of that water. I am waiting on a status report from the Travel Director. Over."

The Galleon was a triple-level ship with slot machines and a galley on the main level. Table games were located on the top level. The below deck level was used for storage, employee activities and breaks.

The sewage had in fact been stopped, but this also meant the no one could use the restrooms.

Mohammed Al Rashid was searching frantically for his escapees in the lower storage rooms, but with no success. He called one of his men on his handheld portable radio. Since his men served as security, the ear buds were not conspicuous. Four in all, the armed men left their posts and followed their directives to search the boat for the two men that were supposed to be locked up.

Jimmy Fred and Chars were drenched and the smell was nauseating. Moving cautiously, they were able to make it up a ladder leading to the main deck. The excitement could be heard from the betting floor. The bells and clanking of coins falling into the reservoirs was an exhilarating sound to many. Trying to remain undetected, they located the bathrooms. Before they could reach the men's room, one of Rashid's security force could be seen headed in their direction. Jimmy Fred said, Quick, in here." In here, meant the women's room. Fortunately due to the restroom prohibition, it was unoccupied. They could hear the armed man enter the men's room. The banging of swinging stall doors could be heard thru the wall. A loud conversation ensued because a man was taking care of business in the last stall. The security guard demanded that the door be unlocked and evidently the man was refusing. Chars hoped the man would hold out for a long time.

They heard the guard say, "No one is supposed to be using the restrooms. You can not flush because the water had to be turned off."

Chars could not hear the response of the man, but it evidently was sufficient to stop the interrogation.

Meanwhile, Jimmy Fred was looking for an escape route and Chars was washing his face, hands and arms in the sink. On the door there was a loud "Bang, bang, bang."

Chars jump nearly four inches off the ground. Jimmy Fred quickly retreated into the closest stall and locked the door.

The security man said loudly in a Middle Eastern accent, "Excuse me, I am a security officer and I need to check the bathroom."

In his best woman's voice, Chars said, "Just a minute. I will be out in just a minute."

"Lady, I am coming in. No one is supposed to be using the restrooms and I need to check for two men," he said opening the door slowly.

"No men in here; please don't come in. I am not decent," said Chars as he moved behind the entry door. He lifted a large stainless steel trash can above his head.

Opening the door he said, "Lady, I am sorry but I must check,".... He never finished his sentence.

Chars crashed the can on top of the man's head sending him to the tile floor. Upon landing the man's forehead received a nice crack as well. The blood from the split began a slow path toward a nearby drain. The man's 38, blue steel revolver slid into the stall where Jimmy Fred had retreated. When he emerged, Jimmy Fred was aiming the gun at Chars.

"All right, Mr. Reynolds, I am going to use you to get me off this boat.

Get the clothes off this guy," Jimmy Fred said, pointing his gunning at the fallen security man. Jimmy Fred stepped over the man, and with his rear end next to the entry door, started undressing. Careful to keep his gun trained on Chars, he lifted one leg out of his pants leg."

A man's voice said, "Everything okay in there?"

The door opened, bumping Jimmy Fred off balance. When Jimmy Fred tried to break his fall, he lost control of the gun. Chars quickly reached down and picked it up. The elderly man inexplicably stepped in the bathroom and began apologizing for knocking Jimmy Fred to the floor.

"I am so sorry..."

He realized that Chars was holding a gun and saw Jimmy Fred on the ground struggling with his pants around his feet. His eyes then looked down to the bleeding security guard. The old man may have been not visually acute, but there was little doubt in his mind that he had made a mistake by involving himself in this situation. He immediately put his hands in the air. The door, unblocked, closed behind him.

Chars said, "You can put your hands down."

Still not convinced, the man said, "I lost all my money at the craps table. I don't have any left to steal."

Chars interrupted, "You are not getting robbed. We just need to get off this boat."

The old man said, "You look like shit."

"Yes we do. We are trying to remedy that as we speak," Chars said and indicated to Jimmy Fred to start stripping the guard. "Say mister, I am going to need your jacket."

"No way mister; I am not helping some criminal."

Desperate, Chars said, "Do you read the newspapers?"

"Sure," the man said almost insulted.

"I am Charles Reynolds with the Miami Express," Chars said with a winning smile while trying to straighten his bedraggled hair.

"Sure, now I recognize you. Your picture is next to your column. I'll be darned. What are you doing in the women's restroom?...he paused, "looking like that and..."

237

he paused again, "holding a gun on a man with his pants down,…" another pause, "and what happened to him? Is he alive?"

"I don't know, but the sooner I can get out of here, the sooner I can get help. I was kidnapped by the owners of this boat. I am trying to call for help." Chars said and deliberately pointed the gun at Jimmy Fred's face.

The man did not look convinced at all by the story.

"Keep going, Jimmy Fred," Chars said in a threatening tone.

Chars turned back to the older man and asked, "Do you have a cell phone?"

"As a matter of fact I do. Are you going to steal that too?" the man asked.

"Just borrow," Chars said taking it from him, then dialed 911. He gave the phone back to the man.

"Just stay on the line and tell the cops there is an emergency aboard this boat and to send help."

"The Coast Guard is parked right out side. Do you need more help than that?" the old man asked.

"Jimmy Fred. If we are going to get off this boat alive, now is our best chance. But we are going to have to work together."

"911, What is our emergency?" a voice said on the man's cell phone.

The man looked toward Chars puzzled as to what to say. Chars shoved the gun into his waistband and took the phone.

To the old man, Chars asked, "What's the name of this boat?"

Looking at Chars like he was addressing a idiot, the man replied, "The Galleon."

"I'm Charles Reynolds. I have been kidnapped and I am on board the ship called The Galleon."

"The Gallon?" the operator asked.

"No. The Galleon," Chars enunciated with exaggeration.

Chars handed the phone back to the man, "Just do what you can. I won't need the jacket after all. Jimmy Fred had already pulled on the security guard's pants and was buttoning up the shirt.

Chars said, "Get his earpiece." Jimmy Fred reached down and pulled the blue tooth receiver out of the unconscious man's ear and picked up the radio unit that carried the signal.

As they moved out of the bathroom, the old man yelled behind them, "I don't believe your Charles Reynolds, he looks a lot younger that you do. You are some type of Las Vegas look a like, aren't you?"

Chars sighed and was looking out into the hallway.

"We have to find a floating device and get off this ship."

"What are we going to do, jump?!" Jimmy Fred asked. "You are crazy."

A gun shot from a silenced weapon struck the wall next to Jimmy Fred's left ear. Plaster and wood fragments showered down on top of the two men. Both Chars and Jimmy Fred instinctively ducked low. The shot had come from the stairwell down below so Chars and Jimmy Fred retreated back toward the crowd of gamblers, who were oblivious to the active battle.

"Get in the crowd and head to the front of the ship. Go that way," Chars said pointing back to the crowd.

In the Captain's Enclave, Captain Love said into the radio, "This is niner two Alpha Charlie Two Niner, The Galleon to the U.S. Coast Guard Cutter Sunbird."

"Go ahead, Galleon."

"Thanks for your attention. I just received the all clear and we are headed on to port," Captain Love said, "We appreciate your assistance."

'Roger, Galleon. We will be in the area if you need us."

Chars got several looks from the patrons of the Galleon as he went by on the outer deck, but most were too busy playing the slots to notice. The upper deck was out of the line of site. Life preservers had been strategically hung on the exterior walls. Chars unhooked two on his way to the bow. While walking quickly, he handed one of the white circles back to Jimmy Fred. As they passed a window, the two caught the attention of another security guard who was moving through the inner casino.

The security guard spoke into his microphone, "I have a visual of the two persons of interest. They are moving along the port side toward the bow, carrying life preservers. Waiting for your direction," the guard said into his radio handset.

Chars' plan was falling apart when he saw the Coast Guard cutter speeding off in a northerly direction. Chars waved his one free hand above his head, but with no apparent success. The cutter continued on its way, oblivious to Chars, but the crowd inside did start to notice. Many paused to see what the excitement was about. One of passengers tried to ask a security guard who was closing in on the two men, but was ignored, then pushed out of the way. This caused a couple of the other guests to voice their dislike of the man's treatment. The security guard gave the crowd a menacing look and pulled his weapon. This caused a panic within the casino. People began ducking and screaming. Several moved to hide behind the slot machines and other headed away from the threat.

Al Rashid spoke into his microphone, "We must capture these two, but if you can, do it without shooting them. If you do shoot, make sure you **do not** shoot any guests!"

Jimmy Fred was out of breath and could barely get the words out. "We cannot jump in front of the boat! Why are we going this way?"

"I was trying to get the attention of the Coast Guard, Jimmy Fred. Where would you suggest?!" Chars shouted derisively.

Up ahead a security guard stepped around the corner and blocked their path. Chars pulled the gun from his waistband and fired. The shot sailed high and the man dove back around the corner.

All of the security personnel who heard the shot simultaneously spoke into their handsets, "Shots fired!"

The crowd's panic increased to a fever pitch upon hearing the gun shots. Some patrons were still trying to cash out their machines, while others had abandoned their game without delay. One employee stood on a chair urging the people to remain calm, but someone inadvertently bumped into the man, knocking him off his chair.

A lady in a ¾ length paisley print dress, clearly overdressed for the Galleon, screamed, "They are going to kill us all!"

Another man could be heard yelling, "It must be pirates!"

An excited murmur of "pirates" moved thru the crowd.

Many of the gamblers were moving with no apparent destination in mind. Since the gunfire was outside, it made no sense to go to those exits, so the dining hall seemed to a good choice for many. Several of the more level-headed men were beginning to assume command. One man with an athletic six foot frame yelled, "Get the women toward the back of the cafeteria. You two men over there, let's set up a resistance wall at the door."

The passengers, needing direction from someone fell in line with the plan.

Outside, all of Al Rashid's men had their weapons pulled and were prepared for a fight. There was nowhere for the escapees to flee. Chars tried to get to a set of stairs toward the front of the boat which led to the third deck, but a security officer stepped out of the stair's recess. Chars and Jimmy Fred were trapped.

"What are we going to do?" yelled Jimmy Fred.

"Jump!" Chars said, throwing the life preserver over and climbing the rail. Gun in hand, Chars leapt out as far as he could from the side. On his way down, he tried to point the gun up and fire at the security guards, but the fear of hitting the water overcame him and he had to look down.

"Are you crazy?" asked Jimmy Fred.

There was no answer from Chars, who had already begun his descent.

A member of the security team yelled into his radio, "He's jumping, he's jumping! Man overboard, man overboard. Should we shoot him?

"SHOOT HIM!" yelled Al Rashid.

Upon hearing the "Man Overboard" call, Captain Love killed the main engines and the Galleon began slowing.

Chars hit the water feet first, but it was still a tremendous jolt. He had managed to raise his arms in an effort to go straight in the water, but his momentum slammed him into the water. His leap carried Chars far enough out to avoid being sucked back into the wake. He plunged under water and the initial impact dazed him slightly causing him to lose control of his gun. His momentum plunged him almost twenty feet below the surface. The security force began firing into the ocean in the general direction of Chars' submersion. Fortunately for Chars, bullets do not travel well through water. Most bullets break up after traveling about three to eight feet. The faster the bullet is traveling, the faster it breaks up. Recovering from the impact, Chars could see the bullet trails above him, but none struck him. He was safest right where he was, but couldn't hold his breath for much longer. He needed to get to the surface and began to pull himself toward upward.

Chars' mind momentarily flashed to his boyhood in Indiana. In his mind, he had just jumped off the wood diving tower at McCormick's Creek State Park. He had been terrified the first time just to move to the edge and look over. But after seeing several other boys his age run and jump, he had gathered the courage and sprinted off the edge, flailing and falling at the same time. He instinctively knew to straighten just before impact. He remembered the exhilaration after the jump and the race back up the 30 foot tower to do it all over again. Chars came back to the present and began a quick climb to the surface.

On board the Galleon, Jimmy Fred raised his hands above his head surrendering to the security force. Several of the security force waited for Chars to resurface, but the boat had already traveled past his entry, and he presented no real target. Two of the security force roughly slammed Jimmy Fred up against a window wall. They frisked him and fitted a plastic zip cuff on him. The view through the window provided a substantial level of entertainment to the remaining onlookers inside the casino. The level of panic subsided, but the excitement of the capture and a man jumping over board would provide lots of stories to take home.

One lady said to her sister, "Maybe this was part of the show. You know, like they do in Vegas."

Her partner said contemplatively, "The one that jumped off the boat seemed rather genuine."

From the rear of the Galleon, flashing lights could be seen on the horizon. It was a second Coast Guard Cutter with agents Fairbanks and Terrell aboard. From the other direction, the first Coast Guard Sunbird had circled around was again headed toward The Galleon.

Chars finally surfaced, stuffed the gun into his waistband at the small of his back and began swimming to his circular life preserver. In the distance he could hear the siren of a Coast Guard cutter approaching. He could also see that The Galleon had stopped. He just hoped it did not circle around to recover him.

Chapter Thirty Six

Miami, Florida

Having been questioned and released by the F.B.I., Chars was driven back to Miami by a F.B.I. agent. It was made it clear that Chars was to remain available and only would be released to Jerry because he was a police officer. He was able to convince the agent to stop by a Verizon store, prior to taking him to the Miami Police station. He was not sure where his phone was, but he needed the old one disconnected and a new one with his current number. Sure enough, all of that was handled in a matter of minutes, after paying a couple hundred bucks of course.

"Next stop, Miami P.D.!" Chars announced to the slightly annoyed agent.

Upon arrival to the station, Chars was released to the custody of Sergeant Jerry Reynolds. Chars filled him in on the story, finishing with its conclusion.

"The Coast Guard picked me up and boarded The Galleon."

"You were smart to place the kidnapping call when you did. That Coast Guard cutter was able to turn around. The F.B.I. had been on its way because of Jimmy Fred's disappearance. Evidently they lost him after he left Washington. They picked up his trail again in Ft. Lauderdale. Then lost him again, evidently around the time he boarded The Galleon."

"They sure showed up in the nick of time," Chars said.

Chars phone vibrated. Looking at the caller I.D. Chars said, "I don't know this number." He answered, "This is Charles Reynolds."

"Charles, what did you find out?" Scott Tivy asked.

Chars pointed to his phone and mouthed the words, "This is the guy."

"I met Jimmy Fred," Chars said to the caller.

"Wow, you are good. What did you find out?" Scott Tivy asked.

"Jimmy Fred is an asshole. Besides that, I think he may have been in cahoots with Senator Kaspar from Ohio," Chars said while writing a note to Jerry.

"That confirms it. You have not read the papers today, have you?" Scott Tivy asked.

"No, I was a little tied up over the last 18 hours," Chars commented dryly. Jerry let out a small laugh and raised his eyebrows.

"I did not know the Senator's name for sure, but when I saw the paper, I guessed that he might be the one involved," Scott said, leaving Chars still in the dark.

"What did the article say?" Chars asked.

"He's dead," Scott blurted out.

"Dead? How?" asked Chars and then turned to Jerry, "Senator Kaspar is dead."

Jerry shrugged and said, "Who is Senator Kaspar?" He got up to go find a national paper. Leaning out the door, Jerry said in a loud voice, "Carolyn. Bring me a copy of the U.S.A. Today."

"He fell down a flight of stairs in his Ohio home," Scott said with cynicism. "I told you, these guys don't mess around."

Chars told Jerry, "He fell down a flight of stairs."

Jerry scrunched up his face and deadpanned, "That was clumsy of him."

"And, did you read the news in Arizona?" Scott asked.

"No," Chars said, and held up his hands to Jerry as if to say there is something else.

"There is a story about three men being shot by the State Police in North Scottsdale. One of them was a tribal police officer," Scott said excitedly.

"I'm sorry, can you translate what that means?" Chars asked.

"Topolo," Scott enunciated slowly and then continued. "One got away, but the one that died was identified by the F.B.I. as Luigi Beltran," Scott said as if that should mean something to Chars.

Chars repeated the name to Jerry.

Jerry said, "Hey, that was one of the two guys they picked up here in Miami... that were looking for you," Jerry said.

Scott heard what Jerry said and asked, "Why were they looking for you?"

"We are not sure they were looking for me," Chars said with irritation. He paused. "But in hindsight they probably were," Chars said with resignation. Chars ran his hand through his hair as he was trying to make sense of all this. He knew that if he could concentrate that all the pieces would come together in a discernable puzzle.

"They have tied Raleigh's murder to Luigi Beltran. You want to know how?" Scott asked. Without waiting for an answer, "Luigi was wearing Raleigh's boots. I am telling you, these guys are ruthless," Scott said with fear in his voice.

Chars let out a deep breath. He was trying to filter thru all that this man was spewing out at a frantic pace. He needed to figure a way to get him to calm down.

"You need to go out to Arizona because it all fits together some way," Scott said.

"Why do I need to go to Arizona?" Chars inquired.

"There are two witnesses, but both were shot in the confrontation. One of them is a twelve year old boy," Scott said. "They are both in the hospital but the boy is critical. He must know something and the mob tried to whack him."

"That is terrible. All of this was in the paper?" Chars asked.

Jerry was showing signs of frustration, rummaging thru the U.S.A. Today, with no luck. Chars mimed that act of searching on the internet and Jerry acknowledged.

"Well some of it. Think about how this fits in with the gambling boat down there in Tampa. Look I have to go, I think I have a tail and I need to get lost," Scott said and ended the call.

Chars shouted into his phone, "No, wait!" But Scott had disconnected the call and was gone. "Damn it!" Chars said, snapping the phone shut in disgust.

"He hung up. He said, think how the Arizona deal and the Florida deal fit together," Chars said in a bewildered tone.

Jerry said, "Both involved this guy Jimmy Fred and most likely the Topolo family. What more is there?"

"I assume Jimmy Fred is singing like a bird," Chars leaned back in the swivel chair in front of Jerry's desk.

"Actually, from what I heard, he was the first to lawyer up. The Arabs have been sent to Guantanamo Bay. The President isn't much for lawyers," Jerry said laughing and taking a sip of black coffee.

"Really," Chars said intrigued, "they think they are gambling terrorists?"

"I don't know what the Muslim terrorists would want gambling boats for except to launder money. But I thought they were against gambling and all that," Jerry said.

"You have got me, but I can't believe that Jimmy Fred does not have something to trade. But he may be scared. Having someone try to kill you does tend to work on your bravado a bit."

"The OC boys told me that one of the Arabs was a man called, The Scorpion. The Lauderdale police are furious that the Febees took the catch. There is some talk that they may have actually been the ones to hit Nikki."

"Oh my gosh, this actually may make sense. I need to find out what happened to Dave Coughlin," Chars said.

"I talked to your friend Deb. She said neither Dave nor his boat have been seen for three days," Jerry said. "Maybe he just went on a long fishing trip."

"If that were true, I would feel much better. I think the Topolo people grabbed him, because I asked him to snoop around. That guy that answered the phone was definitely mafia. Jimmy Fred said that he saw David sailing his boat as late as yesterday, but I don't know whether he was telling the truth or not."

"What made you think it was mafia?" Jerry asked.

"He talked like 'what's yuz going to duz?' Sort of like you, but with less class," Chars said

"Thanks a lot," Jerry said and grimaced.

"Why isn't the F.B.I. on this?" Chars asked.

"They are. They were on to Jimmy Fred long before you even knew who he was," Jerry said.

"I don't know if I want to talk to them again, I spent almost an entire day answering their questions and they would not tell me anything," Chars said wearily. "I thought they were going to lock me up for improperly exiting a vessel at sea or discharging a weapon at sea."

"They arrested Jimmy Fred, right?" asked Jerry.

"I don't think they did, but they are holding him as a material witness," Chars said.

"That's good. If the mob gets wind that he has been captured, they might push him down a flight of stairs," Jerry said.

"How in the hell do the Arabs fit into this, Jerry?" asked Chars.

"The question is why would the Arabs all of sudden want to kill Jimmy Fred?" Jerry asked.

"Jerry, you have no idea how bad I wanted to kill him after being with him for two minutes. The guy is a complete asshole," Chars said.

"Okay, setting aside the possibility for a minute that the Arabs want to kill Jimmy Fred because he is a jerk, can we come up with another reason?" Jerry said sarcastically.

"I asked him that question," Chars said.

"And what did he say?" Jerry asked as if he were dealing with a child.

"I don't really remember," Chars said with embarrassment. "But he did not give me a real answer. It was some obscure answer. I really don't think it meant anything. I think he said something like, the Arabs liked Tampa better than Ft. Lauderdale. He may have just been shooting bull. It is hard to know if anything he said was true."

Jerry went over to the office refrigerator and pulled out two bottles of water. He was hoping Chars would notice, but Chars was concentrating too much to have observed Jerry's selection of water over soda. He sat the water bottle in front of Chars and took his seat back at the round conference table.

"Okay, Jerry said thinking about some possible angles that would make sense, let's say they buy the boats to make money to send money back to Iran or Spain or somewhere to fund Islamic terrorists. Jimmy Fred gets wind of it and threatens to turn them in. They know you have been asking questions and they decide to drop you two off for the sharks on their way out to sea."

"The only way that Jimmy Fred turns them in is if he is not going to get his cut," Chars said with disgust. "But some of that works. I think we were on our way back, but I am not sure. Jimmy Fred definitely believed we were going to be dropped at sea," Chars said.

Jerry said, "If they did not intend to drop you at sea, they were just trying to get you off the streets. You may have been close to stumbling on a story."

Chars said, "Stumble is an apt term."

"This is ridiculous. Let me call Agent Eads and see what he will tell us," Jerry said animatedly.

Chars frowned but reluctantly nodded his head.

Jerry dialed and the phone began ringing.

"Wait, I got a better idea," Chars said holding out his hand in the stop sign.

Now it was Jerry's turn to frown. He fingered the end call button and returned his undivided attention to Chars.

"This whole thing started going down hill when Nikki was killed. Jimmy Fred said that he thought the Arabs killed him," Chars said.

"Did you tell the F.B.I. that?" Jerry asked.

"They did not ask. They wanted to know what story I was working on and I told them that I was investigating the Tampa Bay license mess, not gambling boats. The topic of Nikki never came up."

Jerry thought a moment. He said, "That just doesn't make sense considering they were so hot to trot on you just a few days ago. So maybe they already knew how Nikki's death fit in and did not figure that you knew anything that they didn't."

Chars said, "I think I will take deep throats' advice and go to Arizona. Maybe they have the answer."

"You don't even know who that is," Jerry said.

"I bet I could find out without much trouble. The guy has given me so much personal information I could probably locate a name and where he worked without a lot of trouble."

"And how would you do that?" asked Jerry with a disbelieving smile.

"Search the Scottsdale paper looking for a low level bureaucrat that disappeared suddenly about two weeks ago."

"Chars, you should have been a detective," Jerry said giving Chars a big smile.

"Well, we can at least start with the most recent activity; that being the story about a mob guy getting himself killed yesterday or late the day before."

"Before I go anywhere I want to talk to Johnny Brebowski," Chars said.

Jerry keyed the microphone on his desk and said. "Carolyn, please get Johnny Brebowski on the phone."

Turning his full attention to his computer, Jerry began searching online for the story. Sure enough an article out of the Scottsdale paper had made the AP wire.

"Here you go," said Jerry and he read the headline out loud, "Gun battle leaves 2 dead and 3 wounded."

Mumbling, Jerry skimmed until he got toward the end of the article. He put a hand up for Chars to pay special attention.

"Here, here, listen…"

"I am listening, Jerry."

"Another disappearance possibly related to this series of events was that of County Clerk, Scott Tivy. Tivy has not been seen, or heard from in over two weeks. Authorities and family members are worried that Tivy was killed because he may have possessed some type of incriminating information regarding the casino agreement.

With a look of satisfaction, Jerry said, "Your man is Scott Tivy."

"Sounds very likely," Chars said thoughtfully.

"Mr. Brebowski is on line 4," Carolyn said over the intercom.

"Mr. Brebowski, this is Sergeant Collins of the Miami P.D., I have Charles Reynolds in my office. We are discussing among other things, Nikki Nikolaos."

"Let me talk to Chars," Johnny said. Jerry made a face mocking how important Chars was because he knew a high priced lawyer like Brebowski on a first name basis.

"Hey Johnny," Chars said.

"Chars, do you need a lawyer, cause I can send somebody over there to help you out."

"No, but thanks. You never know when I will need to take you up on that offer. The F.B.I. questioned you about Nikki's death. Did the topic of Arabs come up?" Chars asked.

"The F.B.I. was more focused on Topolo out of Chicago. I told them that I did not believe that it was a mob hit. They were convinced that I was covering for another client of mine. Which I probably would be, but I told them the truth. Why do you think this has something to do with Arabs?" asked Johnny.

"I had an opportunity to spend some time with Jimmy Fred."

"What a fucking abortion Jimmy Fred is. It is no secret that he was brokering all these deals. He would be a good suspect for Nikki's death."

"Johnny, Jimmy Fred said the Arabs killed Nikki."

"Interesting, but Jimmy Fred has never had honesty as a problem to overcome. Jimmy Fred and truth were about as far apart as an Ethiopian and his next meal."

Johnny waited for Chars to laugh, but once he decided that the show of humor was not forthcoming, he continued.

"Nikki had me contact the Feds. He thought he had come across some kind of information that he thought he could bargain with. He did not tell me what it was, but it definitely had something to do with the boats. The fact that the Justice Department was making him sell his business because of some puny felony conviction a couple decades ago was eating his lunch. He was very upset about one of the buyers and their plans for the boats," Johnny said.

"Didn't you oversee the contracts?" Chars asked.

"Jimmy Fred had some other lawyer do the work. I looked at the contracts and they seemed to pass muster. I wanted Nikki to cut and run. He needed to sell in order to avoid fines and a jail sentence. The money was real and the companies seemed real, so I signed off on it," Johnny said.

"So Nikki got his money worth?" Chars asked.

"I think he did. But Nikki was not happy, because he thought Jimmy Fred was getting too big of a cut. Nikki and Jimmy Fred were friends, but Nikki thought Jimmy Fred was always trying to "Jew him" out of his money. Secondly, he thought the final price was lower than it should have been because he had to sell and everybody knew it. I told the Feds all of this. Look, I am due in court in 15 minutes. It was good to talk to you," Johnny said.

"Johnny, aren't you Jewish?" asked Chars.

"Okay, poor choice of words," Johnny laughed a little.

Chars briskly asked, "Did Nikki mention anything about what he wanted to trade with?"

"Not to me. The only thing he told me was that he wanted someone at the meeting from Justice and Homeland Security. I was just supposed to present the carrot and set the meeting, which is exactly what I did. Because I could not give them any details, there was not much interest. They thought that Nikki was pulling a stunt of some sort. Then when he was killed, the F.B.I. came to see what we were talking about and of course, I did not know. Hey

Chars, good to hear from you. If you want to talk later give me a call at home. If I am not in court on time the judge will hold me in contempt," said Johnny as he ended the call.

Chars bolted upright as if a current of electricity were shot through his body. "I think I know why they wanted the Tampa boat."

Chapter Thirty Seven

Miami. Florida

It had been almost 24 hours since Chars had checked his email or voice mail. Maybe it had been 48.

There were two calls from Patti, both of which said, "Call me," in that annoying voice that she used when she had something she wanted to bitch about; which was all the time. Chars' face looked like he had just gotten a whiff of a foul odor and he wanted to spit on something.

Chars moved his neck side to side making a popping noise. He called in hope of getting voice mail, but no such luck. As soon as Patti found out Chars was on the phone, she put him on hold. In record time, the one and only Thom Stanton was on the line, all business.

"Chars, where are you?" Thom asked in a demanding tone.

"Gee Thom, it is so nice that you are concerned about my health and whereabouts. How are you, too? I am in Miami and I have been a little tied up," stated Chars with unabashed impertinence.

Chars wanted to add, '*do you have any Feds in your office today, shit head*?', but didn't.

"Chars, you have missed more time than anyone else around here and you never check in. What are we to think?" he asked, but did not wait for an answer.

Chars thought this all sounded rehearsed but listened without interrupting. *Besides*, Chars thought, *maybe the guy will bust a vein.*

"You are gone days at a time; weeks without showing up at the office; and days without even checking in. I am afraid I am not able to condone this type of deliberate insubordination," Stanton said. He waited for a response, but there did not seem to be any. Stanton figured that Chars was on his heels now and could not speak. In fact, Chars was trying not to laugh at the ridiculous effort to appear angry. Stanton was just not that good of an actor. Patti was sitting at her desk pretending not to hear, but taking in every word with a deep sense of justice flowing over her. She could not control her glee and was self-righteously nodding her head with every point that Stanton made.

"You have ignored repeated memos not to make your own travel arrangements and you continue to waste the paper's money on your personal jaunts," Thomas continued with the seriousness of an executioner.

Chars had heard enough to realize where this was going, so he finally interrupted this diatribe. If Stanton anticipated Chars' response would be asking, no pleading for forgiveness, Stanton was mistaken.

Chars said, "I understand Thom. I hereby tender my resignation upon notification that the General Manager signs off on it,"

Chars knew that Sam Orenstein, his former boss would see right thru the resignation. Stanton had pissed Chars off for the last time, and it was time to send this putrid little man a little wake up call: You don't mess with Charles Reynolds.

Stanton was taken aback. He thought, *this was so easy. Why hadn't I done it before?* Then the thought occurred to him that this might be a trap. "Please put it to me in writing by the first thing in the morning. No make that, by the end of the work day today. Upon receiving the letter, I will forward your last paycheck," Stanton resorted back to a familiar refrain from previous experiences when he was required to let people go. He had gotten fairly good at firing people over the years, but Stanton never before felt this good about firing anyone, as he did right now. He would have a resignation letter in hand. He had no intention of asking for permission on this one. The General Manager would not be able to reverse the decision. Besides, Stanton thought, let Sam try to overturn this decision. Stanton decided right then he would walk out and have every justification for doing so. He thought to himself, *You have to pick your battles and this was one worth fighting.*

While listening on the phone, Chars pulled up the resignation letter that he had saved from the last time that he was going to resign. He quickly corrected the date and attached it to an email, sent it to Stanton with a BCC to Sam Orenstein.

"Will an emailed resignation be acceptable?" Chars asked with a faked solemnity.

Stanton looked over at Patti, who gave up any pretense of not listening to every word. She gave a grave nod of her head, indicating that it probably work. Stanton was not so sure.

"I will accept the e-mail, but I will need a hard copy with your signature."

Stanton heard the "ding" of his computer indicating that a new message had been sent to his company e-mail account. Stanton's eyebrows raised and he signaled Patti to go look at the e-mail.

"Chars, I am sure you will land on your feet," Stanton said, stalling for an extra moment. If the resignation was a joke, he wanted to keep Chars on the phone.

Patti looked up from Stanton's desk and gave him a big thumbs up.

"Yeah, thanks a lot Stanton. You are quite the prize," Chars said, and ended the call.

Chars attached his latest series about Tampa, his kidnapping and trip aboard The Galleon to another e-mail just to Orenstein. He typed in his message, "This story will go to the New York Times as a free-lance report today at 4:00 p.m. Think they will be interested?" Chars smiled and hit send.

Chapter Thirty Eight

Tampa, Florida

On the way up to Tampa from Miami, Jerry and Chars had gone over the various scenarios.

"Jerry, I appreciate you going with me on this one," Chars said as he gunned his Nissan 300ZX across the Sunshine Skyway Bridge.

He decided to come in on the St. Petersburg side and land in West Tampa. He had called Debra again, but received no answer.

"Not a problem, Chars, I needed to get out of the office anyway," Jerry said.

Chars' phone vibrated. Checking the number, he answered, "Charles Reynolds."

"Mr. Reynolds this is Agent Eads, Miami of the F.B.I."

"What can I do for you Agent Eads?" Chars asked.

Looking over at Jerry, Chars gave a wry smile.

"I was wondering what your connection might be with a Scott Tivy?" Agent Eads asked.

Chars was taken off guard by the question. He only recently found out that his informant was Scott Tivy and giving up that information went against what he thought to be protecting his source.

"Should I know him?" asked Chars, unashamedly avoiding the question.

"We thought he was dead. But yesterday around 3:00 p.m., somewhere north of Biloxi, Mississippi, his bank card was used to withdraw money from his bank account," Ron Eads said in an irritable voice.

"And was it this Scott.... What did you say his name was?" Chars asked and smiled to Jerry conspiratorially.

Ignoring Chars' improvised ignorance, Eads said, "A photo shows it probably was Scott Tivy who made the withdrawal. We would very much like to communicate with Scott. I called to hereby advise you that Scott Tivy is now considered a Federal fugitive and that you need to notify us the next time you communicate with him."

"And if I still don't know who Scott Tivy is?" asked an impertinent Chars.

"I will consider any effort to conceal his whereabouts or to harbor this fugitive a crime, and it will likely lead to a loss of your freedom, Mr. Reynolds," Eads stated with only a modest amount of emotion. "If he calls you again, I want you to ascertain where he is and promptly advise the F.B.I."

"How would you know if he had in fact called me?" Chars asked with a modicum of anger in his voice.

"How we know is irrelevant, but I would suggest that the next time you talk to a Federal agent you use more care to tell the whole truth," Agent Eads said in measured tone.

"Really? I will be filing an official complaint with the F.B.I. about you tapping my phone without due cause. You are trampling over the constitution Agent Eads and I plan to make sure you are put in danger of losing your freedom."

Jerry had both hands covering his face. He was listening and was hoping that Chars would just stop. But he knew better, Chars was not one to back down. He also had a bad habit of escalating an argument when he thought someone else was out of line. He could have easily agreed to call the guy if he hears from him.

"I am sorry, Mr. Reynolds, but the Patriot Act has opened all kinds of doors for surveillance. Since this has to do with national security and possible terrorism, you'd be surprised at the level of attention we can muster," Eads said with a confidence that made it apparent that he was not fearful of some reporter's complaint about suppression of the press.

"I will tell you what I am going to do, Agent Eads. If, and that is an unknown, if I talk to someone who I know to be Scott Tivy, I will promptly notify your or the nearest office of the F.B.I.," Charles said with a defiant smile.

"You need to understand that Mr. Tivy's life is in danger and despite your smugness, I will pursue this issue aggressively if you fail to proactively cooperate," Mr. Eads retorted.

"You are going about this all the wrong way Agent Eads, and I am going to give you a chance to avoid being identified as a number one asshole in my next column. It will be such an exfoliation that you will be looking for a skin graft," Chars said calmly.

Jerry was now shaking his head with his eyes closed, head against the head rest saying, "Don't do this Chars, you are taking this to the next level."

"Mr. Reynolds, in light of your obvious defiant behavior, I am entering in the F.B.I. system a "C and D" on you. I am ordering you to surrender to the nearest local authority, and advise them to contact the F.B.I. I will have instructions in the computer for the agent that receives the call," Eads said tersely.

Turning to Jerry with the receiver open, Chars said, "Sergeant Collins, Agent Dick Head says I am supposed to turn myself into the nearest authority, and I deem that to be you. Further, you are supposed to call him. I am saving you the time. Here is Agent Dick Head now."

Jerry shot Chars a look that said, I am going to strangle you.

"Agent Eads, I understand that you have issued a capture and detain order on Chars. Other than the fact that he can be a jerk, do you think that is necessary?" Jerry asked with some disdain.

"Is Mr. Reynolds surrendering himself to you?" Agent Eads asked.

"Yeah, I have him in custody as we speak," Jerry said and rolled his eyes. Shall I just go ahead and shoot him now?"

"Sergeant, this person does not realize that he likely holds valuable information that could save an asset of the F.B.I. I don't take kindly to his flippant attitude toward the life of this man," Eads said with a raised voice.

"Hold on," Jerry said and addressed Chars, "Do you have any idea where his man is?"

"No," Chars said in a pout.

"Agent Eads, I think what we have here is a failure to communicate. First of all, he does not know where this man is. Secondly, I know Chars feels like his newspaper sources are confidential," Jerry said in an effort to turn this conversation into something marginally productive.

Agent Eads said, "Well Sergeant, I think he may have some critical information and it is my understanding that Reynolds was forced to resign from the Miami Express, so it seems that his argument is a moot point."

Jerry narrowed his eyes and shot a look over at Chars that caused Chars to ask, "What?"

"I will be with him. If your man calls, I will make sure to have Chars call you. I will assume responsibility for him in the meantime. Look, he has another call beeping in. We'll let you know if it is your man."

"You did not tell me you were fired," Jerry said accusingly.

"I wasn't. Here, give me the phone so I can answer the call waiting," Chars said reaching for the phone while keeping his eyes on the road.

"There was no call, I just made it up to get that guy off the phone," Jerry said. "You can't just be messing with those guys like that. They can make your life real miserable."

"He is a piss ant," Chars said. He adjusted in his seat to try to get the circulation back in his legs. They were passing through St Pete and on their way to West Tampa. Chars' phone vibrated. He opened the phone and answered. He then realized he had received a text message.

It read: cr emrg– at c - 26,-085, dnt call this num - dc

"I don't know who this is? What do you think this means?" asked Chars.

He handed over the phone to Jerry so he could look at the cryptic code.

Jerry frowned and said, "We could call my daughter, she knows all the abbreviations for text messaging."

"Well CR would be me and the emrg is emergency. What are the other words?" asked Chars.

He was driving in heavy traffic now and stopped his thought process to attend to people jockeying for position. A car in front of Chars slowed dramatically causing Chars to brake quickly. Jerry's gaze jerked up, fearing they were going into the back of the car. Jerry returned his thought to the message after deciding that Chars was not in fact going to kill him in a car accident. He let out a breath and looked again at the message.

"If it is an emergency, why don't they call 911? Doesn't anybody call the police anymore? What is easier than 911?" Jerry asked rhetorically.

"You could send a message back for me, asking to clarify or something like that," suggested Chars.

"I don't know how to send a message," groused Jerry. "I can barely read the numbers on the phone, much less type on the little buttons."

Jerry had a point. One of his beefy fingers probably covered multiple buttons.

"Read it to me again," Chars asked.

Jerry squinted down at the phone's display. Finally giving in, Jerry shifted to his left and reached into his jacket pocket. He pulled out a small pair of reading glasses and sent a look of death toward Chars.

"Don't even say a thing," Jerry said in a threatening tone.

Chars looked over and said, "You look distinguished."

"Yeah right. Okay, it says Charles Reynolds emergency, then at c. What does the letter c stand for?"

"Could be a location or a city or a place. Maybe it is the letter a, t and then the letter c," suggested Jerry. "Then it says twenty six and O eighty five. Looks like he signed this dc."

"What if dc is Dave Coughlin?" asked Chars.

"That would be good news, don't you think?" Jerry asked.

"That might explain the emergency thing. I have no idea about the numbers. We need to get this to somebody that can help," Chars said.

"I guess Agent Eads is out of the question," Jerry said.

Within thirty minutes, Jerry and Chars arrived at the dock where the Wampus Cat used to be docked. Chars tried David phone and it immediately went to voice mail.

"I am going to ask some questions down this way, if you head the other direction, let's meet back here in 30 minutes," Chars said to Jerry after to parking.

A sedan inconspicuously pulled up at the edge of the parking lot. Ahmed el Fayed watched as Chars and the police sergeant went in opposite directions. "The fact that the reporter is back in Tampa is a concern to us. He should have never escaped from the Galleon. Go to Mr. Reynolds. Tell him you have information on Mr. Coughlin or whatever you have to, but get Mr. Reynolds to follow you back to the town home. By choice or force," el Fayed quietly said.

"If he refuses?" asked Samir Nadr.

"If you cannot do what I ask, then kill him," el Fayed said with mild irritation. "I very much want to question him, but he must not escape. Be alert, his friend is a police officer and he will be looking for Mr. Reynolds in a short period of time. Now go quickly."

The brothers, Samir and Jabbar Nadr exited the vehicle and hurriedly made their way toward Chars. Samir went on the boardwalk in front of the restaurants and shops. Jabbar went behind to flank Chars. El Fayed signaled the driver to go to the town home, where they would wait for his quarry.

Jabbar and Samir were dressed casually and therefore fit in nicely with the bay crowd. Jabbar moved quickly around the back of the buildings and worked his way in front of where Chars was going to be. Since Chars might recognize Samir from the hotel abduction, he followed at a safe distance. Jabbar took up a position next to a Kosher hot dog vendor. He would use the Jew to catch the infidel. The good fortune made him praise Allah. He struck up a conversation with the man just as Chars was approaching.

Chars ordered a bottle of water from the vendor, but decided to pass on the sausages. He and Jerry would meet up and have some lunch. Chars wanted to go back to the restaurant that Dave had taken him to on his last trip, Frenchy's.

Speaking to the vendor, "Say, you might be able to help me. There used to be a boat docked here called the Wampus Cat. I am trying to find a friend of mine, named David Coughlin. Do remember seeing it?" Chars asked.

Solomon, the sole proprietor of "Love that Dog", was a cheery man, and eager to please. "Yes sir, I saw David pull out a few days ago. I believe David said that he was hired on for a charter up to the panhandle."

Jabbar was now wishing that the old man did not know so much. What story of additional information could Jabbar possibly fabricate to lure Reynolds to the town home?

"I remember it as well. I know someone who knew the charter party, if you don't mind paying for information," Jabbar said hurriedly.

Solomon gave the interloper a look of disgust.

The man's comment was a little out of the ordinary. Chars had not really been asking for confidential information. It seemed strange, but maybe the man did not speak English well.

"Okay," Chars said drawing the word out showing his suspicion.

Jabbar realized he had come on too strong. He tried a more subtle approach. "If you don't care to know it is okay by me. I thought you were interested in finding your friend," he said. Jabbar turned and started walking in the direction of town home.

Chars hesitated a moment and then said, "Say, wait up." Jabbar silently praised Allah. Chars moved quickly up beside Jabbar and asked, "How far is it that you are taking me?"

"Just around the bend up here not far at all," Jabbar said enthusiastically.

Chars pulled out his cell phone and speed dialed Jerry. "Hello," Jerry said in his gruff voice.

"Hey, I've got a lead on Dave. Seems that he took out a charter a couple days ago. Give me about fifteen minutes and I'll still meet you at the car. I don't think it will take very long. We can go get some lunch," Chars said.

He was a little out of breath because Jabbar seemed in a sudden hurry. Either that or Olympic Race Walking was his preferred activity.

"Hey Chars, be careful. I've got a tail and you might also," Jerry said looking over at a man holding up a newspaper. Jerry knew it was not the F.B.I. No one in U.S. intelligence was that unprofessional. Jerry turned so as not to tip the man that he had been tagged. Jerry decided to go look for Chars, but needed to lose this guy first.

Jabbar knocked on the door and entered without waiting for an answer. He motioned for Chars to follow. Chars cautiously entered, but saw no one other than Jabbar, standing there with a dumb smile on his face. The smell of camels or unwashed bodies caused Chars to stop just inside the door. Jabbar quickly moved to shut the door behind Chars.

"Come in, come in," Jabbar said eagerly.

"Mr. Reynolds," Ahmed el Fayed said as he stepped in from an accompanying bedroom.

"Yes?" Chars was a bit startled by the man's sudden appearance and answered with a question.

"You have been searching for answers. I am here to give them to you," el Fayed said with a bit of an ominous tone and downright evil smile.

Chars immediately knew he was in trouble. This had to be the same group that kidnapped him before. It was likely that they were looking for or had kidnapped Dave Coughlin.

"Great, but I can't think of anything that I need to know right now," Chars quipped.

"I see. You are the clever one aren't you, Mr. Reynolds? I have heard that about you. What is your American term, smart aleck?

Chars shrugged innocently and said, "That seems a bit harsh. Say, were you the hosts on The Galleon? I did not get a chance to fill out a customer comment card. I have a few suggestions to offer."

"Quite so," Ahmed said with an amused smile.

This man had tremendous gall. He must not have any idea that his life would end shortly or he would not act with such bravado.

"You are here to find your friend. We will take you to him now," el Fayed said gesturing toward the patio door.

"Great," Chars said slowly, trying to plan an escape.

He decided outside was an improvement in his situation and exited after Jabbar but before Ahmed.

Docked at the back of the town home was a 27 foot Chris Craft Cabin Cruiser.

"Nice, said Chars, "I guess all that sand has made boats very attractive to you. You know I think I will just try to get in touch with David on my own."

Chars took a step away from the direction of the dock. Ahmed quickly removed a semi-automatic 8000 Cougar Beretta.

"If you would like to live to see another day, please continue toward the boat," el Fayed said firmly.

"I see how it is. I suppose you were able to get a license to carry for that." Chars asked sarcastically.

That comment earned him a push in the back with the butt of el Fayed's weapon. Emboldened by the reaction, Chars thought maybe he could provoke the man enough to get a slight edge. He also was hoping that Jerry might be on his way.

"Did Jimmy Fred get that for you?" Chars asked fishing for information and trying to stall.

Ignoring the question, el Fayed said derisively, "Welcome aboard, Mr. Reynolds. Today you will be a part of the greatest story to hit the United States."

Below Chars could hear the Crusader 270 engines turn over and rev up. Chars was led to the lower cabin. Jabbar turned and frisked Chars. He removed his phone and keys.

"Say, I never got my wallet back from my gambling trip. Do you happen to have it?"

Seeing that he was not going to get an answer to that question, Chars just stood trying to figure out what to do next. Obviously Jerry was not going to make it in time.

"How do you feel about being part of history, Mr. Reynolds?" el Fayed asked in an almost ebullient tone.

"Living thru history in the making? Sounds great," Chars said disingenuously.

"Let's make sure he has no access to our plumbing," el Fayed said and moved to join Samir on the captain's deck.

Chapter Thirty Nine

Meridian Point Hospital, Scottsdale, Arizona

"Hamish, don't you worry about Cowboy. I have been looking after him ever since the state trooper dropped him off," Mavis said, standing next to the hospital bed. The surgeons had removed one slug from his upper arm without complication. He lost a substantial amount of blood, but not life threatening. His voice was still raspy from the oxygen tube being inserted during his surgery.

"Thanks Mavis, it shouldn't be but a day or two. Have the doctors said how the boy is?" Hamish asked.

"I am so sorry Hamish. This was my fault. I shouldn't have called Amos, but I thought he was one of the honest ones," Mavis said with tears in her eyes.

"You mean he did not make it," Hamish said despondently. He closed his eyes not wanting to cry.

Quickly, Mavis reached down and said, "No. No no, I am sorry. I did not mean that. Stevie is progressing. I thought you knew. He is out of intensive care and I think they will take him off critical late today. They may move him to a children's hospital in town. I meant that I am sorry for my part in this," Mavis said and snatched a tissue from a nearby box.

Hamish opened his eyes, let out a sigh of relief and closed his eyes again. Hamish sipped some water to help his dry throat. When he shifted, a stab of pain went thru his shoulder causing him to grimace.

"I would like to see him. I will cover any of his costs. Make sure you tell them that. Whatever he needs, he is to get," Hamish said, with tears now welling up in his eyes.

Mavis looked around to see if anyone was in earshot and said, "One of the detectives told me that they identified the dead mafia guy. They have evidence that he is the one who was responsible for a news reporter's disappearance. They said that the guy was wearing the reporter's boots. The boots had the initials, R.A. branded on the inside. How creepy is that?"

"Really creepy? That is news to me. The Police have not been in here today and they really did not tell me much before surgery. Just asked a lot of questions, that's all," Hamish said.

Mavis continued the news cast of the latest tidbits, "They still have not found the one that got away and Stevie's mom is still missing,"

"Who's watching the store?" Hamish asked, then followed with, "Besides Cowboy."

"My daughter is taking care of the store. It will be fine and yes Cowboy is on that detail," Mavis said smiling.

Two doctors congregated outside the room, looking presumably at Hamish's chart.

Mavis picked up her things and said, "I had better go check on Stevie. He is two floors up. You take care Hamish. When they release you, I will drive you to the Lazy C."

"Thanks Mavis. And about Cowboy, don't go spoiling him with a bunch of food, I will never get him to come back to me."

The older physician stepped into the room with the younger apprentice in tow.

"Mr. Cain, seems as if you have has an exciting arrival in the United States," said Doctor Elijah Stone. "I am Dr. Stone and this is Dr. Quintero."

Hamish nodded a greeting. "Are you also taking care of the boy?"

"I am not the primary, because we have a pediatrician who looks after the younger patients. But I did look in on him around noon and he was resting comfortably. I was told that you were looking after him or something like that," the doctor stated interrogatively.

"Well sort of, but I will take responsibility for him. Has his mother shown up?" Hamish asked.

"I did not see the mother, but I was just there for a few moments," said Dr. Stone.

"What is due to happen to Stevie now?" asked Hamish.

"Well, to first catch you up to date: Dr. Pat Marshall removed a small caliber bullet from the boy's left kidney. Evidently, he was slumped over something or maybe he was in the fetal position when the bullet struck straight on," Dr. Stone said.

Hamish knew that Stevie must have been shielding Cowboy when he was hit, but said nothing.

The doctor continued, "Of course the bleeding was significant, but the damage will repair over time. Dr. Marshall does not feel that removing the kidney will be necessary. So, like you, rest and recovery time are prerequisites to getting back to a normal schedule," the doctor said, and began perusing his charts again.

"As far as you are concerned, your general good health and condition works in your favor. The gunshot wound will heal nicely. You will have a scar to show friends, but no permanent damage. The scarring tends to cause some complications later on, but that is the price of surviving a gun shot wound. I will prescribe rehabilitation of the shoulder and arm, but that should not pose any problems for a man such as yourself. Bottom line, you should be back to chasing kangaroos in a month or two."

He gave a smile at his own little joke.

"I hope that this incident will not cause you to harbor a long term resentment of our fair city.'

"Thanks doc, I really appreciate you taking care of me and the boy," Hamish said sincerely. "Even though the crime rate seems to be bit on the high side, the doctoring seems to be top notch."

Both doctors smiled at the comment. Stone asked, "Are you feeling up to some questions from a couple detectives? They seem fairly anxious."

"Sure, send them in."

Officers Jon Carmel and Greg Lang entered the room. Lang was in casual clothes, but Carmel was in his State Police uniform.

"G'day mates," Hamish said as cheerily as he could manage.

"Mr. Cain, we are very glad to see you're recovering well," Officer Lang said.

"I am knackered, but otherwise doing well. Nice of you blokes to stop by and check on me. Any more details?" asked Hamish.

"We had hoped to be able to ask you a few more questions to help piece this together," Office Lane said. "Our Federal Bureau of Investigation has shown significant interest as well."

Carmel said, "I was impressed with how you handled things, Mr. Cain."

"It was a piece of piss. The dog and the boy did the heavy lifting," Hamish said modestly.

The two officers looked at each other and smiled.

"We are still trying to track down the man who escaped in the rental vehicle. We did find the rental car. The boy's mother was inside the trunk," Carmel said gravely.

Hamish's shoulders dropped as did his head.

"Have you told the boy?" asked Hamish.

"No, he's still not out of the woods yet, but we expect to do so later today or in the morning," answered Lang.

"The perp must not have had time to dump the body. He was bleeding and it is possible that we could locate him through the medical facility search network, but that is not likely," Officer Lang said.

Jon Carmel said, "We just need to go over the sequence of events again to see if there is something that might help us track down this guy."

Hamish went thru the sequence of events right up to the time that the officers called out to Hamish to surrender. Of course, now they realized that Hamish had not thrown down his weapon because Amos had already turned against them. But they had reports to fill out and needed the whole story. They agreed that Stevie's life was saved because he was not at home.

"The man that I shot and killed was named Luigi Beltran. We have traced him back to the Topolo family in Chicago, although that would be difficult to prove. We think that Amos was on the inside of a deal that gave minority ownership of a casino to the family through a shell corporation. We have notified the F.B.I and as well the Arizona Organized Crime Unit. They will probably want to get a statement from you at some point as well. The good news is that Beltran was linked to a disappearance of a local reporter," Carmel said.

Of course Mavis had already given Hamish the scoop, but he thought it would be rude to already know what the officer was telling him, so he only nodded comprehension.

Hamish interrupted with a question, "Might the reporter's body be the same body that the boy saw in my lake?"

"We also had a city bureaucrat disappear about the same time as the reporter. So it could have been either one. We are just not sure, but it would sure help to find out.

"I may have something that might help, but it seems sort of inconsequential. I have it at the Lazy C and you are welcome to it. Stevie was more than a bit brassed off when Amos would not stop and pick it up. I had completely forgotten about it. It was a tag of some kind that was just in the sand by Respite Lake. Stevie could probably tell you more, but he said it had something to do with the body. Mavis thought it might be part of a car license," Hamish said.

"We would very much like to take a look at it."

"Officer Carmel, when it is time to tell the boy about his mum, I would like to be the one to tell him," Hamish said sadly.

Chapter Forty

40 miles Northwest of the Tampa Coast

Arriving along side the Wampus Cat, the cabin cruiser was tied off. Charles was plasti-cuffed and herded on board. Charles noticed that David was at the helm. He could also see a man standing nearby holding what looked to be a small automatic weapon. Once the transition of passengers had been accomplished, unlabeled boxes of supplies were moved from the cabin cruiser to the Wampus Cat.

"Hey Chars," Dave Coughlin said with a dejected smile that reflected his current situation.

Dave was carefully skillfully descending the stairs. Dave's hands were now cuffed and his escort appeared close behind. Dave approached and sat next to Chars on the wooden bench. Chars tried to give David an encouraging smile, but both men were fairly certain that their situation was grim. Both showed their guilt for having involved the other.

In Arabic, the captors talked about the logistics of having two prisoners and whether to let them sit together or even talk. It was evident they determined Chars and David to be no great threat because they allowed them to do both. It may have been that it was easier to keep an eye on the two if they were sitting next to each other. Speaking in quiet tones, Chars and David began the process of figuring out how to survive this ordeal.

"Sorry to bring you in on this," Dave quietly said.

"It is me that should be apologizing to you. If I had not sent you on a fact finding mission, none of this would be happening," Chars whispered regretfully.

"I think this all had to do with the license deal, but that is just it. I don't know what is happening." Dave stated as a matter of fact.

Chars looked around to see if anyone was paying attention to them. One of the men stood nearby with his weapon casually pointing toward the boat deck. He was looking out on the horizon. Chars thought he could probably knock the man overboard, but he too would likely go over. Chars was not sure at this point if he would survive another dip in the drink. He would do it of course if he had no other choice, but not right now.

"I don't know either. I thought the mafia guys had kidnapped you. I did not realize that they were Arab. I can't make the connection." Chars said in a very low voice.

Showing some excitement, but still responding softly, David said, "You are right about the mob guys, Chars! They came on board at first and asked for a charter. But I knew something was not right and when I started asking questions, they pulled guns and took over the ship. How stupid did they think I was? They were in suits and asking for a charter.

Chars gave a little laugh.

"I knew it was you that called. The big guy answered the phone. When he hung up, he called someone else. Evidently they were real upset with you. He mentioned your name and told whoever he was calling that the FBI showed up at your door. Do you have the FBI helping you?"

Chars gave another laugh.

"I wish I did, but I think they thought I was holding out information and may have been involved somehow. I am afraid I should have been more forthcoming, but at the time I was not sure what was going on," Chars said with a tone of regret. "Then what happened?"

David continued, "Yesterday, they tied me up and threw me below. Not more than an hour later, these guys showed up. The mob guys are gone! The Arabs untied me for a while and had me sail out to the gulf. I didn't argue because, well, at least I am not tied up anymore."

Chars nodded his understanding, but said nothing, allowing Dave to continue with his story uninterrupted.

"They had me teach two of the guys how to operate the boat. I asked questions, but they wouldn't tell me what they were doing," Dave said with a bewildered tone.

"I wouldn't expect them to, but have you overheard anything, anything at all?" Chars asked quietly.

"They only speak to me in English. They speak Arabic when they talk amongst themselves. They made me send that message to you," David said apologetically.

"The message I got was from them?" Chars asked with surprise. "And I walked right into their trap."

Chars thought how clever it was to send a coded message. Chars took the bait because he had to decipher the information. Chars thought he was the clever one, just as they had planned. They knew that Chars could not resist the challenge. If it had been too easy, he would have just called the police or been suspicious of a trap. Chars did bring Jerry along, but when they split up, the Arabs had their chance. They had once again outsmarted Chars by putting the decoy out by the hot dog stand. Chars asked the questions and the boys just reeled in the catch. Chars knew that Jerry would immediately alert the locals about Chars disappearance if... Chars had an awful thought, if they did not capture him or worse. Chars thought back through their last conversation and remembered that Jerry said he was being followed. Jerry knew he was being followed, so it was not likely they would have been able to get the drop on him. Chars felt better about the situation feeling certain that Jerry could take care of himself. At least he hoped so. He returned to his own situation knowing that he had been played like a fool and he was disgusted with himself.

"What about other boats or supplies?" Chars asked.

"They brought supplies, and of course," he paused, you." He continued, "I could see everything when I was up top, but I was only allowed to captain the ship long enough for the two Arabs to learn themselves. I have noticed that they have been receiving increased radio transmissions. But that could have been from the cabin cruiser that you just came in on."

Samir and Jabbar were busy bringing on some more supplies and what looked to be a couple floor mats rolled up. One of the men on board jumped across to the deck of the cabin cruiser, fired up the engine and headed back to the direction that it had arrived.

"I am not sure, but since the one guy said something about being part of history, I think they are planning something big," Chars said.

The motors of the Wampus Cat roared to life and the big vessel began moving in a southerly direction. Then,

Chars and Dave both held on as the boat turned abruptly and headed west.

"Have you noticed that they don't even care if we are talking? That means that we are not going to be alive to tell anyone," Chars said evenly. "Have they brought any weapon or explosives on board?"

"Not that I have seen, but there have been several heavy boxes that they have taken below," Dave said.

The Wampus Cat had traveled almost a full hour before cutting its engines. The waves of the ocean were very calm resulting in very little movement on deck. Voices up in the captain area could be heard, but not understood by Chars and Dave. A cloud could be seen approaching from the South. It looked dark and dangerous. The Arabs were obviously discussing what to do.

In Arabic, el Fayed said to the crew, "The authorities have captured Jimmy Fred. It is very likely that he will tell them enough about us that our mission will be jeopardized. Therefore, we must move up our plans. Our brothers are on their way. You will leave to do the work of Allah as soon as the boat is ready and the explosives are armed."

Samir asked, "The prisoners will stay on board?"

Ahmed el Fayed smiled, "It will be the final chapter for our fisherman and the reporter. We will need the fisherman to guide us in to the bay. He will also disarm the local authorities and make it more likely that you will be able to get within the restricted area. Mr. Reynolds final story will not be written by him, rather about him."

Both Samir and Jabbar solemnly nodded with approval.

Following the attacks of 911, a security zone was established that encompassed all waters in the vicinity of MacDill Air Force Base. The secure area extended from a point at 27 degrees 50.20 N 82 degrees 32.14 minutes west and then south-easterly 1000 yards from shore to a point at 27 degrees 48.90 minutes N/82 degrees 28.20 minutes W; then circling 1000 yards from shore to a point 27 degrees 51.51 minutes N/82 degrees 29.18 minutes W. The Coast Guard was charged with monitoring this area; issuing warnings; and intercepting any vessel without the proper authorization from the Captain of the Port or his designated representative. If necessary, the Captain of the Port would notify the public via Marines Safety Radio Broadcast on VHF Marine Band Radio, Channel 13 and 16 (157.1 MHz). Many people were naturally concerned about what effect the new safety zone would have on local traffic, but an agreeable procedure was devised in order to placate most everyone.

El Fayed came down the steps and approached Dave and Chars.

"Are you comfortable?" el Fayed asked his two captives.

Rather than answer, Chars instead used the opportunity to ask a question. "Could you take these cuffs off? They are killing my wrists."

"I am sorry Mr. Reynolds, your last exploits make me unlikely to discount your resourcefulness," said el Fayed. "Mr. Coughlin, please stand?"

"Yes," Dave said struggling to his feet with his restraints.

El Fayed removed his pistol from the small of his back and pointed it at Dave.

"Turn around, please," commanded el Fayed.

It appeared that this would be an execution. Chars was frantically trying to think of something that would stop this. He knew of nothing to say and knew he would be next. Pointing the pistol at David's head, El Fayed pulled out a knife and sliced thru the cuffs with the knife. Chars exhaled and closed his eyes for a moment.

Speaking to Dave, el Fayed said, "You are needed up in the captain's area. Mr. Reynolds, please don't try to escape. I would be forced to kill you."

"They are going to kill us anyway Dave, so you might keep that in mind before you decide to help them," Chars said irritably.

El Fayed slapped Chars with the back of his hand as a reward for his insolence. Chars was knocked over on his side. He used his tongue to check his teeth. They were all in place, but Chars tasted blood from a cut on the inside of his cheek. El Fayed and Dave climbed up the stairway leading to the upper level. About twenty minutes later, from the Captain's deck looking toward the eastern skyline, David could see a small spot appear. For the normal person, the spot appeared to be moving slowly, but to David's trained eye, he knew the vessel was approaching very quickly.

"David, said el Fayed, "That boat will be meeting up with us."

David shrugged and said, "Okay."

As it approached, the roar of the dual 560 horsepower motors could be heard. David looked at the approaching boat with awe. Despite the gravity of his situation, David's mind appreciated the utter coolness of the 38ZR Donzi cigar boat as it came into full view. Samir left the top deck and quickly positioned himself to tie off the arriving boat. Once alongside, the crew got off the boat boarded the Wampus Cat, and gave Samir a big enthusiastic hug. There were smiles and they appeared to be congratulating each other. Samir returned to watch David allowing El Fayed to come down and welcome the new arrivals. The greetings were more formal, but still enthusiastic. "Al-salaamu alaykum," was the greeting all around.

The group then went to work transferring six slender crates to the quarters below of the Wampus Cat. Dave watched the activity from above. The 38 ZR Donzi was a sight to behold: 1200 horsepower with accommodations and sitting area in the oversize hull, made this a favorite of the filthy rich and drug runners. The crew carried the cargo below deck. Chars asked el Fayed for permission to use the bathroom. El Fayed narrowed his gaze at Chars but decided that would be acceptable. He indicated to Chars that it was acceptable to piss over the side of the boat. Chars nodded agreement even though he was hoping for a trip to the bathroom below. Chars was cut free to allow the use of his hands, but was closely watched. Once he finished peeing over the side of the boat, his hands were again cuffed behind him. Having little need for a Captain of an idle ship, Dave was escorted back to the bench by Jabbar, and a new set of cuffs were applied.

After two hours, the crew from below reappeared on deck. El Fayed and his team laid out their mats and faced Mecca for their seldom missed Salaat. Chars took the opportunity to try to sleep. When the prayers were properly completed, the men went below deck again.

Later, under the cover of darkness, el Fayed said goodbyes and boarded the Donzi with its crew in tact. The engines roared to life and the boat was gone in an instant.

Chapter Forty One

Meridian Point Hospital, Scottsdale, Arizona

Stevie Small Feather had successfully endured the operation to remove a small caliber bullet from his kidney. He had regained consciousness about an hour earlier. He was propped up in the bed eating a prescribed breakfast of Jello and Cream of Wheat, neither of which were Stevie's favorite, but he did seem to be hungry. The attending nurse's name tag read Priscilla Thatcher, R.N. She was a fine looking lady in her early thirties. She was tending to the various liquids that were being diverted into Stevie's arm. She reached over and stroked Stevie's head while delivering encouragement. Stevie, clearly enjoying the attention, gave her a weak smile. He liked her smell. Every time she moved about the bed he could smell a flower, even though he did not know what kind. Her nurse's outfit was attractive as well. The front showed very little cleavage, but when she adjusted Stevie's saline tube, her breasts brushed against his shoulder. Stevie felt a little tingle below the sheets so he brought his knees up a little to hide his body's reaction. He thought it unfair that the thoughts of a boy were so easily revealed. His body had an emotional flagpole that moved to attention whenever certain thoughts entered his mind. It seemed to be happening more and more.

"Stevie, I will see you tomorrow. My shift is over, but Nurse Terri will be in here to check on you."

His throat was sore from the tube the doctors used during his surgery. He spoke in a croak more than a voice. He managed, "I bet she is not as nice as you."

Priscilla stopped, realizing that this little boy was flirting. She smiled and said, "You are so sweet to say that Stevie." She gave him a warm smile and then saw evidence of the boy's obvious excitement under the thin blanket. "I can tell you are already getting well." She raised one eyebrow and shook her head in amusement. She mussed his hair and said, "Be good, Stevie Small Feather," and left the room.

A few minutes later, dressed in a hospital gown, Hamish made his way into Stevie's room. He was still moving rather stiffly, but managed a broad smile as he came thru the door and gave a brief knock on the door frame.

"You are sort of young to be hitting on the nurses don't you think?"

Stevie gave Hamish a mischievous smile that had no hint of embarrassment.

Stevie looked intently at Hamish and recognized a look of sadness. He knew something was not exactly right.

"Hello, Hamish," he said in his new raspy voice.

It was the voice of a little boy that had been seriously injured. That physical injury would be nothing compared to the emotional wound that Hamish was about to deliver.

"Hello, mate," Hamish said with a hint of sorrow. "Seems you are a hero. I owe you for saving Cowboy's life."

"He's okay?"

"He's hanging out with Mavis at the store."

A new nurse entered after a perfunctory knock on the door frame. She moved over to the sink and began washing her hands. Stevie thought to himself, *she is as wide as a house. I want Priscilla back.*

The lady finished up at the sink and turned to the two men.

"Hello boys, sorry to interrupt, but I just need to check on a couple things. My name is Sarah and you are?" she said in a light Irish brogue.

Stevie croaked out "Stevie."

"And I am his friend. I am Hamish."

Sarah was busy moving around the room. She was quite agile for a big woman. She checked the charts and the fluid levels and put a hand on Stevie's forehead.

Addressing Hamish, Sarah said, "I heard about you. You are from New Zealand, right?"

Hamish gave a small smile and nodded that he was.

Stevie asked almost in a whisper, "What happened to Amos?"

Sidestepping that question for moment, he asked "Have the police been here to talk to you?" He did not want to tell the boy the truth, but it had been quite evident at the ranch house.

The nurse interjected, "I was told that Stevie has not been awake long enough for the police to be bugging the lad." She continued, "As soon as the boy started regaining consciousness, the doctor told us to get you. He said you had something to talk to him about."

"Yes, I do," Hamish said and sat on the edge of the bed. "Stevie, the police told me... he paused. Gathering his emotions, he restarted, "Your mother was shot by those men. She was very brave in defending your home against them, but they killed her."

Hamish paused not knowing whether to be quiet or continue on. Stevie was silent. He was evidently asking the questions in his mind and answering them. He had not reached a question yet that he did not have the answer to until he got to the question, why? Stevie stared past Hamish as if he were looking at a spot on the wall.

Moving his eyes toward Hamish he said, "They were after me. It was because I saw the body."

He was not asking because he knew the truth. He covered his face with his hands and began to cry. The nurse came to the other side of the bed and put her hand on his shoulder. Hamish sat quietly by while the little boy who had been so brave, allowed the grief to unashamedly pour out. It was obvious that Stevie felt responsible for the fate of his mother. His curiosity had led to her death. They had shot her while searching for him. With Hamish sitting on the edge of the bed, Stevie wept until all his energy was spent and he fell into a restless sleep.

When he awoke again, Hamish had been replaced by the State Police. Stevie was subdued, but told the entire story from beginning to end, leaving out only the presence of his friends.

When Amos entered the story, Stevie's sorrow turned to anger. *How could Amos have been with the bad men? There must have been some misunderstanding.* But Amos' actions at the ranch house and the explanation of police left little doubt that Amos had been on the take. Stevie again began to cry, thinking that Amos had something to do with his mother's death. Stevie's thoughts turned to Sean. Sean's anger would be fueled by shame as well. The nurse stepped in to shield Stevie from any more questions, insisting the officers come back later.

After the police left, Hamish returned.

"I heard you were awake," Hamish said with a bit of enthusiasm.

"The police were here. They told me about Amos," Stevie said choking up little.

Without speaking, Hamish sat on the bed and Stevie leaned into his embrace. Hamish held him as another wave of confusion and sorrow overwhelmed the boy. Hamish thought about the death of his parents; he remembered the sense of hopelessness and despair that losing a parent brought. Hamish made his decision right then and there. If Stevie needed a home, he would be the one to provide it.

Chapter Forty Two

Twelve Miles West of the Tampa Bay Coast

Captain Dave Coughlin, under the supervision of Jabbar, dropped the mid range trawling nets of the Wampus Cat. Chars was cut free so that he could assist Dave in completing the task. If this were a normal outing, Dave would have several of the crew dedicated to each of the two nets. Today they would only drop one of the nets, and the catch of the day itself would not be important. The impression that it left on the harbor officials would be the vital part. Samir and Jabbar decided that a boat with a catch would raise less suspicion. So the next three hours would be spent completing that deception.

At the helm of the ship was Samir, having received his crash course in operating the trawler. The Wampus Cat, making its way back to Tampa Bay, would arrive about the time of a shift change at MacDill.

"We cannot allow this boat to go into Tampa Bay," Dave said quietly while working alongside Chars.

"Do you know what they are going to do?" Chars asked as nonchalantly as possible.

"I think they..." Dave was interrupted by Jabbar.

"Let's keep the conversations to a minimum. Just concentrate on your fishing," Jabbar said, while pointing a semi-automatic rifle in their direction.

"What is your name?" Chars asked in a pleasant voice.

"My name is Jabbar," he said with pride.

As in Kareem Abdul Jabbar?" asked Chars looking for some line of sustainable conversation.

"Just because you change your name, it does not mean that you are a true follower," Jabbar said.

"Jabbar, where do you come from?" Chars asked.

"I really don't see what purpose it serves to satisfy your curiosity," Jabbar said.

"None except, I just want to make sure that I get the story correct when I write it," Chars said with a smile.

Deciding whether to play along or not, Jabbar gave Chars an inquisitive look. Jabbar recalled his training from el Fayed. Jabbar had been counseled the infidels will be more cooperative if they are led to believe that they may get out of this alive. The lying to achieve Allah's purposes was perfectly acceptable. However, Jabbar had also been instructed to be careful about providing any information that might compromise the mission. Despite the infidels' inferiority, they could still be clever. Jabbar decided a careful revealing of information might lead to cooperation.

"I am from Saudi Arabia. I am Jabbar Nadr. Jabbar means mighty or brave. My brother Samir is sailing the boat."

Chars wanted to say, "And does Nadr stand for hijacker, therefore giving you the name the mighty hijacker?" but decided not to make the situation worse. Chars knew that if Jabbar was willing to give him his name, assuming it not to be just a lie, they were planning a terminal mission. Chars would try to get some additional information that he could use to get himself out of this predicament.

I presume that you have some reason for hijacking this boat?" Chars asked.

"You are a reporter. I would think you have an idea about your country's infringement of our borders. We will be finished with the boat shortly, and you can have it back," Jabbar said measuring the success of his deception.

"Hear that Dave, you are going to get you ship back when Jabbar here is done with it," Chars said.

Dave looked up and gave an unconvincing smile. Chars was trying to decide how to proceed. Engaging this lunatic in conversation was certainly one way. Chars knew that he was not going to change the man's mind with a reasoned argument. Contact had to be made now, before they approached the bay. It appeared that the only two Arabs left were Samir and Jabbar, unless there were some down below. Chars and David needed to find out what was below to determine how quickly something had to be done. Chars decided more conversation might be worth it.

"So you are Arab, but you are of the devout variety of Muslims. Is it called the Wajabist version?

"You would be in the minority, Mr. Reynolds, if you actually knew our history. What do you know?" Jabbar asked curiously.

"The Saud family was joined by Muhammed ibn Abd- al-Wajab by marriage. Wahabist views are very fundamental not generally liking the Shiites. The Saudi Royal family claims to be followers of Wahab, but deal with the Americans and therefore are weak in their belief. The Sauds try to make up for this perception with funding of activities like this one here.

This stuck a nerve with Jabbar and his face flushed slightly.

"The United States contributes to the Saudi Arabian moral decline and causes our political weakness," Jabbar continued, "In fact, the United States encourages this so that it may have better access to our resources."

Chars was exhaustively searching his mind to find a way to communicate with anyone that could help.

"Dave, how far do you figure we are from Tampa?" asked Chars.

Jabbar seemed uneasy that the conversation between David and Chars had resumed.

"I'd say about an hour at the most," said as he was raising the trawling net to just below the surface of the water. "How good of swimmer are you?"

"Stop the conversation now. You have work to do," Jabbar stood and said in a irritated tone.

His weapon was not aimed at either Chars or Dave, but it was clearly ready if needed. Chars figured that shooting Dave and Chars this far out was still a possibility as it would not likely jeopardize their mission. As we came into sight of the Bay, a shot would likely attract at least some kind of unwanted attention. However, it may be too late to sabotage whatever these nuts had planned.

A jet airplane's engine could be heard in the distance. Dave went to a storage box and pulled out a crank and an extra pair of gloves for Chars. He tossed the gloves to Chars and attached a fanny pack of some sort to his waist. Dave returned to the port side of the stern. Looking toward Tampa, Dave shielded his eyes from the sun on the horizon. Dave calculated time and distance as any Captain should. Jabbar stood to see what Dave might be looking at.

Dave quickly looked at Chars and nodded toward Jabbar. Chars got the message to engage Jabbar in more conversation.

"Jabbar, you know that any attack on the United States is only going to make things worse," Chars said.

Jabbar's head turned and instead of answering Chars stepped up on a storage platform. He intensely looked in the direction of the bay trying to see what these two infidels were trying to distract him from seeing. Dave took the opportunity of Jabbar looking forward, to open his fanny pack and remove a vinyl heat sealed double pouch. By pulling a tab the pouch began dispensing a fluorescent sea dye marker. This fluorescent green dye began to spread over the surface of the water visible to any aircraft that might be in the area. More useful in the night time, Dave hoped that one of the jets flying out of MacDill might happen to fly over and see the signal. Samir stuck his head out of the Captain's deck door.

"Jabbar, what is that leaking out of the boat?"

Jabbar moved to the back edge of the boat and saw a light colored fluorescent green trail that the boat was emitting. He looked over the edge to see a plastic pouch was wedged in a tie line off the stern. He now realized that the conversation had been merely a distraction. He walked over to Chars and swatted Chars with the backside of his hand. The blow knocked Chars to one knee. Dave started to move toward Jabbar, but the Arab quickly turned his weapon toward Dave. Another Arab emerged from down below, answering an earlier question of who else was on board. Jabbar had conveniently left out this man from his earlier inventory.

Jabbar said gruffly, "Abdul, take him below and secure him with no consideration for his comfort. He is much too clever to give any more chances."

"Shouldn't I just shoot him?" Abdul asked in Arabic.

Jabbar reluctantly said, "No, we may need him on board, but put him below and make sure he can not get free.

Chars was pushed and prodded down below. He was forced at gunpoint to put the plasti-cuffs on his ankles and then Abdul used a second cuff to bind his hands. Below deck, it was barely lit but Chars could just make out a putty like substance stuck to the wall of the front cabin divider. Stuck into the tan looking putty was an electric blasting cap, four inch long, silver in color. A set of wires ran around the corner of the divider and to the rear of the cargo hold.

Before he could comment, Obama pulled a black hood over Chars head and gave him a swift kick in the backside. Unable to break his fall, Chars stumbled and hit his head on a counter. The blow momentarily left Chars unconscious.

Jabbar signaled for David to give him his fanny pack. Inside were two more of the fluorescent sea-die markers. He tossed them aside.

"David, pull up the net and secure it in place," Jabbar said will very little emotion.

David did as he was instructed. When he had completed the task, Jabbar signaled for him to move to the Captain's Deck. A small fishing boat could be seen on the horizon. Jabbar and Abdul discussed what to do about it, but ultimately decided that it was no threat. In the far distance, David could see Tampa Bay coming into view as he climbed the stairs. He knew that anything that he did to stop them from entering the harbor had to happen quickly.

Samir took a deep breath and said aloud, "Ensha Allah." He picked up the radio and spoke in his least accented English, "This is South Shore Shipping, the Wampus Cat, seeking permission to enter Tampa Bay."

A quick reply came back, "We acknowledge Wampus Cat. Is this the Captain?

"No, but he is available if you need him," Samir said with a tinge of panic in his voice.

He looked over at Jabbar for guidance, but Jabbar was alternately concentrating on Dave's face and the water ahead of them. There was a pause. Jabbar grabbed Dave by the shirt collar and shoved his semi-automatic Cougar Beretta into Dave's cheek.

"Something is wrong! What is wrong?" Jabbar challenged Dave.

"They are going to want to talk to me," Dave managed with the gun barrel pressing on the side of his face.

Gabriel McQueen said, "Wampus Cat, this is the TBPA Harbor Master; Coast Guard has okayed your approach and passed you to us. Have you been prepped as far as the required clearance of the secure area?

"Yes, Harbor Master," Samir said.

"Thank you, Wampus Cat. Please state your clear status tag and you will be good to proceed."

Samir jerked around because this was new to him. He had not heard about any clear status code. He looked wild eyed at Jabbar. Dave tried to pretend he did not know by shrugging his shoulders. Jabbar whipped the barrel of his gun across Dave's face creating a split along the cheek bone and causing Dave to stumble.

Holding up his hands in surrender, he said, "Okay, okay, okay. I will tell you. It is Frank, Utah, Charlie, Kellogg, Utah."

Samir looked over at Jabbar with questioning eyes. Jabbar gave him a nod.

"Frank, Utah, Charlie…" He stopped and looked over at Dave.

Dave said, "Kellogg, Utah."

His face had a stream of blood running down.

Jabbar repeated into the radio, "Kellogg, Utah."

"Wampus Cat, I read you…," said McQueen. "Excuse me, did you say, Frank Utah Charlie Kellogg Utah?"

Samir looked at Jabbar. Jabbar shrugged and nodded his head yes. "Correct," said Samir.

"You have permission to proceed Wampus Cat. Just stop by and see me when you dock. I would like to discuss our procedures with you," McQueen said.

"I will see you shortly," Samir said and gave Jabbar a big smile.

"Praise Allah!"

Dave was lying on the floor eyes closed in disbelief.

"Get him below and make sure he does nothing destructive," Jabbar said to Abdul.

Chapter Forty Three

Tampa Bay, Florida

Senior Airman Chris Olivares had quickly taken his position, four hundred yards outside the restricted security zone of MacDill Air Force Base. Covered by high switch grass and light camouflage, Olivares was lying on a small sand bar off the northern coast of the inlet leading into Tampa Bay. After spotting the Wampus Cat with high powered binoculars, Olivares used a secure radio to send his message. "Base Command, this is spotter one, I have a visual on the horizon. Confirming our target is headed toward Sand Trap."

"This is Base Command, thank you for the confirmation. As most of you know, less than ninety minutes ago, we began receiving intel that a substantial threat existed off the coast of Tampa. We are on high alert and initiated Operation Sand Trap. Our react team managed to get a scan of the vessel and it is not hot, repeat not hot. The F.B.I. has advised us that this vessel is likely to be wired for major damage. We have reason to believe there are two hostages aboard. We will attempt to disable if possible and alternatively destroy if necessary. We have a green light for the Hornets that are being dispatched, to engage if vessel threatens to enter the secure area," said Major General Sam Coleman.

Assigned to assist in the movement of the teams, First Lieutenant Quincy Edwards said, "This is Sand Trap Command. No nukes is good news, sir. Do we have visual confirmation of friendlies on this vessel? Over."

"This is Base Command. Our observation at 0959 from the E-3A Sentry was that there are two likely hostages on-board. A fluorescent trail marker was spotted which we interpreted as a distress signal by the hostages. They however, are not in sight at this time," Coleman said.

This E-3A Sentry was a specially equipped Boeing AWACS or Airborne Early Warning and Control System aircraft. Less than 50 yards down from the spotter was a long range sniper team moving into position. They also had the Wampus Cat coming into their sights.

"This is Op Team Alpha. We are close to ready; please clear channels for a status check," crackled the voice of First Sergeant Cheston Goudge over the radio.

Managing footing in a marsh directly across from Op Team Alpha, a second sniper team was setting up on the south side of the inlet leading into Tampa Bay.

"This is Op Team Bravo. We are in position and standing by," said sharpshooter, Staff Sergeant Jake Wilker.

Dispatched almost immediately upon receiving the threat, an inconspicuous fishing boat hastily, maneuvered so that it was now shadowing the Wampus Cat. Next to a large fishing poll, and improvisationally covered with a tarp, a state of the art parabolic dish and headset was adeptly positioned by Senior Airman Lee Clarac. With optimal conditions, the long range listening device was capable of hearing conversations almost a half mile a way.

"This is Op Team Charlie checking in. We are in position and are monitoring for conversation," said Clarac.

"This is the 6th Operations Support Field Commander for Sand Trap, we have scrambled the two F-18 Hornets out of Pope," said Major Stephen Miller, referring to Pope Air Force Base. "We are waiting for a go or no go recommendation from Base Command."

"Verifying. This is Captain Wilson Vick of the Hornet Striker One and Two, we are on our way and will be in position to engage the enemy in 12 minutes. Over."

"This is Base Command, Hornet Striker please proceed, but we have not given a go, repeat have not given a go," Coleman said.

"Roger that. This is Hornet Striker One and Two, we proceeding toward target, and will await a green light."

"This is Op team Charlie, we have a positive voice I.D. on the Captain. He is definitely a hostage and has been trying to alert the base of the imminent danger. The Captain gave the hostiles the clearance code, Frank Utah, Charlie, Kellogg, Utah to the Harbor Master."

Every team member smiled at the subterfuge.

Clarac continued, "He was moved below deck right after that. The second hostage has not been accounted for. It appears that the hostiles are unaware of detection, but very nervous."

Coleman said, "All teams, this is Base Command, please be advised we have a Pave- Hawk Helicopter in the air in case we need to pluck some one from the water." Coleman stopped speaking when he saw the Base Commander enter the room with an entourage. Following salutes, the general indicated he was going to take the microphone so Coleman said, "Stand by all teams, I have General Jason Kendrick, Base Commander on deck."

"This is the Base Commander, General Kendrick. I have Special Agent Ron Eads from the F.B.I. and Sergeant Jerry Collins from the Miami Police Department with me. Needless to say we have had a difficult challenge thrown at us here with little time to react. But you are professionals and we do what needs to be done. Based on the information provided by Sergeant Collins and Agent Eads we were able to identify this threat and hopefully we will be able to contain or thwart it entirely. In order to make sure we are all on the same page, I am going to give a quick status report. I will then turn this back to our teams. We have three or more hostiles that have commandeered the Wampus Cat in an apparent effort to attack MacDill and the surrounding area. On board are two civilian hostages that we want to rescue if possible. We know that the vessel does not have nuclear weapons, but may have biological or chemical weapons. Our priority is to the civilians of the Tampa area as well as our armed forces. We plan to initiate a preemptive strike, prior to the Wampus Cat entering the mouth of the bay and the secure area." General Kendrick continued, "I have authorized deadly force to eliminate this threat if given the opportunity prior to a strike from the Hornets. But anything less that complete neutralization of the hostiles or total demolition of this vessel may create a hazardous situation."

Chapter Forty Four

Near Tampa Bay, Florida

Below the deck of the Wampus Cat, Chars was attempting to stand. The hood on his head prevented him from seeing where exactly he was in relation to the stairs or the explosive charge that he saw when he was first shoved into the room. After managing to stand, Chars bent over to try to remove the hood. The pain riveted thru his head from the blow received earlier. He nearly passed out, but leaned against a wall for support. This time more slowly, he leaned forward and gripped the top of his hood with his knees. The material was drawing tight thus preventing him from removing the hood. The door above opened and Dave tumbled down the stairs knocking Chars through the closed door leading to the back room. The blow received from Dave's fall and the subsequent rubbing of Chars face on door, was enough to lift the hood atop Chars' head. He could barely see, but he was able to shake his head from side to side to finally free himself from the hood. *Thank you Lord!* Chars thought.

Chars scooted back up into the front room to check on Dave. Chars listened for breathing and decided that Dave was unconscious but still alive. He could see coagulated blood streaked from a gash on his cheek. Chars also noticed the fresh wound on the back of Dave's head.

Chars managed to stand again. He needed to figure a way to disarm the charge if he and Dave had any chance of survival. Chars leaned over to the wall where the blasting cap was stuck in the C4. It took several tries but he finally was able to use his teeth to pull the pencil like charge free of the explosive. Chars breathed out a sigh of relief. He straightened up and hopped toward the divider wall. He shifted and sat heavily on a side bench. Using his nose he was able to flip the light switch on the wall. The light in the front cabin bled thru the door into the aft cabin. Chars gasped as he looked past the divider. More blasting caps were stuck in C4 down the entire side of the boat. Each cap had wires extending toward the back of the room. After finding another light switch, Chars hopped into the back room only to receive some more bad news. The wires that connected the explosive also were connected at end of the hull to six cylinders the size of soda dispensers. Each cylinder was labeled with a red sticker that read, Caution: Chemical Material, O-ethyl-S- [2(diisopropylamino)ethyl] methylphosphonothiolate –VX.

"Dave, Dave you have to wake up!" Chars said in an urgent whisper.

But Dave did not show any signs of life. Chars would have to get this done on his own. Still bound, he began pulling each blasting cap out with his teeth. With nothing to leverage his weight against, Chars was having difficulty grasping the thin metal caps. The cap on his front tooth gave way and dropped to the floor.

"Shit!" quietly exclaimed Chars.

Frantically Chars began a practically futile effort to remove all the blasting caps from the C4.

Inside the Captain's control deck, Jabbar looked thru a set of binoculars toward the U.S. Air Force base. He did not see any one or anything. That worried him because surely there should be some other fishing boats going in or out of the bay.

"Samir, this is too easy," Jabbar now looked in a 360 degree pattern.

"Maybe Allah is clearing our way for us," Samir said.

"Yes, perhaps. But if they are wise to us, we must be ready to make the call. Speaking to Abdul, Jabbar asked, "You have the phone, yes?"

Cell phones had become quite popular in sending a signal to explode bombs. One speed dial number was all it took and the beauty of it was that it could be done from quite a distance. The electrical power generated by the cell phones' ring was quite effective at activating the bomb's circuitry. Abdul smiled a confirmation, held up the phone and replaced it in his pocket.

"And Abdul, are the two men secured below?"

"Yes, the captain is unconscious and the other is bound securely in the front cabin," Abdul mistakenly said with a slight bow of his head.

"If the soldiers try to prevent us from entering the secured zone, we will increase speed to get as close to the base as possible. Until then just maintain your current speed," Jabbar said nervously looking around.

The Wampus Cat continued on its path toward the entry to the bay. Below deck, Chars had removed all the charges he could see, somehow managed to free his hands and began pulling David up the stairs. He was going to attempt get both himself and David off this boat.

"Sand Trap Command, this is Op Team Charlie, we have audio and a visual on three, repeat three hostiles in the Captain's control deck. We believe the hostages are down below. Both Op Teams have a neutralizing shot if Base Command gives the okay."

"This is Base Command. Op Team Alpha and Bravo, use nearest targets protocol. You have the green light for the shots on all three hostiles, repeat green light," said Coleman.

Within two seconds, from three hundred yards off the portside bow, a shot fired from an Op Team Alpha sniper, penetrated Samir's head without warning. The impact of the bullet slammed the terrorist's body to a wall covered with a spray of blood and brain matter. His lifeless body crumpled to the Captain's Deck floor. A simultaneous, second shot from a team member of Op Team Bravo, sent an identical .50 caliber round from a Barrett M-107 long range sniper rifle, thru the skull of Abdul. His body appeared as if it were yanked thru the door and down the stairs to the deck below. Because Jabbar reacted, Alpha team's second shot, less than one second later, was slightly off target. It exploded the left ear of Jabbar, but did not penetrate his skull.

Jabbar, minus one ear, was violently knocked to floor. Despite the enormous pain, he managed to crawl to cover. He reached for a wad of paper towels to press against his profusely bleeding head. The pain was excruciating and it was all he could do to regain his senses. He had to get to Abdul and make the call. He reached up to the throttle and pulled down. The Wampus Cat's engines' thrust caused Jabbar to slide backwards on the blood soaked floor. Exiting the cabin below with David in tow, the sudden increase in speed actually aided Chars' effort to push an unconscious David out the door onto the deck.

"Sand Trap Command this is Op Team Bravo. We have neutralized 2 of 3 hostiles. The third is wounded but still functioning."

"This is Sand Trap Command to F18 Hornet, please advise status."

"This is Captain Vick of the Hornet Striker One. Striker One and Two are in position and locked on the target. We are awaiting your command."

"This is Sand Trap Command, Hornet Striker One cue but hold steady for green light!"

"Sand Trap Command, this is Op Team Bravo, we are waiting for a clear shot."

"This is Op Team Alpha, looking for an opening."

Jabbar, battling pain and blood loss, crawled thru the Captain's deck door and peered down at Abdul. He had to get to the phone. The Wampus Cat powered on within 200 yards of the Security Zone. Jabbar dove head first down the stairs. He took several hard knocks on the way down, but his goal was achieved. He was still alive and he was at the foot of the stairs next to Abdul. He quickly reached in Abdul's pocket and felt for the phone.

Observing the Wampus Cat from its new position, Olivares said into his radio, "He's on the main deck and he's trying to detonate! Take him out! Repeat, take him out!" said Olivares.

The series of bullets from both sniper teams sent splinters of wood flying, but Jabbar scrambled beneath the shelter of the stairs. He saw Chars emerging from the lower cabin, but just smiled. He opened the phone.

Jabbar yelled, "Alah en akbar!" and pressed the send button.

A bullet hit Jabbar in the throat and the phone fell from his hand.

While lifting David to his feet, Chars heard a phone ring in the cabin below, followed by a series of small explosions. He realized the blasting caps were detonating. Struggling to maintain his balance, he dragged Dave toward the stern of the speeding boat as the bowels of Wampus Cat exploded. Chars felt the impact of the explosion, heat, searing pain, aching cold and then nothing at all.

Chapter Forty Five

Tampa Regional Hospital

Jerry Collins was looking at the doctor's report that had been hung on the end of the patient's steel bed support. Having just exited from surgery to repair a broken collar bone and a tibial shaft fracture, Chars was starting to come out from under the anesthesia. The fracture of the lower leg required a cast just below the knee to extending to the foot. The collarbone seemed to require some more specific attention. His arm was held into place with a shoulder immobilizer.

In a raspy croak, Chars said, "Hey doc, does it look like I am going to survive?"

"If I am your doctor, I say the chances are real poor," Jerry said, pleased that Chars regained consciousness.

It was only after hearing Jerry's voice did he realize it was his old friend. Chars gave pathetic laugh.

"Where am I?" Chars asked

"You are the guest of the Commander of MacDill Air Force base at the Tampa General Hospital."

"Are you a patient too?" asked Chars in a groggy voice.

"Only if they have a psych ward," Jerry said.

"Hey, my front tooth is missing," Chars said, checking out his teeth with his tongue.

He attempted to raise his free hand to his mouth. It was then he realized he was hooked to an intravenous drip.

"You will have to see a dentist to fix that. They can't do that here. You were very lucky. The explosion propelled you and David off the back of the boat. The Air Force had a Pave-Hawk Helicopter in the air and crews pluck you two out of the water."

"How's David?"

"Deb is with him now. He had a severe concussion, two broken ribs and a fractured wrist He is going to be fine. Your body took the bulk of the initial blast. By the way, what did you do below deck to keep the full explosion from happening?"

"I pulled the blasting caps out of the C4," he paused, "with my teeth. I did not think about the blasting caps themselves blowing up."

Jerry was clearly enjoying the story.

"When I tried to roust David, a pair of needle nose pliers fell out of his pants pocket. I was able to cut my plasti-cuffs off. I don't know how, but I was able to drag him up the stairs and out onto the deck. I heard a phone ring and then everything went black."

Chars wore an expression that showed he was remembering the sequence of events.

"The divers recovered 6 canisters of weaponized VX in tact," Jerry said solemnly.

"I saw the VX stuff, what is it?" asked Chars. He was croaking again and took a sip of water from a cup sitting on a swinging tray.

"Weaponized VX is a nerve agent that we think Iraq dropped on Iran. It was not supposed to be in existence, but many think Saddam Hussein moved his chemical weapons

313

out right before the U.S. invasion," Jerry said. "The guys that kidnapped you and hijacked the Wampus Cat were going to float as close as they could to MacDill and set off a ¼ ton of C4. The content of the cylinders was supposed to be scattered toward Tampa."

"Yeah, I got that far on my own. But I did not know how the mob fit in," Chars said.

"Agent Eads, who is a really nice guy by the way, gave me the poop," Jerry said.

Chars give a little harrumph of disagreement.

"Jimmy Fred was taken in after you two escaped the gambling boat. Hey, you are sort of making a habit of the boat jumping deal."

Jerry laughed aloud at the thought of Chars jumping off one boat, only to be blown off another.

"I can see where my best friend might think that was funny," Chars said facetiously.

"Hey Chars, you have to admit, you have gotten the shit kicked out of you this week," Jerry said.

"That seems to make you happy in some way," Chars said. "Just tell me about Jimmy Fred."

"Jimmy Fred puked Tweety. After Nikki found out the company that was buying his boats was a shell company owned by some sleazy people in Morocco or somewhere over there in the Middle East, he was going to the Feds."

"That's why he was killed. It wasn't the mob, it was the terrorists. They whacked him to keep his mouth closed and made it look like a mob hit," Chars said with understanding.

"Jimmy Fred thought the mob killed Nikki. He did not realize that the Arabs wanted the Tampa boats, not the

Ft. Lauderdale boats. He just figured that they wanted to use the boats to launder money or fund whatever activities they were up to," Jerry said.

"And that alone did not bother him enough to mention it to someone?" Chars said with indignation.

"That's what he told me. They liked Tampa a lot more than Ft. Lauderdale."

"When Jimmie Fred gets squeezed by the terrorists, he comes up with the idea of giving them Dave's boat. Which he tells them can be retrofitted to become a gambling ship. Of course they don't care about the gambling, they just want to get close to MacDill," Jerry explained.

"So the mob got mixed up in this because of Jimmy Fred?" Chars asked, but really already had confirmed that in his mind.

"Evidently, Jimmy Fred promised the Tampa boats to the Topolo family and the Arabs," Jerry said with a laugh.

"What was all the bullshit about the licenses out of Tampa Bay?" asked Chars.

"It was a fluke. Dave's boat and the gambling ships were the same size and there was a small allotment of commercial licenses for that size of boat. Jimmy Fred had a guy on the inside that delayed Dave and his friends long enough to guarantee the gambling boats receive their licenses," Jerry said.

"The prick at the Tampa Bay Authority, I can't even remember his name," Chars said with a pained look on his face.

Jerry helped him out, "Ray Jones."

"Yep, that's him," agreed Chars.

The nurse came in with a paper cup with three tablets. She removed the doctor's chart from Jerry's hand and replaced it on the hook. Jerry looked offended but said nothing, she was really cute.

"Mr. Reynolds, I need you to take these, please. The doctors are on the floor and will be in to see you shortly," she said and gave him a lingering look and a precocious smile. Chars smiled back and thought, *if I weren't so exhausted, I would like to play doctor with you.*

"Careful there tiger, your body can't handle anymore abuse," teased Jerry.

"You are telling me. Back to the story, Jimmy Fred was also in on the Arizona deal with the mob as well, right?"

"Yeah, and the FBI wants to talk to you about your source. Turns out it is Scott Tivy. He is a government snitch. They turned him on a felony tax evasion charge."

"So why is he running?" asked Chars.

"The Feds latched on to him when he won a sizable amount of money. He had given a false I.D. and failed to claim the income on his taxes. So the Feds turned him in to an informant. Just so happened they needed one in Scottsdale to keep track of one, Jimmy Fred. Scott never knew his full name, if that was his name. When he found out the mafia was involved he did not want to rat on Topolo. He was worried about the FBI reneging on their deal and decided to rabbit. He is operating on borrowed time and was using you to try to get Topolo and crew put away," Jerry said.

"Before the Topolos put Scott away," Chars finished the thought.

Epilogue:

Tampa Bay Tribune Herald

Express Reporter and Local Fisherman Honored
By Travis Gipson, Tampa Bay Tribune Herald Staff Writer

The Mayor of Tampa recognized the heroic exploits of Miami Express investigative reporter, Charles Reynolds and Dave Coughlin, the owner/captain of the fishing vessel, The Wampus Cat. Both men helped operational forces from MacDill Air Force, the Federal Bureau of Investigations and local authorities thwart an imminent attack.

All three of the terrorists on board were shot by snipers, but one of the Al Queda operatives managed to send a cell phone call that was intended to trigger the explosion of ¼ ton of C4 explosives. The blast alone would have proved enormously destructive, but the fact that the bomb involved a weaponized form of VX [Chemical Material,O-ethyl-S-2(diisopropylamino)ethylmethyl phosphonothiolate] nerve agent could have been disastrous.

Both men were kidnapped aboard the Wampus Cat, but with the help of Sergeant Jerry Collins of the Miami Police Department, eventually managed to alert authorities of their whereabouts of the floating bomb and partially disarm the explosives that were tied to the deadly nerve agent.

Reynolds, an investigative reporter, has won several awards for his hard hitting reporting, but this story could be his most impressive yet. Reynolds was abducted at gunpoint at the Tampa Pier yesterday morning and transported to Coughlin's Wampus Cat thirty miles out in the Gulf of Mexico. Dave Coughlin, captain and owner of the Wampus Cat had an even more harrowing tale of abduction. Coughlin had been misled to believe that the terrorist were hiring his services as a charter. Shortly after leaving the Bay, the terrorist assumed control of the fishing vessel. Over the course of two days, several transports arrived with the materials to arm the boat as a weapon of mass destruction.

Federal authorities are continuing to investigate the plot of three Al Queda based terrorists. Another man's description is being circulated throughout the Gulf Coast states that is suspected of aiding in the attack. From descriptions given by Reynolds and Coughlin, the department of Homeland Security was able to identify the ringleader as Ahmed el Fayed. His likeness and description were circulated almost immediately after the identification, but the high level terrorist has not been captured.

Captain Dave Coughlin has plans to return to the fishing profession, but did mention an interest in running for political office in the Tampa Bay Area.

Reynolds, unavailable for comment, left immediately after the award ceremonies. He was traveling to Arizona to investigate a casino bribery scandal that involved the late Ohio senator, Wayman Kaspar. Reynolds' editor, Thom Stanton, had glowing praises for the award winning reporter, calling him a true professional. Stanton did admit that Reynolds' employment had been terminated in a misunderstanding prior to Reynolds being kidnapped. According to Stanton, Reynolds had once again proven to be Miami's top investigative reporter.

******

Scottsdale, Arizona

"How did you latch on to this story?" asked Hamish suspiciously.

Chars sigh slightly as he gathered his thoughts and how decided how to make sense of all that happened in the previous weeks.

"I began receiving calls from an informant. Come to think of it, an informant, who is still out there somewhere," said Chars almost as if speaking to himself. "I was more concerned with all that was going on in Florida."

Chars shifted his walking cast to try to get more comfortable. In spite of doctor's orders, he was no longer wearing an arm sling.

"Strange how distances seem so inconsequential here in America," Hamish said sitting in a chair thrashed together with bark strips.

Chars said thoughtfully, "Money causes all kinds of theatrics when you think about it."

"Greed and a willingness to break laws always seem to lead to a crooked world, but you were speaking of your informant," Hamish said.

"I don't know what happened to him, but anyway, an acquaintance of mine was killed in Florida. From the information I was getting from this informant, I thought the same group that shot you and the boy, shot my friend. But it turns out that the real culprits were a terrorist group and not the mob at all," said Chars.

"It is all rather complicated. I really had no idea what the mafia was. Still not sure why they would be interested in a place as far away as Arizona," said Hamish.

"There supposedly was a body that was dumped in a lake on your property, can you tell me about that?" asked Chars.

"Not really, I never actually saw the body, so I really couldn't say," Hamish said. "To my knowledge, they have not recovered it."

"You two," Chars clarified, "you and Stevie, are quite the heroes."

"You could add Cowboy to the list, but Mr. Reynolds, I am looking to keep that opinion as far out of the papers as possible. By the looks of you and your injuries, messing with these people is not a good idea. I still feel we may be in some danger. So, I really need the boy's name left out of the story altogether."

"Sort of takes some of the dramatics out of the story, don't you think?" asked Chars

"I am thinking about the boy's well being, not some story written to sell papers," Hamish said without anger.

A bit too quickly Chars said, "I am trying to get to the truth about a connection between the mob and the casinos." He paused and told himself to go slower. He continued, "Could I talk to the boy about what he saw?"

"You feel that it would serve a greater purpose for the boy to somehow identify the body and then you could trace who killed him?'

"I am not sure, but I think that it is likely."

Hamish looked out into the field where Stevie was throwing a stick to Cowboy in between digging their new garden. Stevie was making steady progress despite his recent wound. It would take years to heal, but Stevie seemed to deal with the pain well. Cowboy would return the stick each time and Stevie would pause to give it another throw. Under the boy's baggy t-shirt, an outline of the remnant of a bandage was barely noticeable. Every once in a while, Stevie glanced over to the porch, but did not approach. Hamish turned his attention back to Chars.

"Mr. Reynolds, I understand that you have a desire to know the truth and get your story. What do you think that would do to that boy, if this mafia reads in the newspaper that the boy is the only witness that could possibly identify a body that they would rather not be found."

"So you feel that if I report this, your friend there would once again be in danger?"

"I think you know the answer to that, Mr. Reynolds. The less attention called to this matter, the fewer people will feel like they have to get involved. The State of Arizona has given me temporary custody, but that could change if someone gets the idea that Stevie is in danger. If you write your story, those people that don't want the truth to come out will be left with only one choice: eliminate the witness."

There was a long silence as Chars played through the possibilities in his mind. Chars looked out at the Lazy C, sat back in his chair and let out a sigh.

Seeing the indecision in Chars, Hamish continued, "Mr. Reynolds, I was told that you are a famous reporter. You probably can write your story whether I want you to or not. But that boy out there deserves a life that does not include looking over his shoulder."

"Could you call him over?"

Hamish intensely looked at Chars as if trying to see deep into his soul. Hamish gave a loud whistle. Cowboy immediately broke his chase for the stick and approached full stride toward the cabin. Chars smiled questioningly. Cowboy arrived at the front porch and came to full attention.

"Cowboy, this is Mr. Reynolds."

Cowboy's brown eyes looked from Hamish to Chars and then back to Hamish. Chars did not move. Cowboy slowly approached and gave Chars' leg a complete sniff. He then sat down on the porch, tongue dangling out of his mouth. Chars' eyebrows raised and try to conceal a sigh. When Chars looked up, Stevie was standing at the foot of the stairs leading up to the porch. His look toward Chars was far more suspicious than Cowboys' had been.

Chars looked at the young boy's thin frame and black, collar length hair. Chars saw the intelligent eyes and the look of mistrust.

Chars stood with some effort, smiled and said, "Hello, Stevie. My name is Chars."

Stevie's brow furrowed, but he said nothing. Nodding slightly with his eyes still fixed on this curious man., the little boy stood straight and unintimidated

Looking at the cast on Chars' leg, Stevie asked, "What happened to you?"

Chars smiled and said, "Boating accident."

There was silence as Chars realized Stevie was waiting on him to say something.

"I just wanted to shake the hand of a hero."

With a completely straight face, Stevie asked, "Want my autograph?"

Chars laughed in amusement and said, "I probably should. But I think a handshake will do."

The two shook hands and Chars slowly moved off the porch. He turned back to Hamish and the boy.

"It was my pleasure to meet you, Hamish, and you, Small Feather. The Lazy C is going to be a great home for you both."

Stevie gave a small smile at the use of his Indian name.

Chars paused and added, "And for you too, Cowboy."

Cowboy's ears perked up and he gave a quiet, "whoof."

Chars gave a quick wave, ambled to his car and drove away.

Stevie turned to Hamish. "Is he going to be a problem?"

"I don't think so."

"What kind of a pussy name is Chars anyway?"

Hamish shrugged.

"We are going to have to work on that mouth of yours."

Stevie shrugged and said "Okay."

He then turned to Cowboy, "Let's go play fetch." Stevie let go a mighty heave wincing at the lingering pain. A small stick sailed through the air and the blue healer was at full pursuit within seconds. Stevie let out a sound of glee as he watched the dog break into full stride.

THE END